MW00768949

Rob White is a fiction author, blogger, comic book collaborator and professional dreamer. Rob makes his home in Athens, Georgia, where he revels in the chaos and magic of living in a town full of artists and collaborates with other mad and beautiful souls as frequently as possible. The Pull was his first novel, begun at age fourteen in 1994, completed in 1999 and finally released in print edition in 2013. What you hold in your hands is the first in a series of five novels and a labor of nearly two decades of imagination.

To Cody,

May your journey be filled with adventure and discovery

ISBN-13 978-1484931578
ISBN-10 1484931572

http://followthepull.com/

Rob White

The Pull

Prologue

I dream sometimes. I dream of people I've yet to meet and events yet to come. I dream of battles yet to be fought and heroes yet to fall. Mostly now I dream of a great and terrible darkness that will spring from the heart of an innocent and rise to heights so lofty it will threaten to consume us all. It is a shadow, and all shadows can be cast away with light; and yet I fear that light may not come.

My name is Patricia. In my life I am trapped, but in my dreams I soar. The flight I embark upon, and sometimes endure, is not always a pleasant one. There are nights when I wake up screaming in a voice that isn't mine; but there are also nights where I am so surrounded by the one thing I lack in my waking life that I wish never to open my eyes. Hope. Sometimes I dream of hope.

Hope has a name. More than one, actually. I can never remember that name when I awaken but I know that it is simple and strong, just as he is. He carries something inside of him that will change the world, but he has a path to follow first. A Pull.

There are others of equal strength that will walk that path with him. A woman of scars. A man of chains. A girl of endless warmth and a man of endless malice. There is also a monster behind him. Its eyes are purple and its teeth are sharp.

I see the threads between them, as I see them between all of us. Those threads will strengthen or unravel, I know not which,

I don't know how it ends. I never do; but I do know how it will begin.

It will begin with the voice of a child.

1

"Wake up."

He opened his eyes and breathed in the cool late winter air. It was crisp and clean. He shifted and knew the gentle crunch beneath him was pine needles. He was in a forest. This is where he had fallen. This is where the fire consumed them.

Like a dream, Nick felt the memory of that fire fading fast. It was an unusual color. Purple. It was also alive and inside of him and whispering; always, always whispering. It had been he and The Whisper and someone else here; someone he did not remember.

It was that someone who told him to wake, he thought. In his mind he saw a little girl with golden hair and a brown dress with red sleeves. He thought he knew her name once, but it must have slipped away with all the rest. Her name, what the fire meant, who he was and where he came from. For Nick was alone. His memory and his companions had left him. The little girl with the golden hair was gone. He was alone with only a glimmer of purpose and a name.

He sat up, alarmed at the sense of loss and realization of danger past. He gripped the object in his hand and scanned his surroundings with a cautious eye. There was nothing but trees around him, slightly swaying in the wind, tall and brown and peaceful. He was in a small clearing and he could hear no sounds of life outside of a few birds chirping and the rustle beneath his own body. There was no purple fire here. That danger had fled.

It was then that he saw the object gripped in his right hand, the one that had been in that hand when he awoke. It was long and reflective and sharp. A sword, curved like a clear horizon. The sword was part of him, though he did not remember why.

He saw his reflection in that blade and remembered his face. He was young, about nineteen he thought. His skin was fair and his hair was dark brown, messy and hanging over dark green eyes. His eyes were large and open, he thought they looked both thoughtful and curious. His face was narrow and angular, with a sloped nose and small pink lips. He had no facial hair, and had a sense that he had never seen himself with any. His body was of average height and sleight build, with thin wrists and lean limbs. He was wearing a black long-sleeved shirt and dark jeans. His shoes were canvas and worn, perhaps once black but now a muddy brown.

He had been travelling. He thought he even remembered where. Or rather, what direction, for Nick realized he would not be so lucky as to be able to know his destination. No, what he felt inside of him was a compass of sorts. A memory perhaps, but one that felt more like an urge. Not an instinct but more of a calling. A pull. The pull told him to go west.

Nick rose to his feet and took one more look around him. He was indeed alone but for whatever reason, that did not alarm him. No, what he felt instead was exhilaration. He was here. He was alive. He knew not why that should make him so happy, but it did. The wind on his skin, the sword in his hand, the bird calls floating to his ears and the pull inside of his heart; it was all his.

Nick turned west, and followed The Pull.

The world spun and her heart pounded; her vision was foggy and her gym clothes were doused in sweat, yet her mind was razor focused. Melissa stood up from the bench against the training room wall and took one long last gulp from her beer before flinging the empty bottle into the corner. She recognized the task before her: that punching bag had to die.

She screamed. It wasn't a drunken yowl or the terrified wail of a frightened girl. No, this was a roar, and it was her battle cry. She ran at full speed, covering the twenty feet between the wall and the blue gym bag hanging from the central ceiling. She felt her foot catch on the edge of the floor mat, but didn't allow the momentary drink-induced stumble to interrupt her momentum. She collided with the bag with elbow outstretched and a violent smile on her lips.

Melissa was a great and terrible vision. Her blonde hair whipped through the air as long toned legs and arms thundered into the bag, laying blow after blow after heavy, resounding blow. Her style was fast but also incredibly powerful, and though her blood coursed with alcohol, she fell into it with the ease of riding a bike.

She head-butted the bag and felt the world spin. Suddenly her mind and her periphery were filled not only with the whirling unfocused gym around her...but with her the trash-littered living room of her father's house, the Alabama bar in which she got in her first real fight, the hospital room she lost her mother in.

She roared again, and kicked the bag harder.

Melissa heard the door open behind her but did not want to stop. It was likely one of the other hired goons of this place, security or surveillance or just plain hired muscle. Her employer, Jacob Raven, liked to be surrounded by meat-heads because meat-heads were as easy to control as a mistreated dog on a leash. Dangle a dripping steak in front of it and it will tear apart anything you ask it to.

"Hey Blondie. Get off the bag and off the bottle and get your drunk ass to Raven's office. He's asked to see you," she heard the familiar voice call from behind her.

Melissa let out one final vicious, spit-flying roar, spinning an angry backhand into the swaying bag before walking away from her inanimate enemy and grabbing another beer from the cooler beside the bench.

"I said get off the bottle, you dumb...."

"Make me, Francis," she taunted, not bothering to look at the hulking, 6 foot 3 inch mound of muscle she nonetheless looked down upon. Francis McElroy, greaseball that he was, was Raven's right hand. He earned that spot by being just a bit bigger, just a bit smarter, and most importantly just a bit more obedient than his colleagues.

Francis shook his head in disgust.

"What a waste. You'd be a fine piece of ass if you weren't so pathetic."

Melissa felt herself dash across the room, grabbing her weapon from its resting place on the wall as she went. McElroy had an instant to react, but only that.

"Say that again, jackass. Say anything like that again and I'll shove my staff so far down your throat you'll turn into a goddamn scarecrow."

Francis looked down at the angry woman and her weapon poised so painfully under his chin. It was a six foot fighting staff, one Melissa carried with her everywhere. As fearful as she was with only fists and feet, Melissa was twice as much so with that damnable stick in her hands.

"You're lucky Raven likes you, bitch. Otherwise we'd have kicked your ass years ago. You may be good against five tough guys like me, but what about fifty?" Francis answered bravely. Melissa had to give him credit for that much, the man did not back down.

"Bring every last one you've got," she offered, full of a rage-filled bravado she knew full well would one day get her into trouble.

Francis flicked the staff away, giving her a smug grin.

"One day, Melissa. Maybe sooner than you think. Right now you need to get to Raven's office. For god's sake take a shower first."

Melissa leaned against her staff and gave a smile of her own.

"Jacob can deal with it. The runt didn't hire me to sit behind a desk and shuffle papers."

"He also didn't hire you to drink on the job and trespass into restricted areas," Francis retorted.

That wiped the smile from her face. Shit. So that was what this was about.

"And you've got to stop calling him by his first name. It's Mr. Raven to you just like it is to the rest of us," he continued.

Melissa let out a small incredulous laugh.

"The runt will get my respect when he earns it," she said, walking by Francis and ignoring his suggestion to clean up before visiting her boss.

"You mean that nearly six figure paycheck isn't enough?" Francis asked as she walked away.

Melissa didn't answer.

When she entered Raven's office, the man was sitting behind his enormous mahogany desk eating peanuts and gazing out his office window at the Atlanta skyline below. It was indeed below, as the RavenCorp building towered over every other edifice in the city, just as the man himself, figuratively if not by virtue of physical stature, towered over all other men not only in Atlanta but the nation beyond it.

"What do you want, Jacob?" Melissa asked impatiently. She had tossed her unfinished beer along the way, wanting to have as clear a head as possible for the conversation she knew was to come.

Raven spun around in his leather office chair, greeting her with a broad smile above his neatly groomed goatee. His hair was blonde like hers but carried a more yellow sheen than her honey golden. Between the oddly pointed facial hair, the diminutive height and the unusual shades of purple and white he wore, Raven looked more like a cartoon than a man, and his hungry grin did little to dispel that image.

"Melissa! Damn good to see you! Come, sit!" he motioned at one of the equally leather but significantly smaller chairs facing his own across the desk.

She crossed her arms and remained where she stood.

"Just tell me what this is about, Raven, so I can get back to the gym. I was in the middle of a workout when Magilla Gorilla here interrupted me."

Raven laughed and winked at Francis McElroy, standing with his arms crossed in front of the door, only partially obscuring the fact that he was purposefully barring her exit.

"Well I certainly wouldn't want to pull my personal escort away from her training."

"I'm not an 'escort', Jacob, I'm your bodyguard. I hate it when you call me that. Makes me sound like your call girl," she said with a grimace.

Raven shrugged.

"Well it's true that I didn't just hire you for your ability to beat people to a pulp, but you are correct. Bodyguard, then."

"Thanks," she said sarcastically, "So…."

"So I've asked you here because I want you to stop visiting the guest quarters," Raven said, propping his elbows on his desk and crossing his fingers in front of him. She could see him gaze at her intently, waiting to gauge her reaction.

"Guest quarters," Melissa chuckled, "That's a hoot. Is that what they called them back on the plantation too? 'Send the guests out to the field to pick 'Massa some cotton'?"

"Melissa, don't be dramatic," he said impatiently.

"Dramatic? You have an entire wing of the building dedicated to holding people against their will, Jacob. Men, women, hell I've seen kids barely into their teens back there. Are we calling those guest rooms now? Twelve by ten prison cells with nothing but a toilet and a cot?"

He was still smiling, but Melissa could see anger boiling beneath his calm façade. She had seen that look a number of times before. Jacob Raven was used to getting his way.

"The purpose of the guest quarters and their occupants are not your concern. I told you what areas of the building you were not to visit and you did so anyway. So tell me, why exactly did you decide to stroll into Hall 38 three weeks ago?"

It was Melissa's turn to shrug.

"I got bored."

Raven gritted his teeth.

"You got...bored," he repeated, barely able to contain his anger.

She said nothing, only stared at him defiantly.

Raven looked at her for a moment then finally sat back in his chair.

"You may leave now, Miss Moonbeam; but know that if you wander into Hall 38 again it will mean your job."

Melissa's fists clenched. There was something in Hall 38 she had no intention of staying away from.

"Are you going to send your goon squad to finish me off like some of the other saps you've fired lately?"

Raven smiled again, stretching his arms behind him and folding his hands behind his head confidently.

"Now Melissa, why would you think me so crass?"

"Fine. Whatever you say," Melissa said, shaking her head and turning to leave. She shoved Francis out of the way and threw open the office door, slamming it behind her as she left.

"Keep an eye on her, Francis," Raven said, his voice trailing off and his attention turning towards a black and white monitor on the desk beside him, "I have a feeling Miss Moonbeam may soon become more trouble than she's worth."

Francis nodded and left his boss alone in his office. Raven watched the monitor, tuned to Hall 38 Room 11, where a tall young African American man huddled in a corner on his cot.

"You're not very much now, are you little man?"

Raven stroked his goatee and smiled.

"Perhaps one day I'll make you something more."

3

Nick watched himself walk across the leaves, now oak instead of pine. His legs moved up and down, up and down, forwards and back. His body did not seem new to him; it seemed familiar and solid. What felt new to him was the rhythm. The sensation of locomotion felt oddly alien, not as if he had never walked in his own body before, but had in fact only watched himself walk in his own body. Now that he was in control of those legs the rhythm of them was something he was having to acclimate himself to.

To say the notion unnerved him would be an understatement. The more Nick journeyed west and the more he moved, ate and drank the more he realized that it all felt unusual to him. There was a mismatch between his mind and his body and he couldn't for the life of him put his finger on why.

Perhaps it was simply a symptom of amnesia. Nick's accumulated knowledge seemed to be intact. He knew what amnesia was. He remembered how to tie his shoe and which direction the sun set in the evening and rose in the morning. He even remembered what season it was: late winter approaching the cusp of spring; and yet anything pertaining to himself was simply gone. It was as if he had vanished from his own memory. He, his history, his family, his friends were no longer within reach.

Nick felt a stab in his heart at the thought. He was alone. Truly and completely alone. The bizarre exhilaration at experiencing the world anew was tempered by the ever-growing sense of loneliness emerging from within. He had to find the source of his Pull (in his mind the word was always capitalized, as was Whisper) and hopefully there he would discover he was not alone at all.

As he watched his legs his attention returned to an unsettling observation he had made the day before. The leaves beneath his feet were not crunching.

Nick did not make a sound when he walked.

A day later, two since his awakening in the forest, Nick finally saw the Atlanta cityscape cresting the horizon. The site made him smile, for it was approaching dusk and the last rays of the setting sun were beginning to make a playground of the steel and glass arrayed before him. He remembered that. He remembered how beautiful Atlanta was in the sunset.

He also knew there was danger there. The city had, in his lifetime, begun devolving into something less than what it once was. It was a common trend across the continent since the political upheaval of the last decade. The rise of corporations eventually left politicians with less power as they began to more openly act in service to their financial backers. The people still spoke and votes were still cast, but when term after term proved promises of reform empty and corporate interests dominant, most people simply stopped going to the polls. Apathy spread and a general acceptance enveloped the nation· there was no American Dream for the common man. The most one could hope for would be to get a nine-to-five job that paid for rent in one of the increasingly common low-income housing developments or, if one is lucky, in a small residential rental property in the suburbs.

Home ownership was for the wealthy. So was ownership of anything, really. All was owed to the banks and every penny went to basic survival and endless debt repayment. No one fought it anymore. This was simply the way the world was.

The Peace and Disarmament Act proposed by Congressman and Oil Tycoon Elias Raven and passed unanimously took guns from the hands of citizens and placed them solely in the arms of local police forces. What all feared would then happen followed without pause: corrupt officials began selling those weapons to wealthy international drug traffickers, who then began arming their base-level street thugs.

The eventual result of the Act was that guns were now rare. Most were stockpiled in police stations and government buildings; but those guns that were still on the streets were virtually always found in the hands of violent criminals and organized gangs. The reality of gun control was an open secret. This led even less people to trust their representatives, and the gulf between the common individual and those in power grew even wider.

Nick remembered every bit of this. It was a part of the world he grew up in. He had seen a gun perhaps once in his life, behind a glass case at a museum. He reached his hand behind him and gripped the handle of his sword, shielded through a thin canvas bag he had found in a dumpster the day before. At least he would be prepared if confronted with violence, though he knew not if he could use the weapon.

The terrain he now traveled was hilly; with ups and downs, dips and bobs like much of the Georgia landscape. The land was thickly forested in parts and wide open grassland in others, dotted by many an intruding subdivision or trailer park and the occasional highway. Georgia highways were mostly unpleasant, thickly trafficked lanes of pollution and aggression. Cars were still one of the few things the poor spent their money on, or rather went into debt over. That was another thing Nick remembered: he never liked cars.

He could see another trailer park at the bottom of a hill before him. It was large and would require him to either cut through or go around. He had been trying to avoid society until he got to Atlanta for fear of arousing suspicion. He was a young man, slightly dirty from living in the woods, un-showered and carrying a backpack along with a long covered object he hoped no one could tell was a sword. Perhaps it wouldn't be such a bad thing if the police picked him up. They may be able to help him locate his home; yet somehow something within him panicked at the thought. He had to keep moving forward. What he needed was in the city, and he had to be the one to find it.

As he approached the tree-line bordering the trailer park, Nick could hear voices drifting in his direction, or rather a solitary voice: male and angry from the sound of it. He got closer and saw a large balding man in a stained tank top yelling at something below him. Nick crouched at the edge of the clearing and saw a big brown dog through a chain-link fence. It was a German Shepherd; male, and very frightened of its owner. Nick could now make out the man's ranting.

"And I told her she was wasting the last years of her life spending money on you. Dog food and romance novels, that's all that woman seemed to care about. Didn't seem to give no mind towards saving anything for her own damn children. What, did she want us to live in a goddamn trailer for the rest of our lives?" the man ranted, pausing and motioning towards the dog as if he expected a response.

The man was an obvious example of the dying breed of Georgia redneck. The city and its surrounding areas was now more Detroit than Mayberry, but men like this still held on to what they considered their land by birthright.

The dog sat obediently in front of the man, hanging its head and looking up through cautious eyes. It had been yelled at before, Nick could tell as he crouched less than a stone's throw from the scene, and it seemed to know what to expect.

"'Course she was perfectly happy to spend her golden years in this god-forsaken place. I was going to Nashville! I was going to be the next Alan Jackson and I was going to take her with me, but she wouldn't leave this trailer and she wouldn't give me a dime for it either!"

The man looked at one dirt-covered hand. His other hand rubbed a belly that was barely concealed.

"Not that she ever had much."

The man turned a sideways glance back to the dog. Even from this distance Nick could see the menace forming behind those eyes; menace and the signs of sudden inspiration.

"She wouldn't leave you either," he said softly, rubbing his fat fingers together. "Stay where you is, pup. I got a right fine idea what to do with you."

The man went inside, slamming the screen door behind him. The dog quickly trotted off to lie down next to an old battered dog house in the corner of the yard.

Nick was feeling very uneasy about what he was seeing. Something unfortunate was about to take place. The dog seemed harmless. The man, on the other hand, did not.

Without giving it much thought, he decided to approach, quietly making his way across the grass to the fence.

The dog jumped and let out a low growl when it suddenly noticed the presence of a stranger crouching on the other side of its fence. Nick raised his hands in a sign of truce.

"It's okay," he whispered. "I want to help."

The dog seemed to relax a bit. It still looked concerned, but made no attempt to back away. Nick slowly un-shouldered his backpack, reached inside, and pulled out the rest of the stick of beef jerky he had been snacking on earlier. It was the only food he had eaten since he had woken up; a stash he had found in a brown paper bag on a school playground. A child's forgotten snack, he assumed.

The dog did not hesitate to snatch the jerky from Nick's offering hand. Nick took the opportunity to glance at the dog's collar and tag. The tag was old and scuffed. He had an image of the dog being kicked in the throat on numerous occasions in the past. His sympathy for the animal grew.

All that remained visible on the tag were the first five letters of a word; most likely the dog's name.

BLITZ

"Blitz? Blitzed? Blitzen?" Nick spoke to himself. The dog's ears perked up at the word "Blitzen."

"Blitzen?" Nick said in amusement. "Like the reindeer?"

At that moment the screen door was kicked back open, and Nick looked up to see the large balding ogre of a man standing there, eyes wide with surprise and anger, a shotgun perched in his hands; a gun Nick believed the man had intended to use on the dog.

"What the hell you doin' with my dog, boy?" the man said in a low, hateful voice.

"I..." Nick barely got the one syllable out of his mouth before a shot was fired into the air above him.

"Get out!" the man yelled angrily. "Get the hell off my land!" He leveled the gun directly at Nick.

Nick was off like a light, running for the tree-line with all the speed he could muster. He heard another shot ring into the air behind him, again angled just enough into the air above to avoid taking his head off.

The man chuckled a bit as Nick vanished. "Man but that skinny little shit did run. Probably some junkie lookin' for a fix," he looked down at the dog. "Now let's get this business over with."

The dog watched the man reload the gun. It then looked out into the woods where the boy had run. A decision was made behind those intelligent brown eyes.

"What the...," the man muttered as the dog sprang into action, leaping on top of its dog house and then jumping over the fence.

"Like hell!" the man screamed. He finished loading, then fired a shot at the fleeing dog.

Nick stopped running a few moments after the last gunshot. He had cleared quite a lot of ground between he and his angry assailant, and he didn't believe that the man would chase him this far and likely not at all. His business had been with the dog, and Nick worried that the last shot he had heard might have hit its mark.

He turned away, looking for a route around the neighborhood, his heart heavy for the poor animal.

It was then that he noticed the sound of rustling leaves behind him. Something was coming. Something with more than two feet.

A grin spread across his face when Nick saw the dog cross the edge of the rise in front of him. The dog was panting heavily, and seemed to pant even louder when it saw Nick.

"Well hi there," Nick said, laughing a little.

The dog stopped in front of him and happily gazed up into his face, showing none of the timidity it had shown its master.

"Come for more of this?" Nick said, tossing the dog another chunk of jerky from his pack. The dog caught it easily.

He watched it eat for a moment before turning to continue on his way.

"Well it was nice meeting you, Blitzen. Glad to see you made it out in one piece."

The dog looked up as Nick walked off. It wasn't long before Nick heard the sound of four padded feet behind him.

Nick turned back to regard his new follower.

"So you want to come with me?"

He thought about it for a moment. Having a friend beside him, furry or otherwise, might do him good. Being alone in the woods was starting to weigh on him. The dog might wander off at any point between now and Nick's destination, but in the meantime he thought he would welcome the company.

"Ok then...Blitz," Nick said, preferring the amended title on the dog's damaged collar to something that would make him think of Christmas. "You can come with me; though I have to warn you, you may not like it where I'm going."

Blitz, oblivious to the words of caution, trotted right up to Nick's feet and looked up at him in happy expectation.

"Fair enough," Nick said, and turned his attention back to The Pull. Somehow, the fact that he was no longer alone made the walk a good bit easier.

4

Melissa couldn't stay away any longer. She had spent the past two nights parked on the couch in her apartment drinking heavily and thinking about a way out. There may not be a way out for her; she was resigned to that now though she hoped otherwise, but she had to find a way out for Jason, the prisoner she had met in Hall 38.

The thin, dark-skinned boy sitting with his back to the wall on the corner of his cot stared at a spot on the ceiling, almost without blinking, as if staring hard enough would bring the walls around him crumbling down. His brown eyes were heavy and angry. His lips were pursed together and his fists were clenched in front of his knees. His hair was starting to get longer. It was bunched together in neat kinks. The beginnings of dreadlocks, Jason told her. He'd been tired of looking like a kid.

Truth was, he was no more a kid than she was. They were both in their early twenties. What made the difference was experience. Melissa had been through so much and Jason so little that it made the two of them seem years apart. Jason's sheltered life with his mother and older brother had given him little to build off of. He was full of book-smarts, that much was for sure, but he had no experience with girls, with life outside of the city, with the violence people like Raven perpetrated; until now.

Melissa knew that Jason Dredd wasn't really staring at the ceiling. He was staring beyond it, at the images in his head. The same memory that had replayed itself over and over and over again in the two months since he had been brought to this place.

The memory of his brother's betrayal.

Colin Dredd had been his hero. Four years older than Jason, Colin was the man of the house. The captain of their basketball team, the replacement for their long missing father, the one who walked beside him each day on the way home from school, protecting him from the thugs and the pushers. Colin was tall and athletic, and he walked with a confidence that made those around him feel as though they needed to look upwards to look Colin in the eye.

Their family was going through a tough period. The boys had never really known their father, who their mother had said deserted them long ago, not long after Jason was born. Even Colin only had vague memories of him, which the older brother had related were not all that pleasant. Their mother, Bernice, had taken care of them by working back-to-back jobs for nearly two decades. Nurse, assistant teacher, grocery clerk; Bernice Dredd had done it all, turning in far more hours than most people, all for the sake of her boys.

There had once been three Dredd boys: Jason, Colin and Patrick. Patrick was the hyperactive and overconfident middle child, never pausing to consider his actions or question the fact that the world was his oyster. Patrick was gunned down in a seemingly random drive-by that nearly took Jason and Colin's lives as well. It was at that time that Colin changed. The humor seemed to drain out of him. He became obsessed with protecting Jason and his mother. He was hard to talk to after that day, but Jason perhaps looked up to him even more.

The name Dredd wasn't their legal name. Their mother was born Bernice Dreddowski. Her grandfather had been Polish; not to mention white. She took the name back after her husband had left her, but felt like she should change something to reflect the new and stronger person she wanted to be; the survivor that would provide for her family. Colin was the one that came up with the name Dredd. It was a simple shortening of their last name, but it spoke volumes about the seriousness of their resolve. Black families living in the hood tended to not get much respect with a name like Dreddowski; but Dredd? That was a different story.

Bernice didn't like it at first, but when she saw how thrilled her boys were at the prospect of having such an intimidating name, she accepted the idea. Thus Jason Dreddowski became Jason Dredd.

Jason now wondered if that intimidating new name had served to help them or hinder them towards the end. Had Raven become interested in his brother just as much because of the amusingly menacing name as for his skills?

The family had fallen on worse times than usual. Bernice had lost one of her jobs and was having trouble finding another. Their rent was two months overdue and the landlord had threatened eviction more than once.

Colin had been saying lately that he had a plan, but Jason never liked the look on his brother's face when he said it. He looked determined, but also very scared.

On the night Colin went through with his plan, Jason had been watching the Discovery Channel; a show about astronomy, his favorite subject. Bernice was doing laundry. Colin had been out for a couple of hours. Gone for a drive with some friends, he had said.

When the door whipped open with enough force to shake the walls of their tiny apartment, Jason's heart seemed to stop beating. When he turned around and saw his brother standing there with a gun in his hand, all the breath fled from his lungs as well.

Colin wasn't alone. Two big men in suits, also carrying 9mm handguns, followed him in. The gun in Colin's hand was pointed at the floor. His shoulders were slumped, and as he caught Jason's eye for a moment, Jason saw that all the strength and confidence and older brother bravado that he had known and loved was absent from Colin's eyes. This was a different person walking in the door. One that was terrified and defeated.

Jason then got his first look at the man he now hated more than anyone in the world.

Only about five foot six, in a purple vest and shiny black shoes and a cane he seemed to use more for show than for practical use, the man behind his brother walked in with a grin. When he saw the goatee, Jason wondered if his brother had made a deal with the devil.

He knew now that he hadn't been far wrong.

"So this is the rest of Clan Dredd, is it Colin?" said the man with the evil goatee.

Colin didn't say a word, just kept looking at the floor.

"What the hell is going on here, Colin?" Bernice asked, placing her hands on her hips, trying to look as if the only thing she was feeling was irritation, and that those hands weren't shaking with surprise and fear.

Jason just stayed there, frozen to the couch, watching the scene as if it were playing out on the TV behind him.

"Mom just do what he says and we'll all be fine," Colin said to her, though he kept his eyes locked firmly on the floor.

"Yes, Ms. Dredd, please do what he says," the man with the cane said with a snicker. "My name is Jacob Raven. You may have heard of me."

Jason had. He believed most of the literate public must have. The name Raven was plastered nearly everywhere in Atlanta; and now here he was, standing in Jason's living room, with two men pointing guns at he and his mother.

"Your son here has very recently become my employee. You should be proud, Ms. Dredd. He's soon going to be paid likely more than you've ever seen in your life," Raven continued.

Bernice Dredd did not look impressed. "Yeah, I've heard of you. I've read the papers. They say you and your daddy were two of the most powerful men in the country. But they also say that you might also be the closest thing this country's seen to Al Capone in thirty years. You're a drug runner and an arms smuggler, Mr. Raven."

Raven lifted his arms in a comical expression and shrugged.

"These are complicated times, Bernice. Complicated times call for complicated actions."

"Colin, what are you doing with these men?" Bernice asked, ignoring Raven, "I don't know what they offered you, but it isn't worth this. It isn't worth jail time and it isn't worth your life; and it certainly isn't worth pointing guns at your family!" she said, trying in vain to get Colin to look her in the eye.

"Why are you doing this?" Jason spoke up for the first time. He had been surprised to hear his own voice, and he realized immediately that the question had been pointed more at Colin than at Raven or the men with the guns.

A fact which was not lost on Raven.

"He's doing this to give his family a chance...Jason, is it?" Raven said. As he spoke, his eyes narrowed and his voice slowed. Jason had the clear sense that the man was studying him.

The extremely uncomfortable sensation lasted several seconds longer, as Raven stared at the boy, his fingers fondling his cane in a nearly obscene fashion.

"What do you want with us then?" Bernice asked, attempting to direct Raven's attention back to her.

It didn't work. Raven kept studying Jason like a butterfly trapped in a jar moments before its wings are yanked off.

"I said I'd work for him, Mom. I'd work for him and I'd make more money than we ever could have made at the rate we were going. I'd provide for you...if I let him have his say," Colin spoke. There was a desperation in his voice, as if he were trying with all his might to convince himself he was doing the right thing.

"So what is 'his say', Colin? What is all that money in exchange for?" she asked him.

"Protection and compensation at the cost of a simple relocation, Ms. Dredd. You'll be taken care of. You'll be off the streets and under my wing and Colin won't have to worry about you anymore" was Raven's answer to her.

"Take them."

The two men with guns sprang into motion. One ran to Bernice while the other moved towards Jason. There was a struggle. No shots were fired, but he heard his mother screaming in anger. Jason fought back as well. Or at least he thought he did. All that was clear at that moment was the look in Colin's eyes. Colin stared directly at Jason. His attacker went mostly ignored. Jason could do nothing but watch Colin, and ask him wordlessly...why?

"Why didn't you protect us?" Jason said, now sitting in that bland little room in the tallest tower of the farthest castle. Or so he had come to think of his prison, RavenCorp International.

"He thought he was, Jason," Melissa said from the stool propped on the other side of the barrier.

Jason turned to look at her. She watched him embarrassingly try to regain his composure and found it a bit endearing. Jason had obviously developed a crush on her since she began visiting him.

"How could he think that having me and mom locked away in a cell was the right thing to do?" Jason asked, scooting to the foot of the bed to sit closer to her.

"Things are bad out there, Jason. Bad and getting worse. Raven's stupid laws are funneling guns off the streets, but that only means they're going to his hands and back out into the hands of all the wrong people. Crime rate's higher than ever. The police have less autonomy than they ever did. People are living in fear. The world is changing, and it's not for the better. Colin, however misguided, thought he was getting you away from all that," Melissa said very matter-of-factly.

"How did this happen, Melissa? How did our world get so...screwed up?"

Melissa leaned her stool back against the wall of the hallway outside his cell and sighed heavily.

"The rug got pulled out from under us, kiddo. The money disappeared, and when the money disappeared people got scared. They gave all the power to the ones who still had money. People like Raven. And Raven only wants what Raven wants. He doesn't give a good goddamn what the rest of us do."

"And what does Raven want?" Jason asked. Melissa knew he was asking just as much about Raven's intentions for him personally as he was about the world in general.

She paused for a moment, and then shook her head.

"I'm still trying to figure that out."

Raven had kept Jason here, alone in a cell and away from his family, for two whole months. Two whole months with almost nothing but a hard cot to sleep on and a cold porcelain toilet in the corner. TV dinners once a day. Only water from the tap to drink.

The cell was about twelve feet by ten feet. The back wall held a small window that Jason had to stand on his cot to look out of. The cityscape of Atlanta played out far below him. No amount of shouting would be heard from that height. On the opposite wall was the clear Plexiglas screen; bullet-proof. He had exhausted himself that first night trying to break it, to no avail. A small slit adorned the bottom left corner, through which his food was passed by some nameless thug or another. A door was set into the barrier, but it was tightly sealed shut and had not opened since the night he was brought here.

All in all it was a bleak situation. Jason would have given up hope long ago; should have given up hope, if not for Melissa.

One day he had been staring at that wall, much as he had been earlier, though it was depression he was swimming in that morning, not anger. He was staring at that wall and finally sinking into the realization that he might never see his family again, that Raven had some perverted designs for him and that sooner or later he would wind up dead or worse. He was staring at that wall and wondering if his tiny cell held some way of killing himself and ending all of this before Raven could get to him.

Then movement flashed out of the corner of his eye.

A tall blonde woman walked by; strode by with purpose, it seemed. She was carrying a long stick and wearing gym clothes. At first it seemed as though she would keep on walking, but then she did a double take as she passed Jason's cell. She stopped in mid-stride and turned to face him, a look of bewilderment in her big blue eyes.

"Who the hell are you?" she had asked.

All he could think to say was to repeat her question back at her.

"I asked you first," she replied, a slight smile appearing on her lips.

"Jason," he answered. "My name is Jason and I don't know why I'm here."

What followed was three weeks of Melissa's daily visits. Turns out she had just been exploring that day, walking the corridors, bored out of her mind, when she wandered into what she called Raven's, "Guest Wing." She had not expected to find anyone, but there was Jason.

She kept coming back not out of kindness in her heart, which was in short supply, but because something about Jason fascinated her. He was the same age as her, and yet he carried none of the burdens she did. No one had hurt him until now, with the exception of his brother's death and father's absence. He had spent his whole life reading books and watching TV and dreaming of the future. Even now, he still looked at the world with wonder. He was a rarity these days, and Melissa envied him.

When she looked at him and then looked at herself in the mirror...she couldn't help but feel a kind of shame.

She remembered that first conversation. She had introduced herself as Melissa Lunar Moonbeam. Her parents were hippies, she added as her token disclaimer. The two of them had shared a laugh about their equally unusual names. She was Raven's bodyguard. One of them, she said. Raven had a small army of men around him most of the time, but Melissa was special. She was different. Melissa never fully explained how, but she did dispel his fears by saying that it was nothing of the sexual sort.

"I wouldn't touch that little runt with a ten foot pole," she had exclaimed, and then they both looked at Melissa's staff, and shared a laugh.

"Ok, maybe I would."

The staff was Melissa's favorite weapon, though she didn't get to use it as often as she wanted to. It would be awkward to carry such a weapon to dinner parties and press conferences.

"I don't really need it," she had said. "But you should see how many teeth this thing has knocked out."

"Why are you still working for him?" Jason had asked, "You don't seem like you want to."

Melissa shrugged. "You should see my apartment," she said, as if that were explanation enough.

She didn't know where the rest of Jason's family was. Bernice wasn't in the same part of the building as Jason, and Melissa had never come across her during her other explorations of the place. She hadn't heard anything about Colin, though she admitted that most of Raven's business was a secret to her.

"I just walk the walk and talk the talk," she told him, shaking her stick for emphasis. Jason was afraid to see what Melissa's idea of "talk" was.

And then she promised to get him out.

"I'll find a way," she told him. "That slimy little jerk can't get away with holding someone like you against your will, for God knows what reason."

Someone like you. She caught the words as they came out of her mouth, and she also caught the small smile on his face as she said them.

So Melissa was his hope. She was his ticket out of here, and she had accepted the secret responsibility whole-heartedly.

The conversations they had shared had not only been about his capture or about how much they hated Raven. Melissa had asked him once what Jason did for fun.

"You know...before," she had said.

So he told her. For two hours he went on and one about the constellations; about Ursa Minor and Orion's Belt, about solar flares and white dwarfs. As he talked about the passion he had nearly forgotten, Melissa felt something within herself; a yearning to feel so strongly about something the way he did.

"So what do you do?" Jason asked her after he had finally decided to make himself stop going on about the stars and his dreams of going to college and being an architect so he could design a planetarium and how he one day wanted to study anthropology among the tribes of New Guinea.

The light seemed to fade from Melissa's eyes. She shook her head and looked at the floor.

"I don't know...stuff."

In that one moment of vulnerability, when Melissa couldn't reproduce the passion that Jason had just displayed, she unintentionally showed him a bit of who she really was. How lonely she was. How lost she was. That was why she spent hours sitting on the other side of that Plexiglas wall every day. He was, in reality, her only friend.

She wasn't going to let that feeling go. Not for all of Raven's money. Not for anything; which made what she had to say right now that much harder.

"I can't see you anymore, Jason," Melissa said, leaning forward to get as close as she could with that Plexiglass between them.

She could almost see his heart sink.

"Why?"

"Because I think he'll kill me if I do," Melissa exclaimed. She knew he could see the anger burning in her eyes.

"I bribed one of the guards tp let me in here to say goodbye."

Melissa knew word would get back to Raven. In fact, she knew about the cameras, thankfully devoid of audio. She also knew the brute she had bribed would tell Raven why she had come, and she hoped her story of saying goodbye to her friend would be enough to placate him.

Jason's eyes turned to the window over his shoulder. She could tell he was fighting back tears of disappointment and anger at losing his only ray of hope in his place.

"But..." Melissa said softly, a smile forming at the corner of her mouth. Jason turned back to her and she saw his eyes widen in anticipation, "Raven doesn't know everything."

"Is it time?" Jason asked, referring to the vague escape plan he and Melissa had talked about several times before.

"Not yet; but soon. Maybe in another week. There's been talk of a company-wide move. That might be the perfect time."

Jason nodded. She had shared a plan with him last week. It was simple, and it was dependent on whether or not Raven decided to move him at some point, but she thought it might work.

"Have you found my mom yet?" Jason asked.

Melissa shook her head. "No. I'm sorry, Jason. I even got someone to dig around his files for me. She's not in them. Nor does anyone know why you're here."

"Then let's not stay here long enough to find out," Jason replied.

Melissa smiled at the notion of them escaping together, as if they were both prisoners. She thought that in a way it was true.

"I've got to go," Melissa pointed at the camera facing the cell in the hallway. "Big Brother is watching."

"I told you there's no audio," Jason told her. The small camera didn't have the proper microphone sensors on it. At the time she had made fun of him and called him a nerd for knowing that. Now she was simply grateful.

"All the same.... If we're going to make this work, I have to pretend to play by his rules for now." She looked him in the eyes, her anger replaced with excitement. The thrill of the plot. Not to mention the upcoming fight.

She put her hand up against the glass. He placed his on the other side. His heart ached a little at the thought that he might not see her again for a while.

"Hope you like pancakes, Jason, 'cause that's all I know how to cook," Melissa said, and then got up to walk off.

Jason sat back again, this time wearing a grin from ear to ear.

As she walked away, she felt her whole body tingle with excitement and fear. She wasn't afraid of Raven's thugs. She wasn't afraid of Raven himself. No...it was the prospect of not being alone that scared the hell out of her. The prospect of inviting someone in.

5

A day and a whole bag of beef jerky later, Nick and Blitz sat at the foot of a big tree, ready to retire for the night. The view in front of them was now completely dominated by the setting sun permeating and reflecting off the Atlanta skyline. The sounds of nature were quickly being replaced by the rush of cars along Highway 78; people heading into and out of the city, carrying on their daily lives with memories and comforts they had no idea they were so lucky to have.

Nick, with no memories, no comforts, and soon no food, watched those buildings in the distance as the last hint of the day's sunlight played against the glass and steel.

He was almost there.

He had to assume that his Pull would end somewhere downtown. The sprawling city seemed like the perfect end to a road, whatever the truth of Nick's particular road might be. His home could be there. His family could be there. Surely at least he would find someone who recognized him.

He turned to Blitz and smiled as his friend ate one of their last sticks of jerky.

"Enjoy that, kiddo. Pretty soon it'll be the end of it. Hopefully I'll find wherever home is and you and I can finally have a real meal; with Mom and Dad or...whoever."

As he said this, Nick felt another twinge of pain in his heart. He believed he knew that, whatever he would find there, it would probably not be his parents. He had a sense that they would not be searching for him as he was for them. That was perhaps one reason he had been traveling alone through the woods to begin with.

Letting those emotions pass, Nick watched the dog contentedly. Blitz hadn't left his side since his escape from his abusive owner. He supposed that this life, no matter how rough, must be whole worlds better than what Blitz had come from. Food was scarce and the travel was constant, but at least the dog didn't have a boot heel to look forward to several times a day; or a shotgun barrel for that matter.

It was good not to be alone, Nick realized. Perhaps he had his comforts after all.

Blitz suddenly looked up. His ears rose and his attention turned to something beyond Nick.

27

"What's up? I wouldn't have thought hell or high water could turn you away from...."

Nick noticed something. A reflection in the dog's eye. Fire.

He spun around and saw the twinkle of flames a couple of hundred yards away; a small house sitting apart from the nearest subdivision, from the look of it. Nick heard yelling from that direction; a woman screaming at the top of her lungs.

Blitz watched as his friend ran off in the direction of the blaze. The dog decided to stay where he was.

"Jamie! Oh dear god, my Jamie!" the woman screamed, her eyes wide and her hands clenched tightly into her nightgown.

"Momma!" a diminutive reply cried from the second story window of the burning house. The flames had nearly engulfed the first floor, and it would only be a matter of minutes before the second floor would be a raging inferno.

"Jamie!" the woman shrieked again, heading back towards the front porch. She took two steps up the stairs and then halted as half of the overhang collapsed in front of her. There would be no going back in that way.

Mortal terror filled her heart. Not only because her seven year old son was about to die a horrible death, but because it might have been her fault. She had left the gas oven on again, and this time hadn't caught it before disaster struck. A candle left burning on her coffee table had ignited the entire living room. She had only escaped because she had been in the bathroom and managed to crawl out the window.

Jamie could get out that way as well, but she knew her son would be too scared to do it. Jamie was the kind of boy that wouldn't walk from one end of the supermarket to the other without holding her hand.

"Climb out the window, Jamie!" she pleaded with him anyway.

"I can't, Momma. It's too high and there's fire on the roof!"

He was right. There was fire on what was left of the porch awning. There was enough room for him to make it out unharmed, but that literal window of opportunity would be gone in seconds. The fire was spreading too fast.

She slumped to the ground and began weeping. She listened desperately for sirens approaching, but heard nothing. This was a slum on the outskirts of Atlanta, and emergency services were notoriously slow to make their way to the poorest neighborhoods, when they came at all.

She heard nothing until the sound of rapid footsteps approached her from behind.

28

A dark shape sped past her at unbelievable speed. It then jumped fifteen feet from the ground to the roof of the porch and leaped through Jamie's window.

It was a man, she realized. She didn't know how it was possible, but that thing had been a man.

Nick didn't think about the fire. He didn't think about how high the jump was. He didn't think about how he was going to get back out. All he thought about was that boy, and that mother sitting helplessly on the dirt behind him. He was through the window almost before he could realize what he was doing.

The little boy gasped as Nick stood there, one leg on the window sill and the other inside the room, his hand outstretched and his green-brown eyes locked on the boy's.

Jamie looked at those eyes, and suddenly realized he had nothing to fear. A smile crossed the little boy's face.

"Are you Batman?"

Nick smiled back. "Sure. Want to be Robin?"

Her eyes didn't leave the window. The fire would soon cover it from view, but she didn't care. Someone had come to save her boy. A miracle was occurring right in front of her.

The man emerged holding her son. Jamie, amazingly, had a wide grin on his face. The man jumped without hesitation, through the fire, through the air, and onto the dirt in front of her some twenty feet away from the window.

Jamie squealed with laughter. "Momma, look! I got saved by a superhero!"

She took her son from the man before taking the opportunity to examine her son's strange savior.

The first thing she noticed was that he was more a boy than a man; in his late teens or early twenties from the look of it. His dark brown hair hung a bit in his face and his sharp green eyes looked at her with a stunning sincerity. Eyes that peered out above something. A black strip of cloth covering his nose and mouth.

A mask. The man was wearing a mask.

Even stranger still was that she could see the handle of a sword strapped to his thin frame. A curved blade like the ancient Japanese had used, or so she remembered from that Tom Cruise movie a few years back.

"Who are you?" she asked, her voice almost trembling, knowing she should be afraid of this bizarre character in front of her, but instead feeling only a kind of grateful awe.

29

The boy seemed thrown off by the question. His brow furrowed above his mask and he took a step back from them.

"Just…just a concerned passerby," he replied.

"Well thank you, stranger. You saved my son's life. I don't know how I can repay you."

The boy shook his head and looked at Jamie. "Just hold onto him. Hold onto him and remind him…every day…that he has someone that loves him."

She took in the curious response, and then heard the sudden flare of approaching sirens. Fire trucks that would have been too little too late to save her son had the stranger not appeared. The thought threatened to fill her with dread for a moment before subsiding with the satisfied knowledge that a terrible fate had been averted thanks to this stranger.

He heard them too, and began to walk away, back towards the woods he had apparently come from.

"Don't go. You're a hero. Don't you want credit for what you did?" she called after him.

The boy shook his head again after he turned to look at her one last time.

"No. All I want from this is what I'm looking at right now," he said, raising a hand to motion towards her and Jamie, who was still grinning ear to ear and watching his savior like a hawk.

Then he turned again and began running. In moments he was gone. Her heart slowed down a bit, but she kept staring in the direction the boy had vanished. By the time the firemen had arrived, she had forgotten about the blaze behind her.

"Are you ok, Miss? What happened?" one of the firemen asked her as the others began to battle the blaze.

She turned to him, and he was visibly surprised when he saw the smiles on both her and her little boy's faces.

"Well, Mister…have I got a story to tell you."

6

A few short miles from the spot where Nick had just gained his first spark of celebrity, a strange ceremony was taking place in the attic of an old two story house.

Five men stood in a circle, their arms raised and their faces mostly shrouded by hooded robes. One man spoke, reciting unearthly passages very few scholars would be able to decipher.

An arcane symbol was drawn on the floor. Its eight points joining a circle painted on the old wooden boards. The symbol and the circle surrounding it were a deep crimson red. Candles lay at the eight bisected points.

In the middle of this circle, in the spot the five men were surrounding, was a table. On that table was a man-shaped figure made of bronze; a mannequin, faceless and unliving.

The speaking man broke his chant, and then lowered his arms in unison with the other four men. He then spoke in English.

"Bring your wrath upon our enemy, oh dark powers. Engulf his arrogance in your flame. Bring us glory through your servant, and reward us for our obedience."

He stared at the figure on the table. His eyes and the eyes of the four other men were filled with expectation.

A moment of silence passed, and then another moment. One of the men began to shuffle.

"It didn't work," a second, portly man muttered, "It didn't…"

Then the room shook. Their summons had been answered.

The men gasped as the thing on the table sat up.

"I…I command you in the name of your lord," the leader stammered.

The creature ignored him. It looked at its new hands. Its shapeless face was reflected back at it in the polished bronze. It seemed to concentrate on the reflection, and features began to emerge.

The men watched in horror as the monster's fingers grew. Sharp points like knives formed on each of the five digits, and then they continued to grow…and grow…and grow until each hand was covered in sword-length claws.

Its feet morphed into talons; three toes, two in the front, one in the back formed from the metal.

Its face then began to change. The sides of its head began to curve back sharply, almost to the form of bat ears. A mouth began to form, rowed with sharp teeth, each several inches long. Two eyes, almond shaped slits, opened up above the mouth.

Each of the men questioned the wisdom of their actions when the thing's eyes burst into flame. Purple flame. Its mouth widened into a sickening grin, and they could see the fire burn within its maw as well.

The animated shell stood up, its body widening and forming the appearance of thick muscles. The terrifying visage was complete. No man could question that this thing before them was a creature born from nightmares.

"I...I command you," the leader tried again, this time pointing at the circle beneath them. "You cannot cross this boundary unless I allow it. We have a job for you, and when it is done you may return to the depths from which you came."

It looked around, letting its gaze settle on each of the men. They quaked where they stood, but each stood his ground...at least until the creature reached the last one; a diminutive man with sweat coursing down his hooded brow. As the monster's eyes met his, the man whimpered, and took a step back.

The creature looked at the ground and noticed that the man's shoe had erased part of the circle.

As simple as that, it was free.

The leader of the cultists opened his mouth to command the beast yet again, but before he could say a word, a shower of blood hit him as one of his comrades was sliced in half.

The monster spun around with a violent force and decapitated a second man.

The two others attempted to run, but the thing was on them in a fraction of an instant. It simultaneously impaled one through the back of his throat while severing the spine of the second.

The creature grinned, looking down at its new deadly hands with malicious glee.

The leader stood frozen, covered in the blood and gore of the others. The monster turned to him and approached.

"You were supposed to be...ours," he said, his eyes wide and his voice failing him.

The monster just looked at him with that maddening smile. It raised a bladed hand and gently placed a finger against the man's forehead.

The man looked up for a moment, the closed his eyes and began to weep.

"Forgive me, God. I didn't know."

32

The creature then pushed its finger through the man's skull, and the cultist knew no more.

As the body slumped through the floor, the monster removed its finger. It was as if slicing a knife through butter. It turned and scanned the room, locating a television in the corner. It ran towards it and swiped its hand through the air.

The television then lay in two pieces on the floor. Its hard surface had offered no resistance whatsoever.

The thing looked again at the deadly new toys that adorned its hands, and let out a raspy, inhuman laugh.

The animate bronze monster looked up, crouched for an instant, and then jumped straight up, into the roof and through it, landing with a thump on the shingles above.

It gazed through the night air, spread his arms wide, and roared joyfully. For a mile surrounding that house, every living animal suddenly fell into silence. Babies wept in their cribs and the winter air grew colder still, for The Whisper had returned.

The creature scanned its surroundings, its chest rising and falling not for the need to breathe, but simply out of pure exhilaration.

Its eyes caught something; a fire in the distance. Something there hooked its senses. Something familiar.

"The boy," the monster spoke quietly into the night air, its warped, whispering voice coming not from its mouth but simply from the ether around it.

It jumped from the building, creating a huge crater in the pavement below. Then it was running, carving through trees, fences, and anything else that got in his path.

When it came to a highway, the beast did not slow. It leaped from the bank overlooking the road and landed directly on top of a speeding car. The monster jumped off, slashing the roof with its claws as it went. It could hear the vehicle fishtail and smash into another car behind it. The monster began to run, straight towards an eighteen wheel truck moving at a steady pace in the left-hand lane.

The monster's pace grew, its speed increased. It easily caught up to the truck, ran beside it…and the charged directly into and through the cab, slashing steel and iron as it went, landing at a run on the other side. The truck capsized behind it, slid several hundred feet, and then exploded.

The beast continued to run as the flames licked behind it, sometimes dodging cars, other times plowing right through them. It grinned wider. Finally it had a form once more. Finally it had hands with which to grasp and a shell with which to hold its malice. Yes, thought the beast, now was the time.

This is what it lived for.
This is what it existed to do
The hunt was on.

7

Jacob Raven stood over the sobbing form of a young man in a dark room. The man was wearing a plain brown outfit akin to hospital scrubs, a set of plain khaki pants and shirt with no shoes. The room was barren. The only light in the room was from a stage lamp Raven's man had brought in, directed solely upon the boy.

Raven himself was wearing rubber gloves, rubber shoes and an apron over his nice clothes. His business here had been messy. He took one glove off and threw it at the boy, then another before taking a step back.

"You disappoint me, Phillip," he said to the sobbing young man, "I wanted so much more for you. With your family gone and your old life behind you, I gave you the tools to shape yourself into something new; something beautiful!" Raven guestured in the air, thrusting his arms up as if in reverence to what could have been.

"I came in here to punish you," Raven continued, careful not to step in the pool of blood that had formed next to an overturned chair in the center of the room, "To punish you and in doing so give you one last chance to burst out of your shell and be the strong, violent, powerful man I want you to be."

Raven dropped his arms and sighed, shaking his head in disappointment.

"But instead," he gestured towards the boy, "you're still...this."

The boy cradled his bruised and bloody head in his hands, weeping softly and rocking back and forth on the floor.

"So if you won't be strong, Philip," Raven said, pulling a 9mm handgun from his waistband beneath the apron, "Then what use are you to me?"

Raven raised the gun, but then froze. He felt something. A new presence in the room. They were not alone.

"May I have the pleasure?" came a voice from a shadowed corner.

Raven lowered the gun.

"Yes, but please stop scaring me like that."

A tall man dressed in black stepped out into the edge of the light. He wore a dark suit with a black shirt and tie beneath it. His hair was salt-and-pepper black. His eyes were brown. For now.

"I knew you would fail, Philip," The Dark Man said, and then raised his hand into the air.

As he did so, something terrible occurred. Philip, still crouched on the floor, suddenly jerked up as if yanked to his knees. As the dark man's hand continued to rise, Philip was pulled to his feet. Higher the hand went, and soon Philip was no longer on his feet, but hovering inches above the ground clawing at his neck, his horrified eyes bulging.

"And…" The Dark Man said.

His wrist twisted suddenly to the right. There was a loud cracking sound in the room, as if someone had pulled a limb from a tree. Phillip spasmed for a moment, then was still.

"…one less thing to worry about," The Dark Man finished.

Raven watched as the boy crumpled to the floor. He felt a shudder threaten to run through him. He denied it, instead looking at his advisor, who looked entirely too pleased with himself.

"Really, Jacob, this hobby of yours is getting old," The Dark Man said condescendingly.

"It won't end until one of them passes the test," Raven said, pulling off the apron and tossing it to the floor. He looked at the boy's body in disgust.

"What makes you think one of them will?"

Raven thought for a moment.

"I just haven't found the right one," he said, determination in his voice.

"At least try a girl next time. Why do they have to all be boys?" The Dark Man asked.

Raven was getting tired of his mentor's tone.

"What do you want?"

The Dark Man's arms crossed over his chest. Raven noticed two things at that moment. One was that something serious was on his friend's mind. The other was that his eyes were now green.

Raven never failed to find that unsettling.

"Something has happened," The Dark Man said, "Something has changed in this city. I felt the threads being pulled two days ago. Hard. Then again tonight. Something is tugging at the fabric of reality. Something powerful."

Raven's eyes widened.

"Are you suggesting…."

"I don't know," The Dark Man interrupted, "But I think we need to start putting things into motion."

Raven was stunned. His advisor had never talked like this before. He had almost expected the man's premonitions and prophecies to be nothing but the dreams of the mad.

"What should I do?" Raven asked meekly.

"Watch the news. Listen to your ears on the streets. Look for things to start happening; extraordinary things, for good or ill."

He approached Jacob, standing several inches above him. Raven could feel the strange dark power emanating from the man.

"There will be one who will rise above. Man or woman, I do not know. Whoever they are, we need them. When you know who they are, bring all of your forces to bear to bring them to me."

"And where will you be?" Raven asked.

The Dark Man turned, "I'll be in touch," he said, before walking back to the shadowed corner he appeared from.

Raven watched the man disappear into the darkness. He watched the corner for several seconds before he realized that his visitor was gone. Raven was alone in the room once more.

This time he did shudder.

A moment later Raven walked out of the room, slamming the door behind him.

"Clean it up," he told the guard sitting at a desk outside. The man shot to his feet.

"Yes sir," he said, quickly entering the room behind Jacob.

Raven walked past the man's desk, his mind whirling, only barely hearing the news report on the small television on the guard's desk.

He took two more steps, and then froze.

Raven whipped around, sliding into the guard's chair and starting at the television.

"He was like some kind of superhero," the black woman being interviewed said, holding a child, "Normal people don't wear masks and normal people don't jump over flames twenty feet high to rescue little boys. No...this young man was something more, and I owe him my son's life."

Raven's fingers gripped the arms of the chair tightly.

8

Melissa marched down the hall, aggravated that she had been placed on escort duty. She had arrived and been told by the executive staff handler that she was to accompany some kind of military tracking specialist and his aide this afternoon.

Just what she needed, babysitting duty in the middle of one of the most stressful periods of her recent life. Her mind was completely occupied with how to free Jason and then get the two of them safely away from Raven. Truth was, she knew her plan was underdeveloped, and even with her considerable skill she was afraid that such a task might be beyond her. Nevertheless, she had to try. Jason's life might depend on it.

She entered the room at the end of the corridor to see a stuffy, crew-cutted middle-aged man in what looked like an officer's uniform, complete with decorations. Next to him was a young woman with black hair pulled back into a pony-tail. Her skin was fair, her eyes brown and she was dressed a bit more casually in slacks and a white blouse.

"You must be…," Melissa said, extending a hand in greeting.

"First Sergeant William Cross. United States Air Force," the man replied gruffly, firmly shaking Melissa's hand. He seemed to look her up and down as he did so. Melissa thought he looked disappointed.

"Expecting Raven himself?" Melissa asked.

"No Miss," Sergeant Cross said, "But I did expect someone a bit more…professional."

Melissa looked down at herself, still holding his hand. She was wearing a grey gym shirt and black sweatpants, her usually "around the office" attire. In other words, her "I don't give a damn about appearances" attire.

"Yeah, well it's always been my philosophy that only small men dress big, Mister Cross," she replied sharply, squeezing his hand just enough to make him grimace.

"It's Sergeant Cross, Miss Moonbeam," Cross returned through gritted teeth.

Great, Melissa thought; making friends already. She turned to the girl just in time to see her stifle a laugh.

"So is this your granddaughter?" Melissa asked, releasing his hand.

Sergeant Cross glared at her a moment before answering.

"My daughter, actually. Introduce yourself, Stacy."

Stacy cocked a smile and waved enthusiastically.

"Moonbeam. What an awesome name" Stacy said.

Melissa liked this one much more than her old man.

"Thanks hon. You always follow your dad around on Fridays?"

"Stacy is my aide-de-camp," the man answered for his daughter.

"Your aide-de-what?" Melissa asked, feigning confusion.

This time Stacy did giggle. Cross directed his glare towards her.

"Relax, chief. I'm just messing with you. You and Giggles here can come with me."

"Wonderful," Cross said sarcastically, shooting a disapproving look at his daughter one more time before the two of them followed Melissa down the hallway towards Raven's monitoring station.

An hour later, Melissa was sitting in a chair in the back of the monitoring station watching Sergeant Cross go over video feeds from around the city. Melissa hadn't been briefed on what exactly Cross would be looking for, and she had to admit she was more than curious. Raven rarely contracted outside help, and to bring in a military specialist simply to look for someone, or at least she assumed it was a someone, signified an act of desperation on Raven's part.

"Any idea what your dad's looking for?" Melissa asked, leaning over and whispering in Stacy's ear.

"Nope," Stacy shook her head. She was laying out some papers from her father's briefcase on a side desk, "I'm guessing it's some kind of criminal. Serial killer or bank robber or something like that. That's usually what he gets called in for, to find a bad guy."

Melissa crossed her arms. There was no way it was that simple. Raven wouldn't bother with a simple criminal, even a serial killer. The safety of the people in the city mattered little to him, and he was doing less and less to hide it these days. No one looked to Raven for protection, for good reason.

"So you're his bodyguard?" Stacy asked.

"Basically," Melissa answered.

"You must be pretty tough to guard the most powerful man in America."

Melissa shrugged, "I do kick ass; it's true."

Stacy flashed a smile.

"But don't let Raven fool you," Melissa went on, "He's just a little chump with a big ego."

Stacy looked surprised.

"How do you keep your job with an attitude like that?"

Now Melissa smiled.

"Because I kick ass, remember?"

Stacy laughed quietly and shook her head.

"So you can still laugh after following Mr. Grumpy Pants around all day?" Melissa asked her.

Stacy's smile faded a bit. Now she shrugged.

"He's my dad. He's not all bad. He taught my sister and I how to shoot. How to fly."

"Fly?" Melissa exclaimed.

"Yeah," Stacy nodded, "I'm the one that flew the chopper that brought us here."

Melissa was impressed.

"So you carry a weapon?" she asked Stacy. Since the Peace and Disarmament Act, guns were rare.

"Not a gun, and not openly. I only target shoot. Crossbow," Stacy answered.

"Cool. Haven't seen one of those in years."

"Most people haven't," she went on, "Which is why I decided to pick it up. Good way to let off steam."

Melissa smiled.

"I know what you mean."

Melissa was impressed with herself. Two allies in as many weeks. She was on a roll.

9

Nick sat on a bench in Centennial Olympic Park, his knees folded up in front of him and a newspaper propped up on his thighs.

"Masked hero rescues boy from burning building," Nick read. "In a scene that seemed straight from a comic book, seven year old Jamie Young was snatched from the jaws of death when a masked stranger jumped through the second story window of his Decatur home last night after the house had burst into flames. The cause of the fire is still under investigation, though authorities are claiming it an accident at this time."

Nick paused.

"Masked?"

He hadn't been wearing a mask. Had he?

He read on. "The hero came out of nowhere, said the grateful mother. He had a black mask on his face and a sword strapped to his...."

Nick's heart almost stopped. Had he brought the sword with him? He had no recollection of "strapping on" the weapon, which still didn't even have a sheath, nor of putting on any mask. All he remembered doing was simply running towards the fire.

He put the paper down, frustrated by the lack of information about the boy's condition and over-emphasis on the so called, "Masked Hero." His mind whirled. He supposed he might have wrapped something around his face to keep from breathing in the smoke, but if so, why didn't he remember it? And how could he have forgotten bringing the sword with him? Why on earth would he have thought he would have needed it?

Distress filled him. There was something more going on than simple memory loss. Who was he? Had he been trained to do those things?

Nick shook his head, and decided it wasn't worth worrying about at the moment. He had more pressing things to concern him, like where Blitz had disappeared to, and why his Pull wasn't giving him a specific place to go.

When he had returned to their camp after saving the boy last night, Nick had discovered his furry friend was gone. He had looked around for him and called him for the better part of an hour, but the dog seemed to have wandered off with no intention of returning. Perhaps the fire had scared him, or perhaps he had simply gone off in hopes of finding better food. Either way, Nick was greatly disappointed.

He had awoken early today and walked those last few miles into the city proper, hoping with every step that his memories would return when he got there. He passed one tall building, then another, and then passed three huge hotels and still nothing. His Pull was now flailing in all directions at once. It was as if he was where he needed to be, but even his instincts didn't know what to do then.

He did have to admit however that it was a comfort to be among other people. Those few days in the wilderness and outer city perimeter had left him feeling quite alone, despite Blitz's presence. Having no memories and no idea if anyone would be waiting for him only compounded the problem. The people in the park paid him no mind, but he was still relieved to be surrounded by them.

So Nick found a bench, plopped himself down, and had been sitting here for the past three hours, trying in vain to think of what to do next. He supposed he could always check himself into a hospital citing amnesia, but something told him that wouldn't be the right thing to do. Whatever it was he was looking for, he had to find it himself.

And it was maddeningly close. Whatever or whoever it was, it had to be nearby.

Nick got up, slung his things over his shoulder, and decided to wander the streets until he felt something familiar.

Eight hours later, Nick was no closer to the source of The Pull. He recognized streets and the names of buildings. Restaurants he had a sense he had eaten at before. A run-down aquarium that his instincts told him he had never had the pleasure to visit. But nothing carried the ring of "home" to it. Nothing felt any more familiar than anything else. No person he passed on the street seemed like family. No car he saw drive by felt like one he knew. He was lost, just as sure as if he had never been here before in his life.

He wondered if perhaps he hadn't been homeless to begin with; maybe headed towards Atlanta simply to find a better place to scavenge before…whatever happened to him.

That didn't feel right though. He definitely had a sense that there was something specific he was looking for. He would just have to keep looking until he found it.

It was getting late, and Nick supposed he had better find a place to crash for the night. Perhaps he would have better luck in the morning. Or perhaps that hospital would sound more appealing. He spied a dead-end alley between two hotels with a dumpster and a pile of discarded newspapers. It was as good a place as any to curl up and wait for sunrise.

Nick had noticed a lack of police on the streets, and an over-abundance of homeless and what looked like roaming street gangs. Atlanta was getting worse, that much was certain. In another five years or so, the city would pretty much be reduced to the order of RavenCorp…and the chaos of everything else. Atlanta may be the source of it, but the general lack of effort from those in authority had infected the country. Guns or no guns, the streets were a dangerous place.

He reached the end of the alley and placed his things on the cold hard ground. Before he even had time to think of how he was to sleep on the bare concrete however, he heard two sets of footsteps approaching behind him. He turned and saw a pair of young men, clean cut and wearing designer jeans. Frat boys out for a night on the town, he sensed. One of them was holding a baseball bat. Nick suddenly began to wonder if he had picked the wrong alleyway.

"Look at this, Jimbo. I think we found our first bum of the evening," said the one whose hands appeared to be empty. He wore a baseball cap and a thick jacket with a falcon and the number 18 on it. Football player, Nick thought. Great.

"He's just a kid," said the one with the bat. "Probably a fag, though."

The one in the cap nodded. "Definitely a fag. Look at the hair."

He reached into his pocket and pulled out a small object. He pressed a button on it and a six inch blade popped into view.

"Let's show this fag what we do to homos around here."

The boy started towards Nick.

"Leave me alone," Nick said, reaching down towards his long canvas bag.

"Sure I'll leave you alone, homo. After I put a few scars on your pretty face," the boy said, and then took a few more quick steps and swiped the knife at Nick.

Nick's sword was in his hand by the time the boy had taken another breath.

He caught the hand holding the knife in his left hand, then in one quick motion pulled the boy towards him, meeting the boy's face with his right elbow. The surprised young man's head rocked back violently. His knees buckled beneath him and he was out like a light.

Nick looked down at the boy, amazed at what he had just done and how quickly he had done it. His motions had been ninety percent instinct and ten percent fear.

The other boy stared at his fallen friend for a minute, and then turned hateful eyes towards Nick.

"You're going to pay for that, faggot" he said, before holding the bat above his head and charging.

Nick braced himself, as nervous about what he might do as he was about the threat of the bat.

The attacker did not get far however, for before he took a second step, Nick watched him jerk suddenly and seem to be yanked back, as if he had reached the end of an invisible cord.

The boy seemed confused for a moment. His eyes went wide and the bat dropped to the concrete with a clunk. His arms went limp and his eyes rolled back in his head.

Nick took a step forward out of concern. That concern was soon replaced with horror when he saw a three and a half foot long bronze blade erupt from the boy's chest, followed by a spray of blood.

A massive figure rose up from behind the boy, and as it rose, the boy's body was lifted into the air. Nick watched helplessly as a second blade emerged beside the first.

Nick couldn't move. What he was witnessing could not be real.

The two blades were whipped apart with violent speed. The boy's bottom half flew against one wall of the alley, and his top half bounced into the other, slumping to the ground with a wet thump.

Blood was everywhere. Nick's jaw hung open and he began breathing heavily, his senses reeling from the mind-numbing display of terror that had just taken place in front of him.

H then looked up at the boy's murderer, and his breathing stopped altogether.

A metal monster towered above him at the entrance to the alleyway. Six and a half feet tall at least, its broad shoulders nearly half that width. At the end of each arm were five long blades, each at least the length of his own sword, each appearing to be razor sharp.

Its face was a leering demon visage sporting a jack-o-lantern grin. Its eyes peered at him. No pupils nor irises nor human anatomy altogether was visible in those eyes. Only purple fire.

Purple fire

Nick breathed in sharply and took a step back. The familiar assailant sprang into action and flew towards Nick. He barely had enough time to raise his sword and block the thing's bladed hand a moment before it had cleaved into his skull.

The monster paused for a moment and looked at the sword, as if in confusion, then it battered it away with its other hand. Nick attempted to raise his weapon back up, but the thing was too fast. It picked him up and charged like a rhino towards the back wall of the alley, slamming him roughly into the brick. Nick grimaced in pain, and opened his eyes to see the monster's purple glare inches from his own. A finger pierced the brick on either side of his neck, pinning him in place.

He looked into those eyes. Those eyes that he knew. It had been one of the few memories he had woken up with. Purple fire. The thing that had attacked him in the woods. The thing whose Whisper he could almost still hear.

Nick remembered. It hadn't just attacked him. It had been…inside of him. Inside of his head and whispering things. Horrible, unspeakable things.

"You…the Whisper…. You did this to me. You make me forget."

The monster watched him. It seemed to study him and take in his words. Something Nick had said had made it pause. Instead of tearing his head off it now seemed to be…thinking.

And no, Nick wasn't certain that this thing had been responsible for erasing his memories. In fact, he seemed to remember defeating it. And it had been doing much more than attempting to steal his past.

It had been trying to eat him. Eat him from the inside of his soul.

The monster let out a sound that Nick could only describe as frustration. It pulled its hands away from the wall, allowing him to slump to the ground.

Nick sat there, feeling as helpless as a fawn being pounced on by a wolf. The thing watched him for a moment. Its metal visage had somehow transformed into a scowl, but as Nick watched, that terrible smile returned to its face. That smile spoke volumes to Nick. As it looked at him, Nick heard a voice inside his head. The words were discordant and distorted, as if from a machine missing proper human inflection, and their whispered tone was all too familiar.

"You are not like the others. You are strong. You are,"

The monster leaned closer to Nick's face.

"…mine."

The demon, for that's what Nick believed it must be, seemed satisfied enough at its victim's recognition. In the span of a second it turned from him, darted up the brick wall of the alleyway, and then disappeared into the darkness, leaving a raspy, inhuman laugh behind it.

Nick would remember that laugh for the rest of his life.

47

10

Nick watched the dance of the police lights reflected off the brick and concrete buildings two blocks away. His vantage point from the roof he now sat on offered him no clear view of the alley below. He preferred it that way, for the only thing to see there would be a young man lying in two pieces on the asphalt surrounded by a swarm of police.

He assumed the other boy had been taken to a hospital, where he would no doubt wake up and tell someone he had been attacked by a skinny homeless kid. That same skinny homeless kid would be the prime suspect in the murder of his friend. Nick wasn't sure if the first attacker had enough time to see the sword before Nick had knocked him out cold. If he had, the police would have a suspected murder weapon, for after all, the demon's blades had been shaped just like Nick's sword.

A demon. Was he even sure that's what it was? True, the thing seemed to have no eyes nor face beneath that bronze helmet; just a constantly moving mass of fire. Fire that was a color no fire on earth should be.

Then there was the laugh. Part machine, part child, part raving lunatic. Again, nothing that nature could ever duplicate, as far as Nick knew.

Nick seemed to have had a small sense of communion with the thing, that Whisper from his memories, as it had pinned him to the wall and stared into his eyes. He had a sense of what it was thinking. He had a sense that it wanted to hurt him, but also that it craved the pleasure of his fear.

But that wasn't all. The demon had been nearly as confused as Nick had. Something about the encounter had startled it. Something about Nick's sword, and about Nick himself. Like it had expected him to be someone, or something else.

Nick lay down on the rooftop, his arms spread wide, staring into the stars above.

"Who the hell am I?" he spoke to the night air.

Who carries a sword around? Who puts on a mask to save a little boy? Who runs up walls and fire escapes and rooftops without giving it a second thought? And who gets stalked by monsters?

"No one normal," he said, gripping that strange sword in his right hand, feeling the oddly comforting weight of it like the weight of his own mysterious and apparently deadly importance pressing in on him.

"No one safe to be around."

What if his Pull was something more than simple subconscious memory? What if he had been programmed by someone to go and carry out some horrible task here in the city?

Nick sat up, his face wearing a look of concern and discomfort. Suddenly he felt very uneasy in his own skin. Suddenly he felt very unstable…and very alone.

"Maybe I should run from this," he spoke to himself. "Maybe I should go back into the woods, get as far away from everyone else as possible, and wait for that thing to come back for me."

He looked up at the stars. His heart ached still with the desire for a home and for a place to belong and people to belong with. But it ached also with the guilt of possibly being something…dangerous.

"Maybe the best thing to do would just be to run away."

"No."

Nick's breath caught in his chest. He spun around at the sound of the voice, not knowing whether to expect the demon or another person or simply nothing at all.

Instead what greeted his eyes was a little girl; small, in a red and brown dress with black tennis shoes. One white sock pulled higher than the other. Her hair was long and golden blonde and her eyes were blue and vibrant. She seemed to stare at him without blinking.

Nick calmed a bit, but also realized that he was still frightened. Something about the little girl's presence was…intimidating; and familiar; like an echo of a distant memory.

"Who are you?" he asked in a quiet voice.

"Familiar question, isn't it?" the girl replied. "You've been asking yourself that since you woke up."

Nick tilted his head in a questioning look. "You know me?"

But then he remembered the voice that had spoken to him in the forest. The first sound he remembered hearing. The one that had told him to…

"Wake up," she said, as if reading his mind.

Nick had a sense she had done just that.

"Are you real?" he asked her, wondering if he was crazy.

"As real as you," she answered.

He stood up slowly. Whoever and whatever this child was, she probably had the answers he was looking for.

"Who...who am I then?" he asked her, resigned to the fact that this was someone that knew him, as well as someone who wasn't natural. Like the demon and perhaps like him; another wondrous and strange event in a chain of them that had started since he had woken up in those woods.

"You know, Hero. You're just not ready to remember," she smiled at him.

"What did you call me?" he asked.

"What you are, in a sense. You are that and you are other things. And you are meant to be much more."

He looked at the gravel beneath his feet.

"Tell me...in words that make sense. What am I doing here? Where am I meant to go?"

She walked towards him and knelt down, peeking up into his down-cast eyes. She giggled a little when he looked back at her. He was comforted by that sound. Whoever this little girl was, she was someone he felt he knew, and who obviously knew him. Familiar and powerful. Powerful in a way that might give him direction.

"Follow The Pull," she said, her face becoming serious once more. "Trust it. And trust that sword in your hand, and the mask in your pocket."

Nick felt in his pocket. Sure enough, the small piece of cloth met his fingers as he did. He could have sworn it had not been there earlier that day; but there it was now, almost calling for him to put it on.

"What was that thing that attacked me?" he chose to ask next.

The girl's eyes seemed to shift. She looked haunted now, and concerned.

"Something that tried to hurt us once and failed. It's going to keep trying, for as long as you let it. You can't let it succeed."

"But how can I stop...something like that?" he asked.

"Let what's inside come out, and you can stop it, when you're ready."

Nick let those words sink in. What's inside. What on earth did that mean? What exactly was "inside" of him?

"I have so many questions," he said to her.

"And you'll continue to have them. For a while, anyway until you find the source of The Pull. Then...all will be clear," she grinned at him, showing slightly crooked teeth; the teeth of a child who's climbed more than her share of trees and probably fallen out of one or two of them.

Nick smiled back at her then. He couldn't help himself.

"Thank you," was all he could think to say. As vague as she was, her words were making him feel stronger.

51

"Who are you?" he asked her again.

"Someone close," she replied, and then turned around and began walking away.

"Wa...," Nick began, wanting to ask her to stay. As he opened his mouth he heard a scream from somewhere off to his right. A scream followed by laughter and the revving of engines. He looked to his right to find the source of the sound. A line of cars and motorcycles was turning a corner about a block away. Around that corner was where the noises were coming from.

When he turned back to the little girl, she was gone.

He ran to the edge of the roof. There would have been nowhere to go in that direction but off the side. When he peered over the edge, all he saw was a homeless man shamble by far below. The girl had simply vanished.

Another mystery among the dozens that now confronted him.

Nick stood back up and looked back toward the source of the scream. His heart told him to look that way. His instinct told him he was needed.

"Follow The Pull," Nick said, and began to run.

This time he was aware of everything. He felt himself pull the mask over his face. He felt the wrapped fabric handle of the sword in his hand as he gripped it tighter.

Nick approached the edge of the last rooftop. He stopped his run in mid-stride, momentum seeming to have no hold over him. Below him was a large parking lot sandwiched between two buildings. A huge chain-link fence stretched between the buildings, sealing off the rear entrance of the lot.

Fifteen or sixteen muscle cars and motorcycles crowded the parking lot. Engines roared and music blasted. Several people were leaning out of their windows and yelling. Young men and women, most of whom had piercings and tattoos covering what wasn't covered by leather and torn denim. Street gang, Nick thought. Mohawks and dyed hair adorned nearly every head he looked at. Kids whose fashion style was stuck in the 80's, but whose taste for violence and anarchy was very much rooted in the same place as any other street clique. Their lives sucked, so they took it out on authority. Or in this case, an elderly couple pinned against the chain link fence.

An old man in a brown sweater stood with an arm protectively around his wife, a short stocky woman who looked like she was hyperventilating while clutching her husband's arm with an arthritic claw. Her eyes spoke volumes of terror. The man looked braver than his wife, yet scared nonetheless.

Nick scanned the crowd, looking for a leader. It didn't take him long to find one.

Near the front of the crowd of cars was a red convertible. Four people sat inside; two in front, two in back. The man in the driver's seat had slicked back blonde hair and wore a sleeveless denim vest covered in band patches. He stared at the couple with ice and venom in his eyes. This was the leader, Nick thought.

Beside him was a girl with dyed red hair. Her facial features were sharp and European. Maybe German, Nick thought. Her skin tone was darker than the others and her eyes were a brilliant green. She wore a spiked collar around her neck and red fishnet sleeves. Despite these tough adornments, she looked at the elderly couple with concern and disapproval. The leader's girlfriend, Nick thought; one that obviously didn't share his malicious views of fun.

In the back seat was a very large, well muscled bald man covered in tattoos. He stared ahead blankly, but Nick thought he could see a similar sense of disapproval in his eyes. Beside him was a small skinny man with spiked hair. He smiled and looked around, but seemed to be content to just huddle there while the others did the yelling.

Nick made his mark. He ran to the right for the top of the tall fence. He jumped down from the roof, caught the iron support bar, and then ran horizontally across the fence, his hand holding the bar as he made his way closer to the lead car. When he was close enough, he let go of the bar and pushed off the fence. He soared through the air. No one had seen him yet. That was about to change.

Nick, masked and with his sword in his hand, landed soundlessly on the hood of the red convertible.

The man in the driver's seat's eyes widened. He looked at Nick for a moment in a state of shock. Slowly that look spread to the eyes of others around him. Nick heard a few gasps. A few of the radios went silent. Nick took the opportunity to speak.

"Leave them alone," was all he could think to say.

The driver's eyes narrowed then, and his shock was quickly replaced by anger.

"Get off of my car, dickhead."

The others continued to stare at the strange figure standing on their leader's car, but the leader himself seemed unimpressed.

"Turn your gang around and leave these people alone," Nick reiterated, keeping his eyes locked on the man's.

"Or what, Ninja Boy?"

Nick didn't know what to say. He wasn't used to making threats. He didn't want to hurt anyone. He was hoping the sword and the mask alone would be enough to scare these punks off. If not for their leader, he thought that might have worked. Most of them were still stunned by what they were seeing.

The girl in the passenger seat caught his eyes. Her face had turned from a look of confusion to a look of concern again; this time for the boy on their car that had perhaps bitten off more than he could chew. And for a moment…Nick almost thought he saw a flicker of recognition in her eyes.

"He's right, Sam. I don't know who the hell this is, but it's below us to torture an old couple. Let's get out of here," she said, her eyes flicking back and forth between Nick and Sam.

Nick nodded to her ever so slightly, in silent thanks.

She nodded back, and the hint of a smile reached the corner of her mouth. There it was again. He was certain of it now. This girl recognized him.

Sam looked at her now, his face showing even more anger than when he had looked at Nick. He looked betrayed.

"What, you want me to leave so you can bone the super hero here? Does his bullshit turn you on, you stupid whore?"

Sam looked back at Nick, sheer hatred radiating off of him.

"That's what this is, isn't it Ninja Boy? You some kind of super hero?"

Nick shook his head. "I just want you to leave these people alone."

Sam laughed. "Yeah and bone my girl. Well fuck you. And fuck you too, Patricia."

He leaned behind him and motioned towards the big guy in the back.

"Kurt, show this prancing fairy what happens to assholes who touch my shit."

The big man looked at Sam for a moment, seeming to hesitate. Then he looked back at Nick, opened his car door, and swung his huge tree-trunk legs out.

Nick hopped down off the hood of his car and lowered his sword.

"I don't want to fight you," he said, trying to appeal to the big man's hesitation.

"Too late for that," Sam said with a laugh from behind the safety of the steering wheel.

Kurt closed the last few steps between him and Nick.

"Sorry kid, but you kind of asked for it," he said, and then took a swing at Nick's head.

54

Nick ducked with little effort. He took two quick back-steps away. Kurt looked surprised, but came forward again with a left hook this time.

Nick pushed the big fist away, using its own momentum to allow it to sail harmlessly past his masked face. If that hit had connected, it likely would have shattered his jaw.

Kurt tried to knee Nick in the stomach, but Nick stepped to the left of the knee with the grace of a dancer. Another fist hit nothing but air, and then another, and then another.

"Kurt, you're pissing me off. Stop dicking around and hit the kid!" Sam yelled from the car.

Nick took his eyes off of Kurt for a second. That second was enough for Kurt to land a glancing blow against Nick's shoulder. Nick spun almost completely around with the force of the blow.

"No!" he heard the girl in the car scream. The next thing he was hearing was his foot connecting with the back of Kurt's head. Somehow he had reflexively turned the spin from Kurt's blow into an offensive maneuver, moving beneath a follow-up punch and positioning himself behind Kurt, where he then proceeded to kick him in the back of his skull.

Kurt grunted and fell to his knees. One hand clutched his head, then the other hand gave way and the big man was suddenly curled up on the pavement, obviously stunned and in pain.

Nick jumped back onto Sam's car and raised his sword again. The crowd seemed to gasp, half expecting him to dive back down and slice the prone Kurt into pieces.

Instead he just stood there and looked out at the small sea of cars and street kids before him.

"I will not let you hurt these people! Turn your cars around and go home!"

"What people?" Sam said, looking up at him.

Nick turned to look at the couple the punks had been tormenting. There was no one there. They must have run away during his scuffle with Kurt. Good, Nick thought, it looked like this little skirmish was worth something after all.

And then his world turned upside down. He felt his legs pulled out from under him and his head slam against the hood of the car as he fell. His sword hit the ground with a clank, and Nick soon followed it to the pavement.

He looked up just in time to see Kurt's fist come crashing down into his face.

"Kurt, stop it!" Patricia screamed.

"Hah hah! Everybody get the fucker!" Sam yelled triumphantly. Several car doors opened and then slammed shut as about two dozen punks decided to kick the shit out of the stranger that had interrupted their fun.

Kurt did stop, but it was too late for Nick. He was already descending into darkness when the first steel-toed boot collided with his ribs.

The last thing he heard was Patricia yelling in protest, and Sam laughing his head off.

11

Melissa quickly moved out of the way, allowing four armed men to rush past her on their way out of the briefing room. She watched them go, wondering what the fuss was about. Flak jackets. Combat shotguns only Raven's men were still issued. Not normal rounds though. Submission rounds. "Beanbag Shells" as the security guys called them. Not lethal, but damaging enough to take someone out. Was there a riot she hadn't heard about?

Reminding herself of her purpose, Melissa continued down the hall to the briefing room adjacent to the surveillance hub. When she entered the room she was relieved to find the very person she was looking for gathering papers off the conference table.

"Well good morning, Rainbow Brite. Fancy meeting you here," Melissa called out as the girl across the room looked up at her.

Stacy smiled her usual radiant smile.

"And good morning to you Miss Moonbeam!"

"That's Sergeant Moonbeam to you, missy," Melissa said in a gruff voice.

Stacy giggled.

"So what was that all about?" Melissa asked, pointing a thumb back down the hall behind her.

Stacy shook her head.

"Don't know all the details, but Dad got a hit on the man he's searching for. Some kind of murder a few blocks from here. Poor kid got chopped up."

"Yikes," Melissa exclaimed, "Any idea yet why Raven's so interested in this guy?"

"No clue," Stacy answered, "It's weird too. He had us looking into a fire across town, and a traffic pileup caused by some kind of animal, and now a murder. I can't make heads or tails of it myself, but Dad only tells me what I quote-unquote 'need to know'."

Melissa watched her straighten the papers up as she gathered them, making sure they were in the correct order.

"So that's your life, huh? Intelligence briefings and stacking papers."

Stacy's eyes narrowed for a moment as she closed the file in front of her. Melissa could tell she had struck a nerve.

"My dad isn't…much of a family man."

"What about the rest of the Cross clan?" Melissa asked.

"Well my mom just follows him around like a lost puppy. My sister is off at University and could care less about us."

"Why aren't you?" Melissa prodded.

Stacy shrugged, "Not quite at the head of my class in high school. I had a lot of friends, but at home I was more of the quiet type. Dad thought I could use more 'real life experience'. Said I was too much of a dreamer."

Melissa watched Stacy's usual cheerful demeanor harden. She decided to change the subject before she pushed too many of the girl's buttons. Melissa needed her in top form for what she was about to ask.

"Stacy I've got a favor to ask you," she said.

Stacy crossed her arms in front of her, cradling the file to her chest.

"Like what?"

Melissa took a deep breath.

"In two days there's going to be a "guest re-accommodation" on the security log. Raven's boys are moving someone. I don't know where yet…" Melissa steeled herself. Trust did not come easy to her, "…but I plan to make sure he never gets there."

Stacy didn't say anything. She just looked at Melissa with unease.

"Stacy you have to know that Raven isn't just any old CEO of any old oil company."

"Of course," Stacy agreed cautiously, "And I also know he's dangerous."

Melissa nodded in reluctant agreement.

"Dangerous or not, however, he has my friend."

Understanding seemed to dawn in Stacy's eyes.

"He's not really a 'guest', is he?"

Melissa shook her head.

"No. Raven is planning something terrible for him. I need to get him out of here before that happens."

"But what will happen to you?" Stacy asked with genuine concern.

She shook her head again.

"Doesn't matter. I have to do this. Besides, I can take care of myself. The question is, will you help me?"

Stacy's lips pursed together and her eyes narrowed. Melissa would have found it endearing if she didn't see the determination behind it.

"If I can. Yes, I'll help you."

Melissa sighed in relief, and smiled.

"Thanks, kid. Now here's what I need you to do...."

He awoke in the dark on a cold hard floor. His muscles ached and his head felt like a split watermelon. His ribs were tender and his fingers felt smashed. Honestly he was surprised he wasn't more injured than he was after that beating. He felt around at his surroundings. His sword was gone; so was his mask. He reached out in front of him and felt cold iron bars; thin, like a....

Nick jumped when something cold and wet stroked his hand. There was something else in the cage with him. An animal. His heart started to race a bit, though he figured the thing would have bitten him instead of licked him just then if it meant him harm. He slowly pushed himself against the back corner of the cage.

Four pawed footsteps followed him as he moved. Nick's eyes were beginning to adjust, and the shape of a large dog came into view. It leaned forward and licked him again.

"No way," Nick said in astonishment. "Blitz?"

Light suddenly cascaded into the room as a door opened nearby. The German Shepherd in front of him was panting happily. His scuffed copper collar glinted under the shop bulbs above him. It was Blitz alright.

"Blitz!" Nick exclaimed, throwing his arms around the dog. Blitz began to pant even harder, obviously as happy to see Nick as the boy was to see him.

"You two know each other?" came a voice from the door of the garage. He turned and saw the girl from Sam's car close the door behind her. Patricia, Nick remembered. She seemed surprised at what she was seeing.

"Sam put you in there expecting that dog to tear your head off. I've been waiting for the last six hours for a chance to sneak out here and check on you," she said, walking towards him.

"Blitz wouldn't hurt a fly," Nick said, getting happily licked in the face.

"Tell that to the four guys he took a chunk out of when they tried to catch him," Patricia said as she hunkered down in front of the cage.

Nick took an appraising look at the dog. He supposed that a lifetime of abuse would make an animal prone to violence. Come to think of it, it was kind of unusual that Blitz seemed as good natured as he was.

"Where did they find him?"

"Wandering around in Cabbagetown. Looking for food, probably. He seemed kind of skittish, but Sam loves big dogs so he ordered some of our guys to catch the poor thing. They did...eventually."

Nick stroked Blitz's head. "Why did you run away that night?"

Patricia watched them for a moment before interrupting the tender reunion.

"Can I trust you?" she said.

He looked over at her. She looked as serious as the grave. She was pretty behind all of that makeup and dyed hair; wearing a plain worn t-shirt and jeans this time. Her green eyes spoke of a person older than her years. They also seemed to be asking him for help.

"Yes," he said to her, "Whatever it is you need, I want to help."

The words just came out of his mouth. He surprised himself by saying them, immediately questioning the wisdom of the impulsive offer.

Patricia seemed a startled as well. "I just meant can I trust you to let you out of that cage?"

Nick smiled, "Yeah. I'm harmless."

Patricia laughed a little. "That's not what it looked like last night."

His face darkened at the reminder. When Patricia opened the cage door, Nick crawled out and sat down beside her.

She seemed to tense up as his shoulder touched hers. Blitz crawled out behind him, walked around the pair, and stuck his furry head right between the two of them. Nick laughed, putting his arm around the dog.

Patricia looked at him. She studied him for a moment.

"I'm not used to strangers getting this close to me," she said to him.

Nick scooted away a bit. "Sorry."

She shook her head slowly. "No...it's ok."

She stared at him for a moment longer. Nick had the feeling that she was trying to figure something out about him.

"I haven't been around other people much lately," he said, trying to break the awkward silence. "Been alone for a while. Well, except for Blitz."

Patricia looked at the dog before looking back at him.

"Alone? Why?"

"Because I woke up in the woods a while ago with no memory of how I got there. Or who I was. Something must have happened to me, and I've been trying to figure out what ever since. I just wandered into the city a couple of days ago, hoping I would find something familiar. So far...nothing." Nick told her, not thinking for a moment that the truth of his situation would be something he should hold back. Though there were certain...facts...he had instinctively omitted. The Whisper and the little girl were two things he wasn't comfortable even thinking about, much less discussing.

"You don't remember?" she seemed surprised yet again. "Anything?"

"Just my name. And obviously I still know all the basic stuff like how to read and talk and all that. I remember things around the city. I just don't know how I learned them to being with." Again, Nick omitted The Pull. It was another facet of himself he was still trying to figure out.

She looked at him with her mouth slightly open. It was if she was deciding whether or not to believe him.

"And the sword? The mask? What's up with that? Why were you running around trying to save an old couple dressed like something out of a comic book?" she asked, still trying to make sense of his story.

Nick just shrugged. Truth be told, he didn't really know the answer to that either.

"Were you the guy that saved that little boy the other day? The "Masked Hero" they've been talking about?"

Patricia caught a hint of discomfort in Nick's eyes as he looked up at the wall.

"The firemen weren't going to make it in time."

Patricia cracked a smile.

"You're really something...," she started, stopping as she remembered that he hadn't told her his name yet.

"Nick," he said, smiling back at her.

"Nick," she repeated. Her voice was slow and quiet; almost a whisper. Nick could tell she was having trouble taking his story in. But she trusted him. He could feel that as well.

"Well, Nick," she started, her face growing more serious, almost fearful. "I think I knew you were coming."

Nick felt his fingers digging into his leg.

"Knew I was...you mean you know me?"

She shook her head.

"Only from a dream."

He looked confused.

"Sometimes I...dream about people. I'm never sure if they're real or not...but then sometimes I actually meet them. There's a few I've dreamt about more than once. There's a blonde girl. She has scars she doesn't let anyone see. Then a boy, trapped in a cage carried by an ugly black bird. And another girl crushed beneath the shadow of her father. I can never see their faces clearly. I only have a vague sense of them. And then...there's you."

61

Nick didn't know what to think. With all the strange things that had happened to him since he had woken up, why should this be any different?

"What was I doing?" he asked carefully.

"Walking down a path," she said, "A dark, scary path. Always walking. I can almost see the end of it but...."

"What is it?" Nick interrupted, "What is it I'm moving towards?"

"Someone close to you, I think. I don't know if they will be close to you or if they already are. Whoever it is, it's someone you need."

Nick stared at her, unsure whether or not he wanted to hear any more. Dream or not, premonition or not, crazy or not, at least he was hearing something. Some kind of answer.

"How long have you been having the dream?" he asked, slightly fearful of the answer.

"This particular one? Only a few days. Past three nights, I think, though I think maybe I've had ones like it before. I don't always remember my dreams." she answered.

Nick said nothing, though his breath caught in his chest. Patricia's dream had started the day he woke up.

"It's probably nothing," she said, obviously trying to allay his fears, "Mom used to say that my dreams were about the kind of people I wanted to meet. When I needed a friend, I would dream about one. When I needed someone to talk to, I would dream that my brother was visiting me, awake and walking and making conversation like nothing was wrong. And when I needed a hero...I dreamed of one."

She smiled at him.

"Because you see, Nick, my dream about you was full of hope. That scary road you were on wasn't so bad because you walked it with such purpose. That sword shining in the sunlight. Your eyes were certain, and always forward. You looked like you could take on anything. There were monsters in your path, I think, but none of it could stop you; because you were The Hero."

"What did you say?" Nick asked.

"I said you were a hero," she repeated, "A hero who helped people. The kind of hero I though only existed in fairy tales."

She looked at him as if admiring a painting, as if he were not a real person but somehow a figment of her imagination.

"But here you are," she said, "Here you are, just when I need a hero."

"You need...me?" Nick said skeptically, suddenly concerned about where this was going.

Patricia nodded, still smiling, but now somewhat nervously.

"Yeah Nick, I think I need you."

Nick felt a flicker of alarm. He didn't want this girl to think he was someone he wasn't, especially if he was as dangerous to be around as he was beginning to believe. Nevertheless…he felt as if he should hear her out.

"Sam is the leader of our little group," she began, "He's the leader because he's the meanest and he's the smartest. He's got this strange power over people. Like he just looks at you and you feel your backbone start to crumble and all your strength drain away. Most people would do anything he says because they're so afraid of him. And they have a right to be. When people cross him, he gets mad. And when he get's mad…," Patricia trailed off for a moment, clenching her arms around herself tighter. "He hurts people."

Nick watched her body language and read instantly that Sam had hurt her. Badly. Probably many times.

"You need me to help you get away from him," Nick said, now knowing full well where this was going.

Patricia looked up at him, and he could see a glimmer of hope already forming in her eyes.

"Not just me, Nick. Kurt and Joey. Some of the others. And…my brother, Benjamin."

Nick waited for an explanation for her hesitance at mentioning her brother.

"My brother is special, Nick," she said.

"Special how?"

She seemed to consider how best to explain.

"For one, he's in a coma. Has been for years, ever since Mom and Dad died."

"A coma?" Nick asked, surprised, "And he's here? Not in a hospital?"

Patricia shook her head.

"It's not a normal coma. He still eats when I feed him. He breathes well on his own. It's just like he's…sleeping. Sleeping and he won't wake up."

"And you're afraid that Sam will hurt him?" Nick asked.

She looked at the ground, "Yeah. I used to think that we'd both be safe here. Better the devil you know that the devil you don't, right? But lately Sam's been getting worse. More violent, more erratic, more aggressive. He puts up with Ben because he wants me, but…I'm afraid of what will happen when that patience runs out. We want out, Nick, and the only way we're going to get out," she looked at him, shocking him with the angry determination in her eyes, "…is through violence."

"We've tried before," she continued, "I have. He did things to me I don't like to talk about. Some of the others have tried too…and well…most of them I've never seen again."

Nick looked down at his feet, his own troubles suddenly seeming smaller. "I don't understand. Why did you get into this to begin with, Patricia? There had to have been better places to take care of your brother."

She sighed. "Because I was young and stupid. Sam seemed somehow…different from all the other guys, and different was what I wanted. Before he passed, my dad was always pushing me to get into medicine and live a normal, boring life. Sam was offering me excitement and freedom. What I didn't know was that I was giving up any sort of freedom I had by following him, and that boring life that I hated so much…. I would give anything to have it back now."

"What happened last night, with the old couple…," Nick began to ask.

"Happens all the time, Nick. He gets off on terrorizing people. Anyone he views as weak. He was just going to scare those folks last night, but sometimes…he does a lot worse."

She looked at him, her eyes pleading.

"He has to be stopped, Nick. The only way to do that is to show him that there's someone stronger than him. Kurt won't do it. Even he's afraid of Sam. But you…. I saw him look at you. He's afraid of you, Nick. I don't know why, but he is. I've seen you fight. You took down Kurt! No one's ever done that before. I need you to take out Sam, for all our sakes."

Nick looked at her. He thought for a moment about what she was asking. She wasn't just asking for him to help her escape. She was asking him to hurt Sam. Maybe even kill him.

He knew that he could do it. That sword, if he could get it back, was enough to scare a demon. He had only seen a small glimpse of his skills, but he had a feeling that if he wanted to he could probably murder Sam, Sam's gang, and just about anyone else he felt like.

But that wasn't who he was. For all the things he didn't know about himself, that was one thing that he did. He didn't kill people.

"No," he said to her.

Patricia leaned back a bit, as if struck. She looked around, taking the answer in, and then moved to get up. She opened her mouth to say something to him, but Nick stopped her by gently putting a hand on her arm.

"I won't kill him, Patricia. But I will help you, and your brother, and whoever else needs it, to stand up to him yourselves. He'll never leave you alone unless you prove to him that you are stronger than him. This isn't about me. I'm just a guy that fell out of the sky last night on top of his car. The person that has to put him in his place is you."

Patricia looked into his green eyes, darker than her own but equally filled with intent. For someone with no memory, Nick knew what he was talking about.

She nodded.

Nick smiled and put his hand back in his lap.

"We'll do it here, then. I'll lure him and the others into the garage. Maybe I can convince Kurt to help us this time. He respects the hell out of you after what happened last night," she said.

Nick chuckled. "Good. Glad to hear there's no hard feelings."

"There never were. Kurt didn't want to hurt you. He just felt like he didn't have any other choice."

Blitz walked over to her lap and sat down with his front end over her leg. She looked up at Nick in surprise.

"Told you he's a pussy cat," he said, grinning.

"I'll find a way to get your sword and mask back," she said, bringing things back to the matter at hand, though she stroked Blitz's soft fur as she did. "Then, when I bring Sam and as many of them as I can in here…. We'll show them that we mean business."

She looked at him again. Their eyes, both filled with possibility, gleamed at one another.

"With your help," she added.

Nick nodded. His reluctance was fleeing. He felt himself filled with a rush of purpose, as if this act was exactly what he was supposed to do. The Pull still hadn't become any clearer in its destination, but for the first time, The Pull didn't matter to him. The demon didn't matter. His fear of himself and of the future didn't matter. All that mattered to him was helping this girl and her brother get away from a tyrant.

They had a fight on their hands. For reasons Nick didn't think to question, he was filled with eager anticipation.

12

Patricia walked out of the garage with her heart attempting to race out of her chest. She told Nick to hide with Blitz until the time was right. If anyone else wandered out there, they would simply assume the stranger had escaped, which was fine by her. All the better to lay a trap later that afternoon, when Sam would already be drunk or high and likely at his weakest.

She walked through the lower level of the old warehouse that was their hangout. It was still early in the day, so most of the fifty-plus gang members were passed out on the floor or on the various torn-up cots and couches spread around the place. Empty beer and liquor bottles were everywhere. She had to step over more than one used hypodermic needle, grimacing as she did so.

Patricia herself hadn't used anything more than alcohol in a while. Sam still tried to pressure her into it, but as long as she still got drunk enough to accept his advances from time to time, he didn't press the issue.

Down a hall, Patricia quietly approached a door, pushing it open carefully, even though she knew the room's occupant would likely not wake regardless of noise.

Her brother, Benjamin, lay in a bed in the corner of the room, next to a window. She had chosen the room for him both because of its relative seclusion and because of the way the sun could shine on his bed for the early part of the day.

She chose to believe he liked that.

Patricia quietly walked across the room to stand beside her brother's bed. Ben was wearing a red and white striped shirt with the sheet pulled up just above his armpits. He was growing like a normal child, so Patricia had to buy him new clothes every once in a while. She had no idea what a boy of ten years old would want to wear, so she hoped she wasn't embarrassing him.

Benjamin was a handsome young man. His skin was a shade lighter than Patricia's dark tone, and his hair, once dirty blonde, was turning a sandy brown. His eyes were green, like hers. She remembered that, though she hadn't seen them open in a long, long time.

She reached down and smoothed out his hair.

"I found somebody, Ben," she said as she stroked him, "Someone who might help us."

She realized as she spoke that part of the reason she liked Nick was because he kind of looked like an older version of her brother. Messy brown hair. Wide green-tinted eyes. Skinny as a rail. If he wasn't so pale, Nick could pass as a third sibling.

"We're getting out of here soon, I hope," she continued, "I'm taking you someplace safe. Someplace far away if I can."

Patricia hung her head, feeling her eyes well up with shame.

"I'm so sorry I brought you here," she said, feeling herself wanting to cry, "I was just so…lonely. You and me against the world and no one else to care about us. Sam just seemed so strong; like he could take care of us. Like he could take care of me."

Patricia's arm dropped to her side. It was her own selfishness that brought her here. It was her own need to be accepted and loved that drove her brother into the lion's den.

But she would get him out. She was about to stand up…finally, and fight for a new beginning for the both of them.

She jumped a little as she heard the door open behind them and familiar footsteps enter. Sam shouldn't have been awake this early, so Patricia assumed he must have not yet fallen asleep from the night before.

"There you are," she heard him say as he shut the door behind him.

Patricia quickly wiped the tears from her eyes and turned to face him.

"Hey. What's up?" she said, trying to sound as normal as possible.

Concern crossed Sam's face as he saw the evidence of her tears. He moved to her, arms extended. Patricia had to fight not to cringe. She knew that look. She knew that the concern in his eyes was only a front, a face he put on when he wanted something from her.

"Come here, baby," he said in that purring, almost cat-like voice she so hated.

As he reached out and took hold of her shoulders, she turned back to face Benjamin. Sam paid no mind however, and she soon felt the weight of him pressing against her.

"You know Daddy makes it all better," he spoke into her ear.

Sam's hands drifted down from her shoulders, groping her firmly.

"Sam, no. Not here," she argued.

His grip tightened, and one of his hands continued its uncomfortable journey down her body.

"But Daddy wants his girl," Sam said.

68

"Sam, NO!" Patricia yelled, squirming in his arms.

She gasped as his arms clamped around her, wrapping her in a vice-grip.

"You don't get to tell me no," he threatened, still whispering in his ear, the seductive purr gone, and replaced by gravelly anger.

Her heart was racing. She knew Sam could feel it, and she also knew it excited him.

"Fine," she relented, "Fine. Let's just…go somewhere else."

His arms loosened.

"Ok," he said, sounding satisfied, "Let's go up to the loft. I want everybody to hear us."

Patricia nodded. She wished she had woken up Kurt to share her plan. She wished she had decided to spring her trap sooner. She wished Nick were here to stop him. She wished she was anywhere but here.

So Patricia followed Sam out of the room and upstairs, choosing to focus on the fact that in a few more hours, Sam would never touch her again.

Nick crouched behind the SUV with Blitz beside him, his sword in his hand and mask on his face. He still wasn't sure he liked wearing the thing, but he was fully aware he would need to be intimidating for the upcoming confrontation. He was nervous as hell, and waiting was only making it worse.

Before he had acted mostly out of instinct. He barely remembered the boy in the burning home. Standing up for the elderly couple had been a split-second decision. Now he was consciously walking into a fight. He was going to hurt people.

Nick took a few deep breaths. He knew he could do it. He had no doubt of that. Whatever training he must have had filled his mind with confidence that he would be capable of handling himself; yet the idea of turning himself into a weapon, even for the benefit of someone as victimized as Patricia seemed to be, filled him with doubt.

He had expected to walk into the city, remember his way back home, walk in the door and be greeted by his family. Or at least find an apartment or house that he knew was his. A job. A car. Maybe even a girlfriend.

Instead he was sitting in a dark garage waiting to cut up a violent gang with his sword. This wasn't right. This wasn't what he wanted.

Even in the dim light, Nick could see Patricia's pain and anger as she crouched in front of him. Her cheeks were red. Her hair was a mess.

She put her hands on his shoulders. Nick almost grimaced from the force of her grip.

"Hurt the bastard," she said, glaring at him, "I'm not asking you to kill him, but I am asking you to make…him…suffer."

Nick was too alarmed to say anything. He just stared back at her.

It must have been enough, for Patricia let him go, took a few steps back…and started screaming.

Beside him, Nick saw Blitz's tail tuck between his legs.

Sam was laying in bed, wrapped in a deep slumber brought on by another long night of drinking and satisfaction. Still, Sam was savvy enough to never allow himself to be unaware of his surroundings. After all, any one of his cronies, or even Patricia could take a stab at him while he was too out of it to defend himself. If Sam was anything, it was protective of his power.

So Sam, as drunk and tired as he was, still awoke with a start when he heard the scream from the garage.

Patricia. What had the bitch done now?

She heard them running. Her heart was beating a mile a minute. Patricia tried to calm herself and focus on the act. She clutched the small bruise on her face. She had to hit herself because Nick wouldn't do it. Nick still looked at her like a deer in the headlights, and odd contradiction considering the mask on his face and deadly weapon in his hand. God, she hoped Nick would snap out of it and do his job when that door opened. After leaving Sam and grabbing Nick's things from the loft while he slept she had quickly warned Kurt as to what was about to happen. She thought Kurt would help…but she couldn't be sure until the time came.

Patricia took one last look around the garage. Nick and Blitz were well out of sight. The comforting weight of a knife tucked into the waistband of her jeans pressed against the small of her back. She was as ready as she would ever be.

Sam rounded the corner of the open double-wide door. Fury was in his face. He stalked right towards her and grabbed her arm, not even bothering to look around. Several others filed in behind him. She heard Kurt's voice among them.

"You did it, didn't you? You fucking let him out," Sam said, his angry stare stabbing her like a jagged razor.

"I was just trying to find out who he was. I guess I got too close and he hit me."

Patricia had barely finished her sentence when Sam backhanded her in the cheek. She went reeling and stumbled to the floor, hitting the concrete hard with one knee. A gasp of pain escaped her lips.

That's the last time, Patricia thought. That was the last time.

"It aint him you gotta worry about, sweetheart," Sam said, looming over her.

"If you hit her again it'll be the last time you have hands to hit with," came a voice from the darkness. Nick stepped out of the shadows from behind a truck parked against the wall. Blitz stood beside him, emitting a low growl.

Shit, thought Patricia. There goes the element of surprise.

The punks turned as they heard the garage door slam behind them. Kurt dusted off his hands and winked at her.

She allowed herself a small smile. Perhaps this impromptu ambush would work after all.

"You took the words right out of my mouth, kid," Kurt said, his eyes locked on Sam.

Sam looked at Kurt and shook his head.

"Useless fuck," he said before turning back to Patricia, "Both of you."

He threw a hand in the air, signaling to the gang behind him.

"Just kill them," he said, and when he did the eight flunkies Sam had rounded up on the way sprang into motion without question. Even against a bodybuilder, a guy with a sword, and an angry dog, Sam's hold over them was infallible.

Two of them charged Kurt, two went after Patricia, and the remaining four slowly and cautiously crept towards Nick.

Nick felt himself move. His hesitation was gone. His doubt and concern was erased. All he felt now was the weapon in his hand and the need to win.

He jumped into the air, kicked off the truck behind him, and flew towards his startled enemies. The sword gleamed with the reflection of the dirty fluorescent lights above for the split second Nick was airborne. That split second was all it took for the four punks to freeze in their tracks with terror.

Patricia got to her feet and pulled the knife from the waistband of her jeans. She held it before her and tried to stand in a defensive position. Unfortunately, her attackers were not as impressed as Nick's had been.

"Who the fuck are you trying to kid?" Sam said, simply standing there as Joey and another member of the gang approached Patricia. "You couldn't even cut me while I was nearly passed out drunk. Remember?"

Patricia did remember. One of the times that Sam had assaulted her. The worst time. She had grabbed a kitchen knife, but chickened out before she could make use the small window of opportunity Sam's drunkenness had given her. The next thing she knew that night was a mouthful of her own blood while Sam had his angry way with her.

That thought was enough to get her moving. Patricia snarled and swiped the knife through the air in front of her. Joey and the other kid backed up a step.

"Whoa. Just put it down, Trish. Don't make this harder than it has to be. Maybe Sam'll go easy on you if you just...," Joey tried to plead with her.

"Don't even talk to me, Joey. I thought you were my friend," Patricia shot back with a betrayed look.

"I.... You know I have to do what he says, Trish," Joey stammered.

Patricia answered him by taking a step forward and slashing through the air again in front of Joey's face.

Kurt was easily holding his own, throwing punch after punch at the two men before him. Each hit they landed on him was met with a much harder one from Kurt. The scuffle on his end would not last long.

Nick was twirling between three of the punks like a deadly human pinwheel. His sword and his feet lashed out so quickly that none of them had time to form a single strike. One man grunted as Nick's heel smacked into the under-part of his jaw. In the same maneuver, a second man was brought to the ground as the sword careened into and through his calf muscle.

The third one, a girl probably not even of legal drinking age, held a switchblade in front of her, her eyes wide as she heard the screams of the man Nick had just cut. Those screams were then joined by those of another voice. She turned for a second to see the dog tearing away at someone's thigh. The man was hopping on one leg and swinging a pipe at the dog. The German Shepherd seemed unfazed.

Nick stood there and wiped the blood off of his sword. The first of the crimson liquid to stain his blade, as far as he knew. As far as he hoped.

"Put it down and get out of our way," Nick said to the girl.

She complied without argument.

Kurt put a fist into the jaw of one of his former "friends". The guy suddenly became a limp rag doll and fell to the floor, joining the other man that Kurt had already dispatched. Kurt shook off his fist, and then looked up to see Patricia still swiping away in front of her. She wouldn't be able to do that forever.

Patricia, knowing the very same thing, kept swinging at Joey, knowing full well that the other guy would be on her before long. Then Joey would join, and then Sam probably would as well. They would beat the living hell out of her.

She smiled anyway. The effort had been more than worth it.

She reared her arm back to take another fruitless swipe through the air. Before she could bring it down, two blurs battered into the backs of her attackers. One was brown and furry and came from beneath the man, barreling the legs out from under him. He hit his head on the concrete and was still. Joey yelped in pain as a silver glint cut through the air behind him, slashing him across the buttocks. Nick stood there, holding back from a second swing, believing that the first would do the trick

He was right. Joey held his bleeding backside and ran past Sam screaming. Kurt grabbed him by the throat and held him there, putting a finger to his lips. Joey obliged, still holding his rear end.

Sam roared in anger and pulled a knife of his own from his belt, this one much larger and nastier than Patricia's.

Nick took a step towards Sam, but before he could intercept the screaming madman, Blitz let out an angry bark and leaped through the air in front of them. He hit Sam square in the chest, sending him over to the ground with a thump. The knife fell out of his grasp, and Nick kicked it out of reach.

Blitz took a snap at Sam's face. Sam clawed against the big dog's fur, but Blitz totally ignored the resistance and bit at Sam again. In moments Sam was wailing. Nick could see a small pool of blood beginning to form on the floor.

"Blitz, that's enough!" Nick yelled.

The dog looked up at Nick. The snarl faded off of his face. He growled one more time, then got off of Sam's chest and walked over to Nick's side.

Patricia took a deep breath, and then stepped over Sam. He was clutching the right side of his face and screaming in pain. She could see that the dog had taken a very sizable chunk of Sam's cheek clean off.

Sam writhed on the floor. His screams slowly tapered off into groans of impotent rage.

"You did this to yourself, Sam," Patricia found the courage to say. "Whenever you look in the mirror you're going to remember each time you hurt someone. Every time you hurt me."

Sam sat up violently. "Fuck you, bitch! You're gonna fucking die for this!" He coughed up a wad of blood as he screamed at her.

73

"No she isn't," Nick said, stepping forward. He pointed his sword directly at Sam's bleeding face.

"She isn't because if you ever come near her again, I'll have my dog rip the other half of your face off."

Patricia smiled, noticing the fear well up in her ex-boyfriend's eyes. It was the first time she had ever seen him truly afraid of anything.

Sam didn't say another word. Patricia looked up and she could see why. Above Nick's mask, his eyes stared at Sam with a vengeful intensity. They seemed somehow darker than before. Somehow more…violent. She realized that if it had been her at the end of that sword instead of Sam, she would have managed to do nothing but cower, much as Sam was now. With one hand still holding his wounded face, Sam's eyes had widened in an almost comical look of intimidation.

"It's time we got out of here," Kurt said, bringing everyone back into the moment.

Patricia nodded, shaking off her sudden unease at the stranger that had likely just saved her life.

Nick lowered his sword and walked towards the door. Kurt pulled it open. The two of them stood there and waited for Patricia.

She moved past Sam, unafraid; but then stopped, looking down at him. It was a powerful feeling.

"Goodbye, Sam. My advice to you is to let it go. Let us go, let your anger go, and let your stupid sociopathic fantasies go. They're only going to get you hurt again. And if you mess with me…so will I."

Patricia then walked on. Her heart felt like leaping out of her chest. The last look Sam gave her as she left was full of hate, but the fear behind it told her that it was likely the last time she would ever see him.

She hoped to God she was right, but a part of her…the part of her that dreamed…knew that she was not.

13

The three of them were not the only ones to leave Sam sitting there in his own blood and shame that day. As they walked around to the side entrance of the warehouse to retrieve Benjamin, they saw four others leave that garage and get into their cars, driving away from Sam and away from a life that it had taken Patricia's bravery to show them wasn't necessary. Joey was among them. Patricia was glad for him.

Kurt and Nick watched as Patrica carefully picked up her brother, cradling him close with a serene look on her face.

"I did it, Ben," she said to him, "I actually did it."

They stayed at Kurt's apartment for the night. Patricia said she and Benjamin would stay there until she found a place of their own. Kurt offered the same hospitality to Nick, but Nick simply shook his head.

"Thanks," he had said, "but I need to keep moving."

He and Patricia stayed up almost the entire night, talking about her future and where it might take her now that she was free of her abusive boyfriend and destructive lifestyle. She had no idea what she would do with herself, but anywhere was better than the place she had spent the past three years and the kind of people she had spent them with.

She expected that others would leave Sam now that his iron grip on them had finally been successfully challenged. Many of them had wanted to leave, but had simply never believed that they could. Patricia and Kurt had now given them the hope and the motivation to do so.

Nick eventually got up to call it a night on the air mattress Kurt had set up for him in the hall. Patricia didn't argue, but wished all the same that he would stay. She wished that he would sit with her for the rest of the night, and then stay with her the next day, and the next. Nick had helped liberate her from her past. A future without him there seemed scary and uncertain. Patricia marveled at herself for feeling so attached to a boy she had only met two days before, and knew before that only in vague dreams; but Nick was no ordinary boy.

All the more reason to be sorry to see him go.

The next day the two of them, three including Blitz, stood at the front steps of Kurt's apartment building. Nick had a new backpack slung over his shoulder, a gift from Kurt, and the long canvas case containing his sword looped over the other. Patricia stood in front of him with her arms crossed. She was afraid that if she uncrossed them she would grab onto Nick's arm and not let him go.

"You don't have to keep doing this, Nick," she said to him, her face calm but her eyes clearly stating her disappointment. "You can stay with us and use this as a temporary home while you look for your real one."

Nick nodded. "I know, but something tells me that my destination is just around the corner, and that if I don't keep moving...I might miss it."

Truth was The Pull hadn't let up. Honestly he wished it would. Staying with Patricia would feel more right than he was letting on. The girl was smart, strong, beautiful...and she needed him. Nick felt stupid walking away from her.

Trust The Pull, the little girl had said. Nick believed that he had to. The force of it was strong inside him, like a harpoon on the end of a cord attached to his chest, being pulled by invisible hands somewhere else.

And then there was the demon. The Whisper, Nick had taken to calling him. If he stayed with Patricia, Nick was terrified that the monster would come back at the wrong moment and hurt her in ways he didn't care to think about.

No, it was better if he stayed alone. There was less of a chance of getting people hurt that way. People he might come to care for.

Patricia seemed to understand. She nodded at him, then reached out and took his hand.

"I owe you, hero," she said with a smile. Nick knew he would never get used to that word, and yet he was hearing it a lot lately. "If you ever change your mind, or if you ever need anything at all...you come find me."

Nick smiled and took a long look at her. Patricia's eyes seemed to be welling up with tears she was fighting back. The moisture made her eyes even more brilliant green. The sun reflected off of her red hair. He noticed the blonde roots beginning to show underneath. So the change was beginning already.

He stepped towards her and hugged her. She hugged him back fiercely. They held onto one another for many long moments. For Nick she was the first human friend he had found since he had woken up. For Patricia, Nick was the first genuinely good soul she had met in years. The two of them were reluctant to let each other go.

But they did let go. Nick stepped away from her. He smiled and gave her a quick wave, and then he turned and began walking down the sidewalk, away from Patricia and away from her life.

Patricia sighed. She wiped a stray tear from her cheek, and then walked back to the front door.

She would see him again, she felt. She still wasn't sure how she knew the things she did, but this time had not felt like goodbye.

Nick, soon stepping around the corner and out of her view, felt the same way.

On the rooftop above them, flaming purple eyes watched as bladed fingers dug trenches on the concrete gutter.

The Whisper was watching and waiting.

He had felt the boy's power during the fight in the garage. Those intense bursts of violent passion pulling the threads of the world like a bullet ripping through a spider-web.

The Whisper still didn't know what it all meant. He didn't know how the boy had survived the attack; one that should have been a deathblow to the boy's soul. He didn't know where that awful sword had come from. He didn't know where the boy was heading. But he did know that wherever it was, he would not make it easy.

He would cut at the boy, little by little. Harm him. Take away from him. Nick was right in leaving Patricia behind. If he had remained with her, The Whisper had fully intended to use her against him.

But there was time. The boy would find others. The boy would let his hope continue to grow. And when he was filled with it, full and ready and ripe like a fruit, The Whisper would tear him apart and eat his soul.

He would succeed this time. Whatever the boy was, whatever he was intended to be, and however powerful he may become, The Whisper would always be stronger.

14

Melissa stood at the entrance to the hallway. One more step into that plain white corridor would mean incredible danger for both herself and for Jason. That step would signal a decision she could not turn back from. The end of a life she had lived for over a year.

It was a life she hated. As good as the money and the perks were, none of it was worth the shame she felt when she woke up in the morning. Lapdog to a deranged modern-day Mafioso. It was not the life she had imagined when she had walked out of her father's dumpster of a house that day. It was not the destination she felt she was running towards. No, this was just one stop among many. One mistake among the trail of mistakes she had made since that day.

But now she wasn't aimlessly wandering from one fight to the next. Now she had a purpose. There was someone that needed her; and she needed him. Jason was a genuinely good soul, something she hadn't encountered since her mother died. She needed direction in her life and he could give it. His friendship might finally make her feel whole again, not to mention the act of doing something that was almost purely for the benefit of someone else. Melissa needed to feel like she was worth something again. She hoped saving her friend would bring that to her; and even if she failed, at least she would have the satisfaction of knowing she had tried.

So this was the time to act. This was the time to stop wandering aimlessly. This was the time to pick a fight that actually meant something.

Melissa stepped forward, and strode with purpose down the hall, passing one empty "cabin" after another. When she came to Jason's, her heart was beating a mile a minute, but when she saw his expectant face, all she could feel was proud of herself for finally making a right choice.

"It's time, Jason," she said to him, her fists clenched by her sides. She would have to say as much as possible in the little time that she had.

"Where have you been? I thought you weren't coming back," Jason said, standing up from his cot and coming to face her on the other side of the clear plexiglass wall.

"I had to wait for the right moment. It's here. They're moving you tomorrow. That's when we'll have our chance to get you out of here."

Jason's eyes widened a bit and a hint of a smile began to form on his mouth.

"I don't have much time. He'll have his men in here before long. Last time he thought I was saying good bye, this time he'll see this as a direct challenge to his authority. I may have to fight my way out," she spoke with a sense of urgency.

The smile faded off of Jason's lips. Concern replaced his look of relief.

"It's okay. I can handle them, but you have to listen," she said.

As the finalized plan came out of her mouth, Jason nodded emphatically. He listened, but remained fixated on Melissa's blue eyes and the fire that seemed to burn behind them. He could stare at those eyes all day if he had the chance. Perhaps soon he would.

"You'll be ready, right?" Melissa finished.

"Oh yeah. I've been ready for weeks," Jason replied.

"Good. Now try not to act like anything's different. You'll be under guard tomorrow, but the last thing we need is for that guard to be doubled. I'm good, but I may not be that good," Melissa said. Jason thought it was the first admission of possible vulnerability that Melissa had ever made to him.

They said their goodbyes, and then Melissa made her way back down the hall. Jason watched her go, and then collapsed on his bed and pretended to be upset. Inside, his heart was soaring.

Just as she had expected, Melissa exited the hall into the small elevator lobby to find Raven and two of his men waiting for her. She stopped, crossed her arms in front of her, and gave him a defiant look.

Raven, leaning against a cane Melissa knew he didn't need, just shook his head slowly and let out a dramatic sigh.

"I figured it would come to this, Miss Moonbeam. You're just too stubborn for your own good. Such things aren't healthy."

Melissa said nothing, but hoped the hatred in her eyes was saying more than words ever could.

"I asked you not to see Jason Dredd again. You disobeyed me. Twice. I've put up with your 'rebelling from authority' complex for far longer than I would with anyone else, but I'm afraid this was the last straw."

She clenched her jaw and readied herself. The two men at Raven's side had probably not been brought to peacefully escort her out.

"You're fired, Melissa. I'd appreciated it if you vacate the premises immediately. Your last paycheck will be in the mail today, and you may keep the apartment and the car as a gift."

Her head tilted slightly in confusion. What had he just said? Had Jacob Raven just offered her severance pay?

"It's a shame, Melissa. I really liked you. You were the most interesting employee I'd ever had, and this place will not be the same without you. Do keep in touch, will you?"

Melissa decided to not look a gift horse in the mouth. She made her way towards the elevator.

"Not fucking likely," she said, still feeling the need to throw one last verbal jab at Raven.

Raven just smirked. "Goodbye, Miss Moonbeam."

Melissa glared at the little smiling man as the elevator doors closed.

Raven waited until the light above the elevator descended to the floor below them before raising a hand to signal to the two men beside him.

"Meet her in the lobby. Make sure she doesn't leave this building in one piece."

The two men entered the second elevator and quickly pressed the button.

Raven grinned, and then turned to make his way back to his office and the surveillance monitor that would give him a bird's eye view of the violent confrontation about to take place.

No one crossed him and survived.

Melissa broke into a run the moment the elevator doors opened. She hadn't truly thought for a moment that Raven was going to let her get away. The sound of rapid footsteps behind her as the second elevator opened confirmed that assumption. The two men Raven had sent after her were among his best. She wouldn't have an easy time taking them on and getting away without at least a couple of broken ribs. If she were lucky.

She saw the woman at the reception desk talk into a headset, and then push a button on her console. The front entrance doors locked with an audible clank.

They were only made of glass, but still, thought Melissa...

This was really going to hurt.

Nick had been sitting on some steps in front of an office building, eagerly scarfing down a sandwich he had bought with the last of the money Patricia had given him. It had been a full day since he had left her standing there in front of Kurt's apartment, and not a moment had gone by when he didn't wonder how she was getting along; or if he had made a mistake by leaving her.

The Whisper hadn't shown his horrible face again, but Nick couldn't shake the feeling that the demon was always close. The Pull was still going haywire, telling him that everywhere was the right direction, as if trying to home in on something that it couldn't quite find.

All he had was Blitz and his new vocation: part time vigilante/protector of the innocent. Nick chuckled with a mouthful of ham and cheese.

Regardless of why he had the skills that he did, helping Patricia made Nick realize that he could use them for something good. At least until he found his way home.

If he really even had a home.

Before Nick could let the depressing thought sink in, something happened across the street from him that caused him to drop his sandwich and jump to his feet.

A woman with blonde hair came crashing through the plate glass door of the RavenCorp building. She hit the sidewalk with a roll, and then sprang to her feet just as two large men in black business suits came running after her, climbing through the hole she had just made. The woman seemed to be readying herself to fight rather than run.

Whoever she was, she needed help, Nick thought. Time to test out that new resolve.

Blitz watched him go, leaping over cars and dodging five lanes worth of traffic, pulling on his mask as he went.

The dog thought about following, but then looked down at the discarded ham and cheese sandwich.

His friend could handle himself.

Melissa grimaced as she felt tiny shards of broken glass dig into her arm and hip. If she ever saw that little runt again, Raven was going to pay for this.

Without a word, Raven's men charged her. Melissa sprang into action, turning a quick spin into a powerful roundhouse kick she hoped would catch them both. One of the men leaned back beyond the swinging foot and the other man dodged just enough to only receive a glancing blow on the tip of his chin.

Melissa kept her momentum going, bringing that same leg back around low this time, attempting to knock the legs out from under both of them. This time the man that dodged the first blow was hit full force, he landed painfully on the broken glass below him. The second man turned his leg in a defensive slant that caught Melissa's leg instead of being hurt by it.

Melissa took a few steps back and prepared to go on the defensive. The man that was still standing took a collapsible baton from his pocket and extended it with a snap of his arm. He came running at her, and Melissa could see that the second man was already getting back to his feet.

These guys were tough, and she had half a plate glass door scattered into a million pieces and digging into her body. This time she may have bitten off more than she could chew.

She moved in and blocked the baton-holding arm with her own while leading with her knee. The man took the knee to the stomach with a grunt, and then grabbed Melissa's hair with his left hand. She kicked out at him and jumped away, ripping a chunk of her hair out in the process. Melissa cried out in anger and pain, and then instantly swung into another kick. This one connected full force, and she felt the crunch of the man's front teeth beneath her tennis shoe.

She smiled. Now she was getting somewhere.

Melissa eyed the second man, who had pulled a stun gun from his pocket and was slowly approaching her. Great, Melissa thought, now I can have a shredded arm and 10,000 volts running through my body.

Then something happened she could not have expected. A dark shape darted into view from the road to her right. It soared through the air and collided with the man's head, then flipped backwards and landed behind him. Melissa's jaw dropped open as she saw it was a man. A man in a black mask.

"What the...," Melissa started to exclaim. She was rudely interrupted when a goon missing his two front teeth hit her in the collarbone with his baton.

Melissa cried out again, turning her attention fully back towards her attacker. She burst into motion, barely thinking about what she was doing. In seconds her fist had connected with the man's throat, and then her hands had trapped the arm with the baton and twisted it forcefully. She heard a snap, and the man howled in agony. She let him drop to the ground, and then put her heel into his head and sent him into unconsciousness.

She looked up in time to see the man in the mask standing over her second attacker. The stranger looked down at his dispatched foe with a look more filled with concern and discomfort than anything else; as if he wasn't fully able to grasp what he had just done.

"Listen, I don't know who the hell you are or why you just helped me, but you need to get as far away from here as possible right now. There's about to be a lot more of those guys all over us, and trust me, that's something we don't want," Melissa called out with a sense of urgency.

The stranger looked up at her. For a moment he seemed dazed, and then he nodded.

"What about you?" he asked.

Melissa pointed down the road behind her. "I'm getting the hell out of Dodge, compadre."

"Let me come with you," the man said without hesitation.

Melissa dropped her arm and looked at him in confusion. "Why?"

"What if they catch up with you? I can help," he said, and his dark green eyes told her that he sincerely wanted to.

She noticed that he hadn't bothered to ask why they had come after her. He just saw that she needed help and wanted to give it.

She made a noise of frustration, and then began to run down the road.

"Come on then!" she shouted behind her.

"Blitz, let's move!" she heard him yell. She turned just long enough to see a big brown dog trot after them with half a sandwich in its mouth.

What the hell had she gotten herself into this time?

About a mile and a half of sprinting later, Melissa shoved open the door of her apartment complex and shuffled inside. Her insides felt like they were about to explode. She looked behind her and noticed the man and his dog follow her in. He had not broken a sweat.

She pressed the button on the elevator, then got in and slumped to the floor in exhaustion.

"I've really got to stop drinking," she said, looking up at him as he walked in behind her.

The man took off his mask and smiled at her. He really wasn't a man at all, she could now see. He was probably only a year or two younger than her, barely at the end of his teens. His features were angular yet soft. His smile was simple and seemingly without motive. His eyes were big and childlike in their sincerity. His messy brown hair hung slightly over his forehead. He was as skinny as a rail. She didn't know how someone like that could have just run a mile and a half and not be throwing up in the corner.

"My name is Nick," he said, extending a hand towards her.

"Nick what?" she asked.

Nick shrugged, "Just plain Nick."

Melissa smiled, "Nice to meet you, Just-Plain-Nick."

"Melissa Lunar Moonbeam," she offered, taking his hand, "My parents were hippies."

Nick laughed, and Melissa couldn't help but smile. His laughter was just as harmless as the rest of him seemed to be. How could someone so unthreatening have taken one of Raven's elite bodyguards out as fast as he had?

"And this is Blitz," he said, kneeling and putting an arm around the dog.

Melissa saluted the dog. "Nice to meet you too, Fuzzy."

Blitz just panted happily in front of her.

Nick's face turned serious. "Why were those men trying to hurt you?"

Melissa pursed her lips, deciding how much she should tell this strange person she had only just met.

"I pissed off their boss."

Nick nodded. "Oh," he said, as if that was answer enough.

Melissa smiled. She was beginning to enjoy this character.

"I'd like to hang around for a while, if you don't mind. In case they come after you," he said to her.

Melissa kept smiling, but she gave him a questioning look.

"And why should you care?"

Nick seemed to think for a minute, and then simply shrugged his shoulders again.

"You some kind of superhero?" she asked him.

He shook his head, and seemed uncomfortable with the question.

"Ok, Just-Plain-Nick. You can stick around for a while. I might have a use for you tomorrow anyway."

He smiled, and then looked up at the roof of the elevator.

"How high up is this place of yours?"

Melissa grinned and pointed a finger upwards.

"Straight to the top."

85

Nick stepped out of the elevator into a huge apartment. Hardwood floors stretched wall to wall, the giant open space broken up only by a few huge pillars set into the floor and a small kitchen in one corner of the apartment.

The décor, however, was far from impressive. Aside from one couch thrown into the middle of nowhere, a stack of dirty clothes piled higher than Blitz was tall, and a large blue mat spread out on the floor to his right, the place was almost empty.

"Welcome to Casa-De-Crap," Melissa exclaimed as she walked across the floor. She kicked her shoes off, and then plopped down on the couch.

Nick nodded, pretending to be impressed.

"Nice."

She laughed, "I have simple needs. Honestly I spend most of my time working out or sitting in one bar or another, drinking my cares away and hoping someone picks a fight with me."

Nick looked at her questioningly.

Melissa shrugged. "What you saw out there earlier...that's two thirds of my life, kid. I'm a professional bodyguard. I live to kick ass, in other words."

Nick nodded and continued to look around. This did seem like more of an occasional place to crash than an actual home. Which made him wonder, what kind of person was Melissa that she would crave conflict so much? He had seen her handle herself with those two thugs earlier. She was very capable. Her body was toned and muscular from head to toe. Not in a female bodybuilder sort of way, but more of in a professional martial artist sort of way. Nick supposed that was more or less what she was.

He watched her begin picking pieces of glass out of her arm and tossing them haphazardly on the floor.

"Shouldn't you have a doctor look at that?" he asked.

Melissa just kept on picking. "Why?"

Nick couldn't help but admire how tough she was. Maybe a bit careless, but very tough.

"Can I help, then?"

Melissa looked up at him with a look of mistrust. "No thanks."

Nick nodded and she went back to working on her arm. So he just sat on the floor next to Blitz and watched her.

She was very pretty. Under different circumstances he supposed Melissa could be considered beautiful. Instead she chose to carry herself with something of a rough-and-tumble demeanor and an obvious air of being above concerns of appearance. He guessed by those observations that she didn't think too often about the opposite sex. Or any sex in general.

Her hair was long and honey blonde. A little unmanaged, but still very pretty. Her eyes were a deep ocean blue and seemed to spark with life and emotion. Much of that emotion was anger, Nick guessed, though at what he had no idea.

She had likely come from a past that hadn't exactly been kind to her.

"Do you have any family, Melissa?" Nick asked.

Melissa's features seemed to darken at the question. She shook her head as she picked another piece of glass out of her arm before beginning to work on her hip.

Ah hah, Nick thought. There's the soft spot. He wouldn't press the issue, but he did mentally file it away.

"Any friends?" he asked instead.

Melissa still didn't look up at him, but did speak this time. "Just one."

"Who?" Nick prodded.

"His name's Jason. He's in trouble and that's why those men were chasing me. I'm trying to get him out."

Nick watched as a visible wave of determination washed through those ocean blue eyes.

"Get him out?" he asked.

"Raven is holding him against his will. Has been for a while now. I want to get him out of there, and tomorrow I'm going to do it."

"Raven? As in Jacob Raven?" Nick asked.

Melissa nodded.

Damn, Nick thought. He had just walked into a much larger conflict than a few street thugs.

"So where are you from, Slim Jim?" she asked.

"I'm not from…around here," he told her.

"Obviously," she replied.

Nick continued to look at her for a moment, and then decided to tell her as he had told Patricia.

"Truth is, I don't know where I'm from."

Melissa stopped what she was doing and just sat there, looking at him in surprise.

"I woke up in the woods a few weeks ago with no memory of where I came from. I wandered into the city because it seemed familiar and have been wandering ever since, hoping to remember something other than my name."

She stared at him with a hesitant expression. He could tell she didn't believe him.

"And the superhero thing? The mask and the sword?" she asked, motioning towards Nick's long canvas bag.

"How did you know?" He was startled. He hadn't shown her the sword yet.

"I've got an eye for weapons," she said, motioning towards the far wall.

Nick turned and saw a large rack adorned with several wooden swords and staves as well as a few decorative weapons, one of which looked very similar to Nick's own blade. One staff in particular stood out, being wrapped at both ends with iron. The wood seemed stronger too. He guessed that was her weapon of choice. He turned back to her.

"I woke up with the sword. As for the, uh…'superhero thing'….I don't know. I just….starting doing it," he said with a shrug.

"So that wasn't the first time you attacked someone in plain daylight with a mask on?" she asked, still in a tone of skepticism.

Nick shook his head, "Not exactly."

Melissa stared at him a few moments more, then shook her head and decided to let it go.

"Weird."

Nick was relieved she had decided not to press the issue.

"So, Nick," Melissa said, going back to working on her hip. "Will you help me get Jason out of there?"

Nick answered without hesitation, again surprising her.

"Of course."

Melissa smiled. "Good."

She wasn't quite sure what to make of this odd character yet, but if he could somehow make Jason's escape easier, he was worth keeping around.

Besides, she kind of liked the creep.

15

Melissa awoke the next morning, though it was actually afternoon as was often her practice, to see Nick sitting in the exact same position on the floor he was sitting in last night. He looked up at her expectantly, sipping on a bottle of water. Blitz was curled up beside him, his dark brown eyes stirring open as Melissa sat up.

"Have you been there the whole night?" she asked him, blinking her tired eyes awake.

"No. I went out to get us something. Hope you don't mind. I borrowed some change off the counter. Coffee?" he asked, pointing to a cup sitting on the floor near the couch.

Melissa grunted, then swung her legs over the side and grabbed the cup, eagerly gulping it down.

Nick watched her with rich amusement. Her hair was a complete mess, all shoved to one side and sticking straight up. She had both snored and drooled on her pillow during the night. Somehow her messy demeanor spread a sense of warm familiarity over him. Maybe she reminded him of a friend he once had. Nick relished the feeling.

Melissa looked over and noticed him grinning.

"What?"

"Nothing," Nick said with a chuckle.

Melissa just grunted again, then put the coffee back down on the floor and stood up. She stretched, then put her hands on her lower back and loudly popped her spine. She shook her head until her hair fell back into place. And vioala...Melissa was ready for the day.

She looked up at a clock on the wall and noticed it was only 12:15. Jason wasn't scheduled to be moved until 6:00 PM, and Stacy would notify her if plans changed. They had plenty of time to prepare.

She walked over to the blue mat on the floor and began stretching. Nick watched her with curious attention.

"We've got time to kill. You want to practice?" she asked him with her head hanging by her knee, her arms stretched to one foot.

Nick thought about it. Fight for fun? Combat was more of an instinct to him than an actual conscious skill. Yet the concept intrigued him.

"Okay," he said, and rose to his feet.

Melissa finished her stretching and walked over to the weapon rack on the wall. She grabbed one of the smaller, lighter looking staves. She then picked up a wooden pole that was about sword-sized and tossed it to Nick.

"Here you go, sword boy."

Nick caught it and looked at it like it was a foreign object.

"You're still not used to using that thing, are you?" she asked, noticing his reluctance.

Nick just shook his head.

"Well too bad. 'Cause I'm a goddamn pro with one of these," Melissa said, and spun the staff in her fingers with ease and confidence.

Nick suddenly realized he may have picked a pretend-fight with the wrong person.

"Heads up, chap!" Melissa yelled, a wide smile spreading across her face as she ran to close the distance between them. Her staff swung high at Nick's head. He jumped backward without thinking, covering ten feet of floor in the process.

"Whoa," Melissa said, but didn't stop her charge.

She came at him again, jabbing the staff out its full length of six feet. Nick stepped to the side, and then rolled under as Melissa quickly brought the staff towards him.

He was on his feet in the blink of an eye, still holding the sword in his hand like a five year old awkwardly holding an assault rifle.

"I know you can use that thing. So use it!" Melissa yelled, swinging the staff over-handed like a hammer. Nick spun to the side, batted the weapon away with his own, then spun again and landed a hit on Melissa's thigh.

She rubbed her leg, but smiled all the wider.

"That's more like it," she said, and then came at him twice as fast as she had before.

What commenced then was a complicated and lighting quick dance of dodging and weaving, strikes and counter-strikes, slashing, thrusting, and parrying.

Nick felt a wave of exhilaration wash over him as he allowed his body to move with all the speed and grace it wanted to. The world spun as his body did, and he was only half aware of what he was doing next. She swung at him and his legs would move. She tried to hit him and his arm would block. He was moving faster than his mind could keep up. Inside of him was some faint and fast instinct that told his limbs how to move next, but Nick was only now becoming aware of it.

"Hah!" he laughed, and then jumped full force over Melissa's head, smacking her in the shoulder with his practice-sword as he went.

90

"Stand still, you little monkey!" she screamed and laughed at the same time.

The two of them were beaming, Nick's legs pumping furiously to continually position him away from Melissa's strikes, and Melissa's arms swinging forcefully, never quite able to land more than a glancing blow on the boy. It was a challenge neither of them had quite experienced before, and the fact that it was coming from an ally instead of an enemy magnified the joy of it a hundred fold.

"No memories, huh?" Melissa asked, following her horizontal swipe with a kick at Nick's chest.

"Nope," Nick replied, arms out wide and body pushed back just out of her reach.

"No family? No lady friend? No job?"

"None that I can remember," Nick said, dancing to his left and taking another shot at her side. Melissa deftly brought the staff down in a diagonal line and deflected the blow.

A wave of déjà vu hit Melissa then as she watched Nick's eyes and his smile and watching him move in synch with her own motions. She suddenly had the very distinct feeling that something just like this had happened before. But how? She had never met the kid until yesterday. Certainly she would have remembered someone as weird as him.

She chose to ignore the feeling. No use spoiling as good a time as she was having.

"So you're just bouncing from one corner of the city to the next, hoping to remember something and doing your weird superhero thing?"

Nick leaned back as the staff sailed a mere inch above his chin.

"Pretty much."

Melissa decided to amp things up a bit. Nick was good. Circus-freak good. But she was the best.

Melissa swung her weapon in a vertical arc in front of her and began to twirl it, mimicking a defensive motion. Nick predictably backed away so as to not get his weapon caught in her maneuver.

But at the apex of the third twirl, she kicked out with her left foot, hitting the base of the staff and sending it rocketing in Nick's direction.

Nick tried to move, but not fast enough. The weapon collided with his stomach with the force of a jackhammer. He doubled over before falling sideways with a thump and a groan.

Melissa caught the other end of her staff, then swung it above her head and held it in both hands. She jumped up and down, whooping and hollering.

91

"And we have a winner! The unstoppable! The unbelievable! The best there ever was! Melissa…Lunar…Mooooooooonbeeeeeam!!!"

She chuckled and walked over to him, holding a hand out and beaming.

"I win, Slim Jim. But don't feel bad. I always do."

Nick looked up at her with a sly smile.

He burst into motion, springing the weight of his body onto his hands and looping his legs out from under him in a wide arc. They came around Melissa before she could realize what was happening and swept her legs out from under her. She landed on her butt with a thump. Her eyes widened and a surprised yelp escaped her lips.

Nick tried to stand, but his stomach hurt too much to do it. He settled on propping himself up on his knees.

"There's a first time for everything," he said, a smile of satisfaction on his face.

Melissa looked at him, her eyes still wide. She shoved him hard with one hand. Nick only laughed as he rolled backwards onto the mat.

"Jerk," Melissa said, recovering her own smile.

They both got to their feet, Nick tenderly holding his stomach and Melissa rubbing her sore behind.

"Ow," they both said in unison, which triggered another shared laugh.

They hobbled close together towards the comfort of Melissa's couch, both of them happier than they could remember being in a long time, if also a little bit more sore.

"Slim-Jim?" Nick looked at her with one eyebrow raised.

"Bite me," was Melissa's only reply.

16

"Another garage," Nick said as he and Melissa crouched behind an SUV.

"What?" Melissa whispered.

"Nothing," Nick said, shaking his head.

They surveyed the massive parking garage beneath the RavenCorp building. A single door was set into the wall about fifty feet to their right. Melissa knew that was the door that Jason and his guard would be coming out of. She knew that because that was the door she had helped a few of Raven's "failed employees" out of. Whenever one of his workforce greatly disappointed him, he would have them escorted out of this door. Melissa helped for a few of the more dangerous men that Raven had fired. They were escorted out of this door, shoved in a van, and never seen again. Melissa cared little, for these were always the worst kind of scum heading into that unfortunate fate. Today she felt a twinge of unease knowing that it was her best friend that would be escorted out that door; hopefully to simply another holding facility, though even that Melissa could not say for sure.

"You can stay hidden, right? And move quietly?" she asked Nick.

Nick looked at her for a moment, and then nodded.

"Good. Head over behind that truck on the far side of the door. Try to weave between the cars so the security cameras don't catch you. I'll make the first move. When their attention is diverted…that's when you'll do your thing, chicken wing."

Nick laughed quietly beneath his mask.

"Good luck," he said to her.

"We aint gonna need it, chief."

Nick smiled, and then began making his way across the far side of the garage, ducking low and pausing between each parked car. Melissa was struck by how utterly silent he was. If she hadn't been looking right at him, she would never have known he was there.

She silently prayed that Stacy would pull through. Jason's escort attachment was scheduled for a dozen armed guards. Why, she didn't know; unless Raven expected trouble, in which case he would certainly get it.

Stacy's job was to call in a sighting of the target her team was looking for. At that point, Melissa hoped McElroy would pull some of the attachment off of Jason's escort to go after whatever poor sap Stacy and her father were charged with finding.

Might even the odds a bit. She was less concerned about the danger to her and Nick as she was about the danger to Jason. At any moment, if the two of them didn't keep the guards busy enough, one of them might scoop Jason back into the building, out of her reach forever.

In a few moments, she heard the door open.

"Show time," she whispered to herself, keeping her fingers crossed.

Stacy ran her fingers through her dark hair, wondering if she hadn't just caused a world of trouble for herself. Her father was barking orders to a growing contingent of men in the conference room outside.

Stacy had claimed to have intercepted a police dispatch about a an armed masked man on 10th and Piedmont, right outside the park. An easy ambush spot if Raven's men could get to him in time.

But of course they would arrive and there would be no masked suspect. She hoped they would just assume they had not made it in time, but she knew there was a chance that her father would check police records to confirm the call-in. At that point...she would be screwed.

Her father was a firm believer in consequences. If Stacy messed up, he reprimanded her for it just as if she were a subordinate in the military. And now with Raven involved....

She only hoped her deception would help Melissa out enough to be worth the potential fallout.

Jason stepped out onto the concrete stairs behind one of his huge escorts. Two more followed behind him. His eyes quickly darted about the garage. He was both hoping he would see Melissa and praying he wouldn't, because if he saw her, so would they. All he had at this point was Melissa's bravado to go by. She said she could fight, but Jason was terrified to see her go up against three of Raven's best. At least several of those men had been called away moments before. Small consolation when he looked at the size of the three brutes that guided him towards whatever fate Raven had in store for him.

If he saw his best and only friend get hurt in front of him, Jason was afraid it would be the last straw in his crumbling psyche. Raven would have won. Jason would simply have nothing to live for.

Determined for that not to be the case, Jason snapped himself back into the moment, and remembered his part to play in their plan.

He began to wobble as he walked down the steps.

"What the...," one of the men behind him exclaimed.

Jason let his feet slide out from under him, and he tumbled down the concrete stairs, barely missing the man in front of him. He grimaced as his hip, his shoulder, and then his head smacked against the concrete. There wouldn't be much acting required from this point on.

He lay on the ground, and began to groan. His hands, bound with plastic cuffs, clenched his stomach.

The two men behind him rushed down the stairs and crouched over him.

"Shit, the kid took a tumble. You think he's hurt?"

Jason began making retching and coughing sounds.

"No shit. He's acting like he broke a rib or something. What the hell do we do now?"

The man in front looked around the garage nervously, and then turned to his two partners.

"Dammit. I'll radio Francis and ask him. He aint going to like this, though; and you damn sure know that Raven isn't."

The man lifted his walkie-talkie to his mouth, but before he could press the button to speak, a voice emerged from close behind him.

"Tell Francis he's next. I owe that asshole for a year's worth of trying to show me up."

Jason looked up. There she was, standing in the middle of the garage about fifteen feet away from them, wearing the same kind of gym clothes she always seemed to, with a long staff propped on her shoulder and a confident smile on her face. God, how he loved that woman.

Apparently one of the men saw Jason's beaming face.

"The kid's faking it! It's a set-up!"

The man in front looked at Jason, scowled, and then kicked him in the ribs.

"Why don't you kick someone that can kick back, jack ass!" Melissa yelled, running at them.

Two of the men ran to meet her. One of them stayed behind and hovered over Jason.

"Fucking Moonbeam. That bitch doesn't know when to quit."

Jason could have split the man's skull right then and there if he had the strength.

Melissa met the first man with her staff, battering him across the face too quickly for him to block. A stream of blood cascaded from his broken nose. The second man met her foot, but only stumbled back a few steps.

Jason watched her recover from the initial strike and set her staff before her in time for the man she had kicked to come at her again. The man with the broken nose made a gurgled sound of anger, and then came on as well. She thrust her staff violently at both of them, causing both to back up a step. They would have a chore of reaching her past that six foot weapon.

He smiled. So she really was as good as she said.

His breath caught a little in his throat as he noticed something move past him in the corner of his eye. Something very fast.

An instant later he was vaguely aware of a shape sailing over him, colliding with the last of Raven's men, and sending him over the rail and onto the ground below.

A man landed next to the prone thug, and then quickly side-stepped around him. Jason's mind reeled in confusion.

Who the hell was that?

The man wearing the mask, as Jason now noticed, pulled a long curved sword from a sheath on his hip

Jason began to wonder if he hadn't hit his head too hard on the concrete floor.

The last of Jason's escorts got up off the ground, dusted himself off, and then pulled a collapsible baton out of his waistband, extending it with a flick of his wrist.

"I heard about you, ninja-creep," the man said, seeming unafraid of his opponent's unsheathed blade.

"Then you should know that's not going to stop me," the man in the mask said, and leaped forward. He sliced the baton in half in mid-air, and then kicked the man square in the chest, sending him smashing backwards into the wall.

Jason's jaw dropped open. That baton was made out of metal.

In the blink of an eye, the masked man kicked his opponent three more times across the chest and face. The man twitched slightly, falling to the ground.

Jason wasn't sure what he had just witnessed. He had no time to dwell on it, however, as he suddenly realized he had not been watching Melissa. He turned to see her standing there, one man crumpled to the floor beside her, the other a few steps away, still clutching his broken nose, but now reaching for something in his jacket.

A gun, Jason realized, and his heart jumped into his chest.

It seemed to be stuck in its holster however, and the man fumbled with it in an attempt to release it from its catch.

Melissa just smiled, and began twirling her staff in the air above her head.

"Melissa, what the hell are you doing! Just hit the guy!" Jason yelled, heedless of the danger of drawing more attention to them.

"She's having fun, from the look of it," the masked man said to Jason's left. Jason looked at him long enough to see him shaking his head in the same exasperation that Jason felt.

Melissa continued to twirl her staff, building speed. The man fumbled some more, then Jason heard a click and saw his arm begin to move outwards.

Melissa sprang into motion, clearing the steps between them with a quick hop and swinging the staff outward with all the momentum she had built.

The man drew his gun just in time for Melissa to smash his outdrawn hand.

A thunderous crack echoed in the parking garage, and the gun sailed a good seventy five feet away, landing harmlessly between a Honda Civic and a Mitsubishi Eclipse.

The sound had not come from the impact with the gun. The man looked down at his hand. His eyes widened as he noticed three of his fingers jutting at three different odd angles. A fourth finger hung off his hand by nothing but a thin strip of mangled skin.

He screamed, and didn't seem to notice or care as Melissa swung her staff again, smacking him in the temple and sending him into merciful unconsciousness.

She chuckled a bit as she looked down at him.

"Show off," said the man with the sword. He twirled it twice in his fingers, as if trying to keep up with Melissa, and then sheathed it at his side and approached her.

Jason stood up, feeling bruised and battered, despite the fact that he had not been involved in the fight at all.

"Holy crap," was all he could say.

Melissa grinned and ran towards him, dropping the staff as she went. She swept him up in a bear hug. Jason was nearly half a foot taller than her, but she still picked him up with ease. His shackled hands pressed into her ample chest and Jason felt even more color sweep into his dark cheeks.

"Told you I'd get you out!" she said, beaming with pride and relief.

"Yeah...you did," Jason said, a wide smile spreading across his face as well.

97

He looked up at the stranger with a doubtful look in his eyes.

"Oh that's just Nick. He's kinda weird, but he's useful," she said, putting him down, but still holding onto his arm and smiling.

Nick lifted a hand and gave a quick wave.

"Nice to meet you, Jason," he said. Jason couldn't be sure, but he thought Nick was smiling underneath the mask.

"What's with the….," Jason began, but Melissa interrupted.

"No time for love, Dr. Jones. We gotta split!"

She jerked Jason forward towards the exit, but then seemed to have an idea and brought him over to Nick.

"If you cut him, I'll kill you," she said to him, enforcing her point with a very serious glare.

Nick's eyebrows rose, but then he seemed to catch her point.

"Oh. Yeah, ok," he said, then drew his sword back out.

Jason backed up a step, but before he could protest Melissa pushed his arms in front of him and Nick quickly and gently slid is sword between the plastic shackles. Just like that, Jason was free.

He stared at his wrists for a moment, reveling in the feeling. He hadn't felt free in what seemed like a very long time.

Then Melissa was dragging him forward again. She retrieved her staff, and the three of them ran out of the garage like kids who'd just egged their first house.

Jason looked over at Melissa's smiling face as they ran, and wondered if now wasn't one of the best moments of his life.

17

Raven's jaw was clenched so tight that he thought his teeth might shatter. He seethed with anger at what he saw on the monitor before him. Melissa and Jason running out of the parking garage, following that damn masked freak.

Raven inhaled deeply, his teeth still pressed together in a furious sneer.

"Why the hell didn't you warn me he would be with her? We could have stopped this and caught him at the same time!"

Behind him, a hand calmly came to rest on the leather upholstered chair Raven was perched in.

"I wanted to see first-hand what he was capable of," came the reply from the man standing behind him.

"Well now you know. And now I have two problems to worry about!" Raven pouted.

"Patience, Jacob. Melissa is not worth your worry."

"And how the hell would you know? That bitch is dangerous; and I know dangerous."

The Dark Man said nothing.

"Fine," Raven said, conceding to his mentor's advice.

After all, this was the man that was responsible for Raven's rise to power to begin with. On his deathbed, Jacob's father and then owner of the company had been about to dissolve RavenCorp. Jacob was in a panic, trying to convince his father that he was good enough to run things. Elias Raven would not hear of it. He had come to regret the lifetime he had spent stepping on the backs of others and building a fortune off of not only oil, but also arms dealing with foreign countries. Jacob was a chip off of the old block when it came to business sense, but when it came to ethics...Raven the younger was seriously lacking.

So just when Jacob believed his life of privilege and his chance for power were at an end, in walked a man whose words and abilities changed everything. Garbed more often than not in head-to-toe black, with salt-and-pepper black hair and eyes that never seemed to be the same color, this odd stranger had promised Raven all the power he craved, and began delivering it when he walked into Elias Raven's bed chamber one night, walking out five minutes later with all the necessary papers passing control of RavenCorp to his only son, signed in Elias's own handwriting.

Elias died three days later, having not said a word since The Dark Man left his room that night. The nurses told Jacob he had died with a look of fear on his face.

Jacob mourned little. He admired his father, but the gain of a multi-billion dollar company greatly outweighed the loss of a parent.

"The cosmic chessboard is aligning into place, Jacob. If we are to control it, we have to allow for certain sacrifices," The Dark Man continued.

Raven nodded again. He was furious at allowing Melissa to feel like she had bested him. He was angry at the new-comer who had interfered with his interests not once, but three times now. But he was most upset about letting the Dredd boy go. Jason was a project Raven had been eagerly awaiting the opportunity to begin in earnest. What he had planned for the boy had been his philosophical aspiration for years, and watching the instrument of its completion walk away from him was almost more than Raven's pride could bear.

"But I'll get him back, won't I? And that bitch will die?" Raven asked.

The Dark Man nodded.

"Soon. Jason Dredd will be back in your grasp, and Melissa will get what's been coming to her for longer than you know. But for now, we need them to steer the boy in the direction we want him. He's very important, that one, as I've told you before."

Raven watched Nick and the others, now entering a parking lot several blocks away that likely contained their get-away vehicle. They may not know that Raven had the entire city under surveillance. They also couldn't have known that it didn't matter. He was going to let them go anyway, though he still didn't fully understand why.

"Soon you will, Jacob," The Dark Man said behind him. Raven's heart skipped a beat at the realization that his mentor had just read his thoughts. It wasn't the first time it had happened, but it startled him every time.

"Soon you will understand everything. And when that day comes…you'll truly be the most powerful man on the planet."

Raven clasped his hands in front of him, and couldn't help a greedy smile from spreading across his lips.

Nick climbed into the back seat of Melissa's old red station wagon. Blitz was waiting for them, panting happily. Their stuff was piled in the back. Melissa apparently hadn't needed much from her apartment.

Jason got into the passenger seat, and then immediately leaned back to look at the dog.

"Blitz," Nick said, pointing at his furry companion.

Jason nodded and smiled a bit, though Nick could still see the hesitation in his eyes.

He remembered he was still wearing the mask. He quickly pulled it off. Jason's concern seemed to fade a bit at that.

Melissa cranked up the car, and then sped out of the lot and drove them away from RavenCorp as fast as she could go.

"What's with the....," Jason motioned towards Nick's mask.

Nick looked at it for a moment, and then shrugged.

"He shrugged, didn't he?" he heard Melissa say from the front.

Jason nodded to her. Melissa just shook her head and sighed.

"Apparently this ding-dong has been going around dressed like a ninja turtle for the past few weeks saving kids from burning buildings and stuff," she said, pointing a thumb back at Nick.

Jason looked at him again, his eyes wider.

"Really?"

Nick looked out the window.

"Yeah, sort of," he said.

Jason watched him for a moment more, then simply said, "Huh," and sat back down in his seat.

Despite the obvious mistrust directed towards him, Nick liked Jason immediately. There was something in the kid's eyes that spoke of an intelligence and curiosity that Nick didn't think was common. Physically he was pretty normal, though tall. 5'10 or 11. Kind of thin, like him. African American. Hair that was teased up into short dreadlocks, obviously unkept from the weeks he had spent in Raven's cell. He was probably around the same age as Nick and Melissa. Late teens, early twenties.

But when Jason looked at him, he suddenly seemed a lot older. Maybe it was because of the intelligence behind those brown orbs, or maybe it was because Jason had already been aged by the trauma of his captivity or the loss of his family. Regardless of why, there was something in him that made Nick sure that Jason was a lot tougher than he looked.

They arrived at a dirty, run-down motel on the east side of town about twenty minutes later. Jason had suggested the place. Its roach-infested hovel atmosphere made him think that Raven wouldn't have eyes in a place like this.

They threw down their things in various corners of the room and on the two double beds. Blitz jumped up on one of the beds. None of them cared enough to chide him for it; they were all so relieved to be in relative safety.

"I'm going out for a minute to make sure we weren't followed," Nick said, mostly because he sensed Jason and Melissa needed some time alone.

Melissa nodded and smiled at him. Blitz jumped down and followed his friend back out onto the second story walkway.

They watched Nick close the door, and then turned to one another.

"We did it, kiddo," Melissa said to him with a grin, sitting down on one of the beds.

"Thank god," Jason said, smiling warmly back at her.

"You didn't think I'd go back on my word, did you?" she asked him, cocking one eyebrow in a sly gesture.

"Not for an instant," Jason replied, sitting on the bed across from her.

"So...why didn't you tell me about that guy?" he asked her.

"Who, Nick? I just met him yesterday."

Now Jason raised an eyebrow, this one considerably less playful.

"Look, he kinda came out of nowhere and helped me get away from Raven's men. I told him I was going to bust you out and he offered to help."

"So you trust someone that just 'kinda came out of nowhere' and you only met yesterday? What if he was hired by Raven to spy on you?" Jason asked, seeming slightly irritated.

Melissa crossed her arms in front of her.

"What's the big deal, Jason? Without him, I wouldn't have had nearly as easy a time getting you out. Where's the gratitude? And besides, there's something about him that seems kind of...."

"Dangerous," Jason finished for her.

Melissa's eyes narrowed.

"I was going to say familiar."

Jason shook his head, "So you trust the guy just because you think you've met him before? That's not like you."

Melissa scratched her elbow and suddenly looked uncomfortable.

"He says he has no memory before a few weeks ago. Says he woke up in the woods one day with that sword in his hand and he's been wandering around ever since."

"And you buy it?" he asked.

Melissa thought for a minute.

"Yes…and no. There's something about the guy that doesn't seem quite right. You're right, he's definitely dangerous. And that no-memory business doesn't feel like the whole story."

Jason nodded, glad he wasn't the only one weirded out by Nick.

"But Jason, when I look in Nick's face,…all I see is…well…a nice guy that wants to help."

He sighed and rocked back on his elbows. Melissa was right. There wasn't a hint of malice in Nick's voice or in his eyes. He was either completely genuine or a really good actor.

"So what's the plan, then?" Jason asked her.

"Well, I guess that's what you and I need to talk about."

When Nick and Blitz came back in a few moments later, both Melissa and Jason were sitting on one bed and staring up at him. They had obviously been waiting.

He threw his sword on the other bed, in the sheath that Melissa had let him steal from the prop sword she left behind. He leaned against the wall and looked at them.

"I think we're in the clear," he said, hoping to lighten the tense atmosphere in the room.

"Nick," Melissa began, "We want to ask you a favor. Jason and I aren't really sure what to do next and we'll probably end up hiding here for a week or two until we figure things out."

Nick nodded, a little surprised by where this was going. When he walked in, they had both looked at him like they were about to ask him to leave.

"So we'd like you to stay," Jason said, continuing where Melissa left off.

"Raven will be after you too, now; and Melissa tells me you have nowhere to go, so…we'd like it if you stayed with us until we all have a better idea where to go from here," he finished.

Nick could tell by the look in his eyes that Jason wasn't entirely confident in what he was asking.

"Thanks, guys, but…," Nick began.

"Nick, just shut up and say yes," Melissa interrupted him.

Nick looked at her for a moment. She was smiling. It was a genuine smile. He realized that, despite the fact that they had only known each other for a 48 hour period, Melissa seemed to understand him better than even Patrica had.

But he thought of The Whisper. What if the demon came back while he was with them? Melissa was a force to be reckoned with, but could she stand up against a monster like that? And Jason; he seemed like a smart kid, but did that really matter if they were ambushed by something that wasn't human?

Then again, Nick knew he could help protect them if Raven and his men did find their hiding place.

He reached inward. The Pull hadn't stopped. It was pulling him....

Melissa and Jason noticed an odd look cross Nick's face.

The Pull had changed directions. It was now trying to draw him away from the city, back in the direction he had come. What the hell did that mean? He hadn't found anything here. No one knew him. He didn't seem to have a home here. Was The Pull wrong all along? Should he even trust it? All he had were the words of a possible hallucination and a gut feeling that may simply be mixed up memories.

"Okay," he finally answered, "I'll stay."

Melissa grinned and Jason nodded.

"Good," she said.

Pull aside, Nick couldn't leave them. Though The Whisper was a constant threat, so was Raven. They were in hostile territory, and he wanted to see them out of it.

If his Pull couldn't be trusted...Nick would have to follow his heart.

That evening, Stacy cringed as she heard multiple sets of footsteps clomping down the hall towards the surveillance center. She had been waiting for hours, dreading what was to come. At the very least, her father would yell and scream and go on one of his violent rants. At worst, Raven would demand she be arrested, and her father would have to comply.

Turns out, things were about to get even worse than she could imagine.

Her father burst into the room, pulled his sidearm from his holster, and held it to her head.

"You lying little bitch."

Stacy couldn't breathe. The words had hit her harder than any bullet from that gun could.

"You've been seen colluding with Moonbeam. Moonbeam just attacked a contingent of Raven's men and freed a valuable asset with the help of our target!"

Stacy said nothing. She just stared at him, getting lost in the rage she saw from her father. Six of Raven's men stood behind him, armed with riot guns.

"How do you plead?" her father asked.

"What?" Stacy managed, not comprehending what was going on.

"The charges brought against you...how do you plead?" Sergeant Cross roared.

"Dad, I...."

"Shut up!" he screamed, "You're no daughter of mine."

Stacy couldn't stop herself. She wrapped her arms around herself and started crying.

"Get this weak piece of trash out of my sight," Cross said, motioning with his gun.

As Raven's men led her away towards an uncertain fate, Stacy did not look at her father.

She couldn't, and she wasn't sure if she would ever be able to again.

18

"You did not just do that," Jason said with his mouth hanging slightly agape.

"What?" Nick replied, with a slightly amused grin on his face.

They were standing on the roof of the motel, both of them having succumbed to cabin fever in the five days since they had been there. Melissa was on a supply run, and the two of them had decided to spend some time outside in the sunshine. The weather was starting to get warmer as the first days of Spring truly took hold.

Jason had suggested the roof, and took the easy way by going around to the back of the building and climbing the access ladder.

Turned out there was an even easier way. When Jason reached the top and walked over to the edge to see why Nick had not followed, Nick met him there by vaulting over the edge and landing in front of him.

"You know that was probably a fifteen foot jump," Jason said, trying to stress to Nick the absurdity of what he had just witnessed.

Nick just shrugged, and sat down facing the city.

Jason sighed, shook his head, and then sat down beside Nick.

In the days that they had spent together, nearly all of Jason's mistrust of this strange boy had faded away. Every word out of Nick's mouth was laced with sincerity. Every look he gave them was honest and kind. Sure, he could leap over tall buildings in a single bound and go 48 hours without sleeping a wink and probably dodge bullets for all Jason knew; but despite all of these things, Nick usually acted like any normal young guy.

Well, that wasn't true, Jason thought. Nick was actually a lot nicer than a normal young guy.

"Where's your house?" Nick asked, looking out over the ghetto below them.

"Over there," Jason pointed a few blocks away at a small ramshackle collection of apartments. It hadn't been much, but it had been home.

Jason thought about his missing mother, and the betrayal of his older brother Colin. Suddenly the strength seemed to drain out of him and his arm slumped back onto his knee.

"You think we'll find her?" Jason asked, trying not to sound helpless but knowing he was probably failing.

Nick looked over at him and nodded his head.

"Yeah. I do. It's only a matter of time."

Jason nodded back, trying to force himself to believe that Nick was right. It had probably been a miracle that he had gotten away from Raven, himself. And that, he believed, was mostly due to Raven's carelessness. What hope could his mother have to escape that madman?

He looked over at Nick. Maybe more hope than I think, he thought to himself.

"You going to help me?" he asked Nick.

"Yeah. As long as it takes. We'll get her out," Nick said with apparent certainty.

Jason smiled, and looked back out over the city.

"So tell me…about this 'hero' business."

He could feel Nick growing tense beside him. Nick hated talking about this, and Jason wasn't sure why.

"There've just been a few times when I was at the right place at the right time to help someone. I'm not a hero. I just did what anyone else would do in those situations. I helped."

"And the mask and sword? Is that something just 'anyone else' would do?" Jason asked him.

Nick crossed his arms across his kneecaps and set his chin upon them. Jason thought he looked about twelve just then; like a kid who was still trying to learn what it meant to be a grown up and do grown up things.

Jason had to fight the urge to laugh.

"Whatever that is…it's from before. Part of who I was before I lost my memory. I woke up with that sword and I put that mask on purely by instinct the first few times. I wasn't expecting people to think I was trying to be…something more than an ordinary guy."

"But you kept doing it?" Jason prodded, determined to get to the bottom of this part of Nick's mystery.

Nick's eyes seemed to glaze over, as if looking at something far away. He nodded.

"It felt right. When I see people looking at me…their fear replaced with gratitude…. It just feels right."

Jason smiled. He did believe that Nick truly didn't know where the mask and sword and his incredible skills originally came from; but whatever purpose they originally had, Jason believed that he was using them for a new purpose. A great purpose.

108

"Maybe I should stop. Seems like every time I do something...people think the wrong things about me."

"Like what" Jason said. "That you want to help people? That there's a person out there that wants to look out for them? That they don't have to be afraid anymore when they walk outside their door at night?"

Nick looked up at him, and Jason gave him a serious look.

"You've been on the news, Nick. They're still talking about that burning building and that elderly couple that came forward and said you saved them, not to mention the people who saw you help Melissa in front of RavenCorp."

Nick seemed surprised.

"They call you a hero, Nick, because that's what they want. That's what they've been wanting. The world is a shitty place these days. Everywhere you look there's violence and murder and destruction. The police are corrupt and useless. The youth of America are moving more and more towards anarchy. Gangs are becoming more prevalent today than they've ever been before. People like Raven are able to hold sway over their lives and have power over whether they live or die. We're sliding back towards the dark ages, Nick, and people are feeling more and more helpless at what's happing and what's likely going to happen to them."

Nick looked back out over the city as Jason went on.

"But you...you put on that mask and you become the thing they've been waiting for; a symbol that it's still possible for someone to care. You send a message that they won't always have to fear. You protect people that need protecting. You save people that need saving, like me. And you give them something they thought they'd never feel again. Hope."

Jason watched him as Nick's features changed. His eyebrows creased and he looked at his hands. He seemed to think very hard for a moment or two. Then his head rose back up, and there was something new in his eyes. Determination.

"Maybe...maybe you're right," Nick said quietly, more to himself than to Jason. "Maybe I am supposed to do something good with this."

Jason smiled, and rose to his feet.

"Glad to hear you think so too."

He turned around and headed back towards the ladder.

"The world needs heroes, Nick. Give them what they want."

Jason walked a few steps, and then Nick called out to him.

"Jason?"

Jason turned around.

"Thanks," Nick said, smiling.

109

Jason returned the smile.

"You're a weird guy, Nick. I won't argue that. But weird or not…I'm glad to call you my friend."

Nick's smile widened as he watched Jason turn back around and head back down the ladder.

Melissa hummed to herself as she stepped out of the car. She continued to hum as she lifted the two arm-loads of groceries out of the back of the wagon. It was mostly junk food. Jason would probably complain, but Melissa didn't know thing one about cooking. Nick probably didn't either. The kid seemed to barely know how to tie his shoes sometimes.

It had been nearly a week since the escape and Raven still hadn't found them. Melissa didn't kid herself, however. Richie-Rich probably knew where they were. The runt seemed to know everything. Yet if he wanted to send his men after them, he surely would have done it by now.

Perhaps in another day or two, Melissa would feel confident hopping in the car with Jason…and hopefully Nick and Blitz, and just drive out of town without fear of being stopped by cops on Raven's payroll. Perhaps…just perhaps…Raven had decided they just weren't worth it.

And after that? Melissa had no idea. Maybe she would finally cash-in her mother's inheritance and her padded bank account, assuming Raven didn't freeze her assets, and buy them a place up in the mountains. Far away from this crappy city and the crappy people that live in it. There they could do what they want. Jason could look at the stars and draw his pictures while Melissa lifted weights and watched bad TV. And Nick…well Nick could do whatever the hell Nick does.

It wouldn't be a bad life, really. No more fighting. No more beating up people because Raven told her to. Truth was, she would probably miss that part. Not the taking orders from Raven, but the thrill of the fight. Maybe she'd start another bare-knuckle boxing circuit like the one she was in for a while in Birmingham. Nick would be pretty good at that too, though not as good as her of course.

Melissa's thoughts were interrupted as she walked up the stairs to the second floor of the motel. She could see what looked like a small manila envelope sitting on the ground in front of the door.

Was the payment overdue? She didn't think so. She thought she had paid them through the week at least.

Her good mood started to vanish as she got closer to the door.

No, no no no no, she repeated over and over to herself. Please don't let it be from Raven.

She put the grocery bags down and bent over to pick up the envelope. Her heart sank when she opened it and pulled out the contents.

It was a single black and white photograph. A girl sat in a chair with a gag in her mouth while a large man with an assault rifle stood next to her and stared at the camera.

The man was Francis McElroy. The girl was Stacy Cross.

"Dammit" Melissa muttered under her breath as she sat back against the railing across from the door.

She flipped the photograph over to see if there was a message on the other side. Sure enough, there was.

8th and Juniper. Tonight. Bring Dredd and your new friend or you know what will happen.

She stared at the writing in plain black magic marker for a good two minutes, damning herself for getting someone else into this. It was Jason's and her problem. Involving Stacy was stupid and selfish. Hell, now she even felt bad about getting Nick into this.

She would go alone. Tonight she would say she wanted to go out for a walk or something, and then she would drive across town and deal with this. It was her mess. She would clean it up.

"Who is she?"

Melissa nearly jumped out of her skin. She looked up to see the top-half of Nick's body leaning over the roof above.

Melissa reached inside one of the grocery bags, grabbed an energy drink can and chunked it at him.

"You scared the hell out of me, you creep!" she yelled as Nick shielded his face, the can smacking hard into his elbow.

"Ow!" he exclaimed loudly.

The door to their room opened and Jason poked his head out.

"Everything okay?" he asked, worry on his face as he looked at Melissa sitting on the ground with the contents of one grocery bag spilled around her.

Melissa looked at Jason and sighed. Guess there was no hiding this now.

Nick jumped down from above. Blitz trotted around Jason in the doorway and began sniffing a bag of Doritos.

"So, who is she?" Nick asked, rubbing his sore elbow.

Jason shut the door and sat down on the ground in front of her.

"A mistake," Melissa said plainly, eying Nick.

Nick sat down as well and began picking up bags of chips and pretzels and putting them back in the bag as Blitz watched in disappointment.

"I had some inside help getting you out, Jason," she said, turning her gaze to him.

"And now that person's in trouble," he said, looking at the picture in Melissa's hand. He grabbed it from her and flipped it over. His eyes widened.

"Oh my god," he said quietly.

"Raven's using her as bait, isn't he?" Nick inferred.

Melissa nodded.

"Yeah, now I've got to go over there and get the poor kid out. Just me though. I'm not risking the two of you because I screwed up."

"Bullshit," Jason said, glaring at her.

"No," she said harshly.

"Nick and I will go. Give them what they want. Then we'll grab the girl, fight our way out of there and run like hell, leave this town behind. Think for a while before we come back for my mom," Jason said.

"Simple," Nick noted, "I like it."

"Guys, don't be idiots. McElroy will be prepared this time. There'll be a lot more than just three guys with one gun between them," she tried to reason with them.

"And you want to go alone?" Nick said incredulously.

She sighed again, rubbing her forehead and closing her eyes.

"At least take Blitz and I with you. They don't know about Blitz. Might be just the wild card we need."

"A dog?" she looked at him.

"Hey, you haven't seen this dog when he's angry," Nick countered.

"I'm going too," Jason repeated.

"No, you're not," Melissa argued.

"Yes, I am!" Jason said, his voice rising.

"Jason, Melissa's right. You're the one they want. Having you walk right into their trap would be way too dangerous," Nick said.

"Because what, I'd get in your way? Get over yourselves, both of you!" Jason said, yelling now.

"What's her name?" he asked Melissa.

"Stacy."

"Well Stacy is in trouble because of me. It was her that called two-thirds of my guard unit away, wasn't it?"

Melissa nodded. Nick's eyebrows rose. He seemed impressed.

"She did that for me, Melissa. She did that probably knowing what might happen because of it. Now I have to stand up for her. My freedom's worth nothing if somebody else loses theirs," Jason said with finality.

"I see why you like this guy," Nick said to Melissa, pointing a thumb at Jason.

"Guys," Melissa said, rubbing her forehead again and sounding pretty close to defeated, "We're so close."

Jason put a hand on her shoulder. The feeling was still new to Melissa. She wasn't used to letting people touch her.

"Then let's just take this one last step. Let's take care of this last loose end. Then we can get out of here. Then we can do whatever we want."

She looked up at him, pain in her eyes. She looked at Nick.

"He's right. If Jason wants to help her like she helped him, we should let him," Nick said.

"Fine," Melissa said, rising to her feet and gathering up the grocery bags.

"But I'm killing you both if something goes wrong."

19

Stacy's tears were gone. She simply felt numb as she sat in the chair with her arms clasped behind her. Her father was unpacking something with his back to her nearby. There were four other men with assault weapons on the catwalk with them. She didn't know if the ammo was live or non-lethal rounds meant to incapacitate. Stacy supposed Melissa would find out soon enough.

She was bait. Stacy figured that out the moment they took the hood off of her. They were in some kind of warehouse or staging room. She and her father were on a raised catwalk above a large room below. Judging by the echoes, she thought it was pretty empty. It also sounded like there were quite a few additional men below, waiting for the target...or targets...to arrive.

Melissa talked like a professional, but Stacy didn't see how she could fight her way out of this one. A twinge of guilt struck her as she looked at the weapons the men carried and imagined them firing at Melissa as soon as she opened the door. Given different circumstances, Stacy thought she and Melissa might have been friends. Stacy could certainly use more of those in her isolated life. As it was though, she supposed she was only a liability. There was a real possibility that Melissa might not even come for her.

She looked at her father, once a man she admired. He was always like this, more or less. Love was a weakness to him. Oh he claimed to love his family, but Stacy had known for a while that he only viewed them as possessions. Like articles of furniture in his home, a wife and children were simply things that a proper military man was supposed to have. Stacy and her sister were born because he felt her necessary.

Now that she had betrayed him, however, she was as much a liability to him as she was to Melissa. Therefore she had to be removed, like a wart or a gangrenous toe. She supposed her mother would mourn her for a moment before shifting back to attention for her husband's every whim. The mourning would be brief, however, for her mother was nothing but an empty shell. She had been for years. Stacy's sister Teresa was so self-absorbed she would hardly know she was gone.

115

Stacy felt very alone at that moment. No family that cared about her. No friends to speak of. She had managed to hold onto herself all these years under a vague hope that she would one day step out of her father's shadow and build a proper life. Now that hope was about to vanish in a flash of gunfire, at her own father's hand no less.

"I brought you a present," her father spoke, his back still turned.

She looked at him and watched as he turned around. The object in his arms was familiar. It was her crossbow. The one he had given her years ago, and she had used for target shooting every day since. It was her release, her excuse to think of what she wished her life could be while those narrow bolts sailed towards their target. With every bullseye she hit, Stacy imagined herself one step closer to a life that mattered.

Instead of…this.

Stacy looked confused as she felt her restraining strap being cut behind her, releasing her wrists.

"You can stand up now," her father said.

"Why are you doing this, Dad?" she asked him, rubbing her sore wrists.

"Because I want to give you a chance to redeem yourself," he said, holding the crossbow out to her.

She stepped forward and took it from him, eager to hold the familiar object. Weapon or not, it had acted as a sort of security blanket for her for a long time, and she was glad to have it in this uncertain moment.

"You failed me, Stacy," he father explained, "You failed me because you're weak and impressionable. That awful woman misled you; but you are my daughter, so therefore I know you must not be entirely foolish and naïve."

Stacy looked down at the weapon, a sudden dread filling her at her father's intentions.

"I'm giving you one chance. One chance to earn my love back. One chance to show me you're worthy of the Cross name. When Melissa Moonbeam walks through that door, I want you to shoot her."

Stacy looked up at him in horror.

"One bolt, straight through the skull. I know you can do it. I've seen how precise you are. Kill her. Correct your mistake, and all will be forgiven."

Stacy stood stock still for a moment, unsure how to process what was happening. When she finally moved forward towards the table and the array of crossbow bolts, her father smiled approvingly.

Stacy picked up a handful of bolts and placed them in her pocket. She then retrieved a single bolt before carefully loading it into the stock of the weapon. She brought it up to her shoulder, holding it in the position her father had taught her, staring through the sight at the big double doors below.

"That's my girl," Sergeant Cross said with satisfaction.

Stacy took one deep breath, and then swiveled to her right and fired a single bolt into her father's chest.

Melissa and the others heard the commotion as they approached the building. The parking lot had been empty and seemingly unobserved, which left them with plenty of room to enact their plan. Melissa would go in first with Blitz and make as much noise as possible; Nick would then follow, attacking from a flank and diverting their attention. Jason would then sneak in last and find a way of attacking Raven's doubly-distracted men, possibly with a weapon from a downed thug. It wasn't the most elegant of plans, but they all agreed it would do.

But now it seemed as if someone may have beaten them to the punch, judging by the sound of gunfire inside.

Nick and Jason flanked the door, staying out of sight. She nodded to each of them, and then shoved the door open with one boot-clad foot.

"Decided to start the party without me? Thought I was the guest of honor?" Melissa yelled, walking onto the large warehouse floor. There were a few crates stacked here and there, but the place was mostly empty. Nearly two dozen of Raven's men were in cover position behind the crates, their weapons aimed at a catwalk at the top of a set of stairs to the left. She could see the bodies of several downed thugs splayed about the stairs. Melissa couldn't see who was hiding behind the metal screen shielding the railing above, but she could venture a guess.

Raven's men turned their weapons at her as she entered, causing Blitz to utter a low growl beside her.

"Melissa, get out!" Stacy yelled from the catwalk, confirming Melissa's guess.

"Not a chance, Rainbow Brite," Melissa yelled back. She charged forward, staff in hand, surprised and a bit disappointed that Stacy had already done half the work for her.

Nick stealthily ran in as he heard Melissa's battle cry. He made a b-line to the left, wanting to secure the hostage before things got any worse. From the look of things, however, the hostage may not need securing.

He counted three bodies, stepping over each as he darted up the stairs, sword drawn and ready for anything…which turned out to be a good thing as he was greeting upon reaching the catwalk by a crossbow bolt fired directly at his face.

Nick leaned back a split second before the bolt would have buried itself in his mouth.

He held his free hand up and lowered his weapon, crouching down low both to avoid gunfire from Raven's men and to show the girl he meant no harm.

She was crouched under a table against a thin metal sheet riddled with bullet marks, which immediately led Nick to realize in relief that Raven's men were using non-lethal submission rounds. The girl stared at him with wide eyes, a large crossbow leveled at him in her arms.

Stacy's dark hair was draped around her face and shoulders, her dark brown eyes were tear-streaked and bloodshot. Her fair skin held a spatter of blood, as did her white blouse. Nick hoped the blood wasn't hers. Judging by the number of bodies around the frightened girl, he assumed it probably wasn't.

"It's okay, I'm with Melissa!" he called out to her, "Stacy, right?"

Stacy continued to stare at him. She did not lower her weapon.

"You can trust me," Nick said, and then remembered the mask. He took it off, and as he did he could immediately see a sense of relief wash over her. Her weapon lowered a bit and her shoulders slumped.

Crap, Nick realized. She was about to pass out.

Nick ran across the catwalk, sliding the last few feet on his knees and catching her as she slumped to the side.

He was afraid to leave the obviously traumatized girl alone, but the sound of Melissa's eager hooting and hollering mixed with the sound of gunfire below reminded him that he could not afford to stay out of the battle for long.

Jason crept in as inconspicuously as possible, keeping close to the wall and sliding behind a crate as soon as he could. His attention was torn between trying to stay out of sight and watching the furious battle take place nearby.

A dozen of Raven's men surrounded Melissa and Blitz with close to a dozen more taking pot shots at them from places of cover around the warehouse. One would think that, surrounded by so many trained killers Melissa would appear to be in more trouble than she did. Truth was, it was more Raven's men who were under assault by her.

Melissa moved like a whirling dervish of bludgeoning fury. Her feet were never in one place for more than a few seconds, and her upper body whipped back and forth with the force of her staff. Bullets sailed past her harmlessly. A smile was planted on her face that grew every time her foot or her staff planted onto one of theirs.

Blitz was bouncing back and forth in front of two enemies of his own, biting and snapping at them as each fumbled around, obviously not trained for an attacking animal. Blitz was big enough to be pretty frightening, and Jason did not envy whichever of the men the dog latched onto first. The dog seemed to understand that these men were a threat to his friends, and he was not about to let them be harmed.

Jason saw three men maneuvering against the crates on the far wall, lining up shots at Melissa and waiting for a chance to fire. He quickly moved around the corner and behind the boxes, shoving with all his might when he got there. The tower of heavy crates came crashing down around and on top of the three men. A gun went off and the bullet sailed harmless through the air as all three of them were buried in broken wood and machine parts from inside those heavy containers.

Nick heard the crash and peeked above the edge of the catwalk. He saw Jason standing against the wall with a bewildered but triumphant look on his face. Melissa was mopping up the last of her nearby opponents, all of which looked like they were trying to run away more than fight. Blitz paced underneath the catwalk, probably wishing in his own way that Melissa hadn't hogged most of the action.

His eyes scanned the other men in cover positions; the ones who had been firing at the catwalk and then at Melissa. All at once they seemed to stop, and Nick saw one of them speak into a small microphone on his sleeve. The other men held their ears, listening to orders from the first man, Nick assumed.

And then he noticed that the speaking man's eyes were locked firmly on Jason.

As he began to piece together what was happening, Nick heard the sound of sliding metal and clinking chains from the far wall near Jason.

The back door was being opened from the outside.

Jason heard the back service door slide upward and open. He froze in place, expecting more of Raven's men to come to the aid of their colleagues.

Instead what he saw was Francis McElroy.

Jason's heart sunk, and he slowly and carefully began to back up as two more of Raven's men entered the factory and leveled M16 rifles at Melissa and Blitz.

Melissa tightened her grip on her weapon. Her remaining opponents backed away as McElroy entered the room, closing the distance between himself and Jason, who was cornered between McElroy and the pile of crates he had just knocked over. She should have realized that McElroy wasn't in the building when they entered, and now she cursed herself for her oversight.

"So what do you want now, Francis? Did Raven have you set this up just to teach me a lesson?" Melissa asked, realizing she should stall for time long enough for Nick to save all their asses.

"Don't flatter yourself, Moonbeam," Francis scoffed, "Of all the people in this room, you're the one we want the least."

Melissa clenched her jaw. She really hated that oily-haired bastard. Jason was trapped. If she lost him again....

"So what are you going to do?" she asked, still hoping Nick, currently hidden from view, had a good angle of attack.

"Well, this, for starters," McElroy motioned with his hand. The two men beside him opened fire.

Melissa ducked and put her arms over her head. Those weren't non-lethal rounds. These were actual, live bullets. Blitz scurried away under some equipment in the corner while Melissa ducked and rolled behind a crate.

She then saw two things at once then. The first was Nick leaping like a panther from the catwalk towards the man on the left. The second was Jason screaming and throwing himself at McElroy.

"Jason, no!" Melissa screamed, but it was too late.

McElroy reached out and grabbed Jason in one huge arm. A white cloth was in his hand, which he wrapped around Jason's screaming face. Chloroform, Melissa feared.

Nick landed on his target knees first. The man smacked to the ground beneath him, his gun firing twice more while Nick pummeled the man's face with his fist and the butt of his sword.

Jason struggled for a few seconds, but then grew visibly weaker. Melissa was right. The chemical was knocking him out.

"Jason!" she screamed, breaking into a run towards him, not minding the gunfire.

The second armed man fired at Melissa's feet, slowing her charge and sending her off to the right, giving McElroy plenty of time to back up through the door and give her one last smug smile as he went, holding a now limp Jason in his arms.

Terror worked its way through her veins like a shot of adrenaline. Several critical moments passed as she dodged and maneuvered around the bullets and debris in her path.

"Get your hands off of him!" she roared, and then kicked off the ground and somersaulted through the air. The man fired at her, but simply wasn't fast enough. Her staff hit the top of his head with a loud thunk.

Nick was already out the door and climbing a ladder on an adjacent building when she caught up.

"Where are they?" she yelled in desperation.

"Up!" Nick yelled back.

She quickly climbed behind him. Nick got to the top, and then stopped in his tracks as a crash sounded out behind them from the warehouse. She could see panic in his eyes. Stacy and Blitz were still back there with some of the men she and Melissa had wounded.

Melissa brushed by him without a second thought, only partially aware that he had jumped back off the rooftop and towards the warehouse. She was on her own.

Melissa heard it before she saw it. A helicopter two buildings away. McElroy was already on board.

She pushed herself even harder and broke into her fastest sprint. A quick jump brought her to the next building.

The helicopter began to rise and pull away, taking Jason from her again.

She screamed in rage and sadness as she approached the ascending helicopter. She dropped her staff and readied herself to jump.

The chopper rose and continued to put distance between itself and the building. Melissa jumped on top of an air conditioning unit and then leaped with all her might.

Her fingers barely brushed the landing skid. The next sensation she felt was the earth rushing up to meet her.

Nick ran up the ramp. The crash had only been Blitz knocking over some boxes as he looked for her friends, but still he was concerned for the girl's safety.

He rounded the corner onto the catwalk and there she was, awake and in shock. She cradled one knee while her other leg and arm were sprawled limply upon the catwalk. Her eyes were wide and her face was pale.

She looked at him helplessly. She looked terrified. He tried to think of some other noble and protective thing to say to her; something to let her know once more that things were going to be alright.

121

"Hi," was all he managed.

She nodded weakly.

"Who are you?" she asked.

Nick pulled off his mask again.

"My name is Nick. I'm a friend."

He could see her smile a little as he took the mask off.

"Thank you, Nick," she said.

He just smiled back, and then leaned down and offered her his hand again. She took it, and then he hooked an arm under hers and pulled her up.

"I'm okay," she said.

He nodded, and walked beside her down the ramp.

She looked out over all of the bodies lying on the factory floor, most unconscious, but some dead, killed in Stacy's panicked attempt at self-preservation, Nick assumed.

She gasped, "Did...did I..."

"No," Nick answered, only partially lying. "You didn't do that. My friends and came to help you."

She looked back at him. He took her hand and quickly led her out of the factory. She had seen enough blood for one night. Stacy regarded the dog with curiosity as Blitz followed them out the front entrance.

"Where's Melissa? Is she okay?" Stacy asked as they both felt the cool night air hit their skin.

"Yes, but Jason was taken. She went after him. They'll be fine. Melissa's a force to be reckoned with."

She nodded, and then leaned against him. She was obviously still reeling from the night's events, both physically and mentally.

"We need to wait for them, and then we're getting the heck out of here before the cops or more of Raven's men show up," Nick said.

Just then Melissa came limping from behind the building.

"Melissa! Are you hurt? Where's..." Nick cried out.

"He's gone, Nick. They got away," she said, heartbreaking defeat in her voice.

Nick didn't know what to say. His heart sank.

"I'm so sorry Melissa. This is all my fault," Stacy said, still leaning on Nick.

"Shut up, Stacy, just...shut up," Melissa chided, waving her hand and not even looking at her.

Nick could feel Stacy flinch, and he couldn't help but feel angry at Melissa then. The girl needed reassuring, but Melissa seemed almost mad at her.

He watched Melissa as she paced back and forth for a moment, then wiped her eyes with her forearm and looked up at him with fury in her eyes.

"I have to go to RavenCorp. Right now."

"Let me get her to safety and I'll go with you," Nick said.

"I...I have nowhere to go," Stacy said.

They looked at her.

"I killed my dad. He wanted me to hurt you but I couldn't do it, so I...." Stacy said, trailing off as a sob rose in her throat.

Melissa looked at her a moment longer, and then shook her head.

"Not my problem. My best friend is out there and he's in trouble. I have to go find him...now."

"Hey!" Nick yelled, no longer able to contain his anger at the way Melissa was acting, "I'm not happy about what happened either, but don't take it out on her! She's obviously been through a lot tonight. You heard her. She has no place to go. Raven owns the cops. She needs us.""

"I DON'T CARE, NICK!!!" Melissa roared, stepping towards him threateningly, "Jason was the reason for all of this! If I lose him again, then all of this was for nothing! If it wasn't for her, we might have made it out of here! The three of us. The way we wanted."

"I'll help you, Melissa, just..."

"I don't need you," she interrupted, turning her back to them and walking away, "Either of you. Stay with your new girlfriend, Nick. I've got better things to do."

They watched her as she stalked off. Nick felt torn, but he knew he was right. Jason needed them, but so did Stacy. He was not about to abandon her in the state she was in. Besides, Raven obviously wanted Jason alive, so he was probably safe for now.

"I'm sorry," he said to Stacy as Melissa went back around the building, likely back to RavenCorp.

"She's right," Stacy said. He could feel her shaking. First her kidnapping, then her father, now this.

"Don't say that," he replied.

She pushed away from him.

"I should have been more careful, and I should have known how far my father would go. It's my fault Jason was taken again."

"So help us get him back," Nick said sternly.

She looked at him for a moment, seemingly unsure of what she should do. Finally she nodded.

"I will. Whether Melissa wants it or not, I will. I'll help you get Jason back," she said, brushing past him, back towards the warehouse, "And then I'm going to take down Raven for good,"

Nick followed her.

"Where are you going?"

"To find my weapon. I think I'm going to need it."

20

"You were supposed to bring both of them!" The Dark Man hissed when McElroy climbed out of the helicopter carrying only Jason.

McElroy paused, a look of panic crossing his face.

"Calm down. I told him Jason was the priority," Raven said. He was standing beside The Dark Man with a pleased grin on his face.

"You did what?!!" The Dark Man said, whirling to face Raven. His eyes flashed red for a moment before fading to blue. They had been green just a moment before.

"Really, for all the power you have, my friend, you still haven't learned restraint. I told them to grab The Hero if they could. Obviously he proved too much for them."

McElroy walked forward cautiously. Jason stirred, but remained unconscious in his arms.

"That kid in the mask attacked Randy like a damn mountain lion. It was all I could do to get out with the black kid," he said, trying to defend himself to Raven's dangerous associate.

"Dredd is worthless," The Dark Man said.

"To you, maybe," Raven countered, "But you need to remember that you're not running the show."

The Dark Man straightened his back and glared at Raven. Raven, however, would not be intimidated this time.

"My work with Jason here is very important," Raven said, "It may prove whether or not our plan is going to work."

"I told you it would work," The Dark Man spat back.

"Nevertheless," Raven said, "I need to see it with my own eyes. Jason is perfect. I'm not going to let him slip out of my grasp again. Not even for you."

The Dark Man shook his head.

"Do what you will...boy...but if the most important piece of our puzzle slips away because of this..."

Raven grinned.

"Come on, friend. Remember who you're talking to. Plans are already in motion to move the playing field to a more suitable arena. The Hero will follow us. Even if he doesn't, I have eyes everywhere. I have also have a lead on...resources that will prove much more capable of challenging him than Mr. McElroy here. When the time is right, you'll have him right where you want him."

The Dark Man glared at Raven a moment longer before spinning around and stalking away, giving them a dismissive wave as he went.

"Fine then, go play with your toy."

Raven smiled.

"You heard the man, Francis. Load Mr. Dredd back onto the chopper. I'll be joining you this time."

"Where are we going, sir?" McElroy asked.

Raven's grin widened.

"It's time RavenCorp found a new home."

Stacy stood in the motel shower, letting cool water wash over her. Blood pooled in the tub at her feet before washing down the drain. She watched it go while ringing it out of her hair. There was something cathartic about watching that blood drain away. She felt as if she were washing something else away from her as well. Quite literally she was watching her old life...her father, her family...go down the drain.

The initial shock of the night's violence had worn off when Nick showed up. She didn't know why, but being near him made it all seem okay. He was obviously the target her father had been tasked with finding. Sergeant Cross thought "The Masked Hero" as the press called him was some kind of left-wing nut trying to make Georgians lose faith in their police force by beating up criminals himself. Stacy had seen the police sketches on the news. They didn't do him a bit of justice.

Why was she not afraid of this guy? Why had she so quickly felt safe instead of threatened when he came bounding up that ramp with a sword strapped to his back?

She thought she knew. Nick was an adventure. Nick was something beyond normal. He said he wanted to protect her and she wanted to believe him.

Stacy wrapped her arms around herself and leaned against the shower wall. Guilt stabbed deep within her. Her father had just died, and here she was thinking about a boy.

What did she really have to go home to now? A mother who worshiped a man who had just threatened to kill her? A sister too wrapped up in her own career to even call Stacy on her birthday? An aunt and uncle she hadn't seen in years?

No. The truth of it was she had nothing, and now that Melissa had walked away from her, the only person that could help her now was sitting in the next room with his dog and his sword. She didn't even know his last name.

Stacy turned the shower off, toweled herself dry, and then put on the sweat shirt and pants that Nick had given her. They were Melissa's. Stacy realized as she put them on that they had a comforting smell. Musky and warm. Old but welcoming. She thought of Melissa's tired face. She realized she wanted to see that face smile again. An expression to match the scent she had left behind.

Stacy walked out of the bathroom and sat on the edge of the bed. Nick sat in front of her with his sword in his lap. He looked anxious, but he smiled when she sat near him. Blitz was lying at the foot of the bed, staring at the door.

"You're worried about them," Stacy observed.

"Very much so," he said; his eyes distant.

"You could have gone with her."

Nick looked at her and shook his head.

"No. I can't abandon a friend, even for the sake of another."

Stacy smiled, "But you just met me."

Nick smiled back and shrugged. Stacy grinned a little at the endearing gesture.

"You're different from other people, aren't you Nick?" she said, already knowing the answer.

Nick lifted his sword a bit. "What gave it away?"

She laughed.

"That's not what I mean. It's not the sword. It's not the mask. It's the rest of you. It's what's behind that mask."

Nick looked doubtful.

"You just met me."

Stacy leaned back and studied him. She wasn't used to guys not taking compliments well.

"Thank you, Nick. For helping me. If you hadn't been there...I'd be dead right now."

Nick nodded. "You're welcome."

"I wanted to be dead. After I shot my father...I wanted them to kill me." She felt the sorrow of loss hit her again. Years of built up emotion, un-returned affection and anger...snuffed out like a candle. One moment was all it took. Now she was alone, for better or for worse.

"Did they hurt you?" Nick asked her. He looked like he was afraid to hear the answer.

"No," Stacy said, shaking her head. "I don't know what would have happened if I had done what my father asked. Raven might have demanded my life anyways. Or maybe he would have locked me up in a room like he did Jason."

She saw Nick wince, and immediately regretted her words.

"I'm sorry. I don't know what Raven wants with him, but whatever it is we'll stop it."

He nodded, though she thought she could see his shoulders slump a bit.

"You're the one my dad was hired to find, you know," she said.

Nick slowly looked up at her, his eyes widening.

"What?"

"Yeah. He had us monitoring news reports and security footage from around the city, waiting for you to show up. Do you have any idea why?" she asked, genuinely curious.

"I...," Nick stammered, his eyes now staring into space. Stacy thought he looked horrified, "No...I have no idea," he finished, shaking his head.

"Nothing you could have done in the past would have brought you to his attention?"

Nick looked up at her again. He now looked helpless.

"I don't know," he said.

For the next few moments, Nick explained his lack of memory; how he woke up with the mask and the sword and how he honestly didn't know where his combat skills came from, nor his home or anyone that might be there waiting for him.

Stacy thought the tale was unbelievable, and yet she could see the truth in his eyes. Nick really didn't know who he was.

"We'll find out what Raven wants with you," she tried to reassure him, "Maybe it'll give you a clue as to where you came from."

Stacy decided to change the subject, as Nick was looking more and more panicked as the conversation wore on.

"So what's the story with those two? Jason and Melissa. Why is he so important to her?"

This did seem to shake Nick out of his confusion a bit, to her relief.

"I kinda thought you'd know more than I do," he said.

Stacy shook her head, "She never told me much about him. Just that he was important and she needed to get him out."

Nick seemed to think for a moment.

128

"Jason's something special. He's intelligent and creative. Loyal to a fault. He seems to still look at the world with optimism, despite what's happened to him. Can't say I blame her for wanting to help him."

Stacy nodded, "You think that's all?"

Nick looked at her and sighed.

"I think Melissa's been alone for a very long time. She doesn't talk about her past, but I get a sense she ran away from something. Maybe she's been running for a while. I don't she's let anyone in. Something about Jason…made her decide to take a chance. I think she wants to stop running, and I think he's a reason to do so. She's going to fight for that. I think she'd die for it."

Wow, Stacy thought to herself. She didn't know if Nick was right, but she had also had the notion that Melissa was a solitary person. All that anger. All that strength. It had to come from somewhere. Something long ago must have hurt her very badly. And for Jason to come along and make her feel like everything could be alright….

Stacy had never felt that way about anyone. She'd had friends; plenty of them in school, but never anyone she really truly trusted. She'd never been in love. Relationships in high school had been fleeting. No boy had ever been able to hold her interest, mostly because none of them looked at her as anything but arm candy.

To be able to fight for someone like that… To be willing to die for someone….

The door opened. Nick shot to his feet and Blitz wagged his tail expectantly as Melissa strode through and threw her long wooden staff on the bed.

Nick looked up at her expectantly.

"Empty," was all she said when she looked at him.

Nick seemed confused.

"What's empty?"

"RavenCorp, Nick. It's empty. They're all gone. Not a car in the parking lot. It's just…empty."

"Empty? RavenCorp HQ? The giant building downtown? How could it be empty?" Stacy exclaimed.

Melissa looked at her in surprise, as if she had forgotten Stacy was still there.

"Don't know why, Princess, but it is. If Raven snaps his fingers, people jump. I watched them evacuate the building. Wasn't but about a hundred people, give or take, considering what time of night it is, but they all filed out and loaded up equipment into big trucks around back. No sign of Raven and McElroy. They must've left via helicopter."

"So Jason's gone," Nick said, obviously disturbed by the news. "Where do you think they took him?"

"New Orleans," Melissa answered.

"What?" Nick replied, surprised that Melissa actually knew.

Melissa sat down next to Stacy and rested her elbow on her knees. She looked tired and beaten, Stacy noticed. Behind those tired eyes was a visible wall of rage.

"Raven was talking about a move to New Orleans for a while before I left. I don't know where or why, but it's the only lead I have."

Nick sat back again. "Then I assume that's where you're going."

Melissa looked at him. Stacy could tell that she expected Nick to go with her.

"Yeah. You got a better idea? We just saved him, Nick. And now we're right back where we started. Worse, even. I can't let them get away with this. I can't leave him hanging. Raven's going to be prepared this time. Jason will be under guard 24/7. But that doesn't matter. Nothing matters. I'm going to save him, with or without your help."

Nick seemed conflicted. The idea of going to New Orleans obviously didn't sit well with him. Stacy waited for his answer with just as much anticipation as Melissa did.

"Then I'll go with you. Jason's my friend too now," he finally said.

Melissa smiled. "You're sure? You're willing to leave behind whatever it was in Atlanta you were searching for?"

Nick nodded. "I don't think there's anything left for me here anyway. Whatever was here…I don't think it's here anymore."

Stacy watched him carefully. Something in his eyes told her Nick wasn't entirely sure of the truth of his statement.

Her heart beat faster. Now was the time to make a decision.

"Take me with you," she said to Melissa.

Melissa slowly turned her head to look at Stacy. Her eyes were wide and slightly angry.

"And why the hell would I do that?"

"She needs us, Melissa. And we might need her," Nick said forcefully.

"For what, Nick?" Melissa asked, her voice dripping with skepticism.

"She can help us look for him. Right, Stacy?"

Stacy nodded emphatically.

"I owe him just as much as I owe the rest of you. He was there, fighting for me just like you were. That's what got him captured. You're right Melissa, this is my fault. So let me make it up to him."

Melissa seemed a little impressed by Stacy's resolve. She looked back and forth between Stacy and Nick.

"She's only going to slow us down."

Nick shook his head.

"You know that's not true, Melissa. The two of us can cover a lot of ground. More than most people. Stacy will give us an extra pair of hands, and more importantly, an extra set of eyes and ears."

Melissa looked at Stacy again, then sighed and stood up.

"Fine. Army Brat can come too, but if she gets in the way, she's gone.

Nick smiled at Stacy with satisfaction. She smiled back, immensely relieved that she would get to stay with these strange and wonderful people.

"So saddle up, boys and girls. We're going on a little road trip."

Jason woke up in a dark room. His heart sank as he realized he was in another cell; this one smaller than the other, with no light source other than the light that peeked in through a barred window in the door. The door itself was ajar at the moment. He could see people carrying tables and large blue mats into the huge room beyond.

He could also see he was not alone.

"Hello again, Mr. Dredd," said Raven, sitting at the foot of the cot Jason was now sitting up on.

"You again," Jason said, scooting as far away from Raven as he could.

Raven laughed.

"Yes, me again. You'll be seeing a lot of me in the near future, Jason. A lot more than you would prefer, I'd suspect."

Jason tried to look around for means of escape. The only way out was the steel door. Raven was between him and the door, and he could also see one of Raven's men standing with his back to them outside the doorframe.

"What the hell do you want with me, Raven?" Jason asked, his voice tired and frustrated.

"Well, Mr. Dredd, I'm going to turn ordinary old you," Raven said, pointing his cane at Jason, "Into something special."

Jason did not like the sound of that.

"You know they'll get me out again," he said defiantly.

Raven grinned smugly.

"They will," Jason continued, "Melissa will stop at nothing to get me back. Nick too. You haven't seen what they're capable of. They'll tear this place apart."

Raven continued to grin.

"No, I'm afraid they won't," he said.

Jason stared at him, wishing he could wipe that annoyed smile off the man's face.

"They won't because they're dead."

Jason suddenly felt the world fall silent.

"After McElroy grabbed you, Melissa and...Nick, you said his name was...gave chase. One of my men was waiting in the helicopter with a sniper rifle. He put a bullet in Melissa's skull before she could get within twenty feet of you,"

Jason could not believe what he was hearing.

"That's...not possible," he muttered.

"It is, Jason. As for Nick; he went into a rampage when he saw Melissa fall. Killed two of my best before the sniper got him, too. Hit him right here," Raven said, pointing at his heart.

Jasons chest hitched and his fists clenched in shock.

"No more Hero," Raven said happily.

"Where...," Jason said, fury boiling behind his eyes, "Is my mother?"

Raven seemed surprised.

"Oh her? Why we killed her the night we took you. Didn't even bother to bring her to the building. I'm sorry, I thought you knew."

Jason screamed in rage, lunging at Raven.

Raven laughed as Jason pushed him over, the two of them rolling onto the floor. Before Jason could take a swing, large hands lifted him off of Raven.

"Good. Good! That's exactly why you're here!" Raven said, getting to his feet and dusting himself off.

Jason struggled to break free of the grip of Raven's man. No matter how hard he pulled, the man would not let go. Jason was just not strong enough.

"You're angry, aren't you?" Raven said, eagerness in his eyes, "You want to get to me, but you can't."

Jason sobbed, yanking towards Raven one more time before going limp in the man's arms, knowing his rage was not enough.

"I can change that for you," Raven said.

Jason looked up at him in disgust.

"For the next several months, this will be your home. It's a bit cramped and dark, but you'll get used to it."

Raven stepped aside in the doorway and motioned towards the big room beyond.

"After tomorrow, this room will be a gymnasium. My men will train here. Once a day, someone will let you out so you can too."

Jason was confused. What the hell was Raven implying?

"We'll feed you and clothe you and keep you from harm. You'll get to walk around the gym and lift weights or do whatever it is muscle-heads do. Around noon each day, one of my men will give you a little green pill. You'll take that pill without argument. It will...help you feel better about yourself," Raven said coyly.

Jason listened intently, his mind already grasping at possibilities.

"If you're good and do as you're told, one day you'll get to see your brother again. Yes, Colin still works for us. He misses you, you know."

Colin? Colin was here?

"So I guess that's that," Raven said, "If you need anything, just yell at the man outside your room. I can't promise he'll listen to you, but he's there in case of emergencies."

Raven took a couple of steps outside of the door. The man holding Jason lugged him onto the cot. Jason did not struggle or attempt another escape as the man backed out of the room and took position with his back to the door again.

"Goodbye, Jason. Try not to be too mad. Life's a bitch and all that. I suggest you try to make the best of it," Raven said, giving a small wave.

The door slammed shut, and Jason was thrust into near total darkness.

He sat on the cot with his back against the wall. His heart felt crushed. His soul felt trampled. He had nothing left.

Nothing but rage.

He would do as he was told. He would sit in his cell and eat whatever they fed him and take whatever strange medicine they gave him without complaint. He would step outside his room when they let him and use whatever equipment they would allow. He would strengthen himself in whatever way he could, for as long as was necessary.

And then, when the time was right...

"I'm going to kill Jacob Raven," Jason said, his small voice echoing in the empty room.

The next morning, Nick stood once more on the roof of the motel while Stacy and Melissa loaded up the car, his gaze not on the city, but on the road back east and the treeline beyond. He could see Stone Mountain peeking above the horizon. Something was out there. His Pull had told him so. Back East. Back the way he had come. It still didn't make sense, and yet he felt it, compelling him even more than before.

133

Then there was the demon. The monster hadn't appeared since the day he first saw it; there and then gone again like a dream. Perhaps it had been a dream. Perhaps The Whisper and the little girl had both been a part of the same prolonged hallucination. That would certainly make more sense than the alternative. After all, if it really were some kind of beast that wanted him dead, why hadn't it come back?

Nick looked over his shoulder. He could see Melissa barking orders at Stacy below while Blitz looked on from the back seat. Poor girl. She was getting the brunt of Melissa's frustrations. He only hoped they could find Jason quickly, and Nick could see the three of them off safely, onto whatever destination they decided upon. He had already made up his mind he would deal with Raven somehow. Stacy was right. The man couldn't be allowed to harm anyone else. His threat would have to be ended somehow. And then....

Nick didn't know what he would do then. The way he saw it, there were two choices; follow The Pull...or follow his heart.

He wanted to stay with Melissa and Jason, and perhaps now Stacy as well. They were becoming close to him, despite their brief time together. Melissa was like a demanding but well-intentioned older sister. Jason was like a bright and intuitive brother, and Nick was already taking a liking to Stacy's optimistic and determined attitude and simple world view. He could make a home with them. He knew he could. That fact made him less interested in his past and far more interested in his future. As long as he knew they would be safe with him, because if they weren't...there was no use sticking around. He'd rather die alone by the hand of some metal monster or whatever threat might come than drag his friends into the eye of the storm that followed him.

So he decided then to try something; something he hadn't tried before.

Nick turned his attention inward, and attempted to summon The Pull.

"Talk to me," he said to the crisp morning air, "Talk to me. Tell me what I need to know. What should I do? Where should I be going? Am I s...."

"You'll never be safe, Hero," came the small voice behind him.

Nick whirled around and there she was. It was the same little girl from that night on the rooftop. Same dirty blonde hair. Same red and brown dress. Same crooked teeth and bright blue eyes.

"That didn't take long," he said, surprised and somewhat disappointed. The girl's reappearance seemed to prove that the events of that night were very real.

"You're not crazy," she said, again seeming to read his mind again, "And I'm always close. I won't always come when you call me, but I'll always be here when you need me."

"Are you...The Pull?" he asked.

The girl seemed to think for a moment.

"Let's say I'm the one who gave it to you," she answered, placing her arms behind her back and swaying a bit on her toes.

"So you know where it's leading me," he reasoned.

"Yes," she nodded, her face very serious, "But I can't tell you."

"Why?" Nick asked, feeling a bit defeated. He sat down on the rooftop, crossing his legs as if in audience.

"Because if I tell you now, you won't be ready when you get there," she told him.

Nick leaned back and sighed.

"That doesn't make any sense," he said.

The girl laughed. The sound of it was comforting, despite his frustration.

"Life doesn't make sense, silly," she said, "Not yet anyway."

Nick gave up on that line of questioning. Whoever or whatever the girl was, she seemed determined to remain as enigmatic as possible.

"You probably know where I'm going next," he said.

"New Orleans. To find Jason and stop Raven," she said, nodding.

"And that's alright with you?" he asked her, genuinely curious.

She smiled.

"As long as you're with the right people, yes, it's alright."

Nick was surprised by that answer. The Pull, and whatever force it represented, was okay with him going off the beaten path?

"But I'm not following The Pull if I go with them," he countered.

The little girl shrugged, still rocking back and forth on her toes like a restless child; a real one anyways.

"You'll get there soon enough," she said.

"How do you know that?"

"Because we're all drawn back to where we came from in the end," she answered.

Nick stood up, still no comprehending exactly what she was asking of him.

"I don't get it. You pulled me west, to Atlanta, and then you're pulling me back to where I came from?"

"You found what you needed to here," she said, as if the answer should be clear to him.

Nick looked behind the girl at the cityscape around her. It was true, he found many things in Atlanta. He found Patricia. He found his desire to fight for others. He found Melissa and Jason and Stacy. He also found The Whisper and Jacob Raven.

Nick looked down at her again. He knew she wasn't going to tell him which of those things his Pull had initially brought him to Atlanta to find.

"No, I'm not," she grinned.

"That's really creeping me out," he said.

She laughed a bit harder this time. Nick wondered if Melissa and Stacy could hear her below, assuming she wasn't just in his mind.

"I know you better than anyone, Hero."

Again with that word. Nick still didn't like the sound of it.

"And The Whisper?" he decided to ask while he still had the girl's attention.

"Close," she said, "He's never left you since he found you again. He's been watching all this time."

Nick's eyes darted around him. The thought of seeing that monster again terrified him.

"Cool name, by the way. Sounds better than "That Purple Fire Thing"," she said, brining his attention back to her.

"You still think I can stop it? If it comes back?" he asked.

The girl winked at him.

"Maybe with a little help."

She then turned and began walking towards the far edge of the roof, likely to disappear as she had before, Nick realized.

"So that's it then," he said.

"For now," she said, looking back at him.

"But if I need you again…"

"You don't, Hero," she interrupted, "Not yet. Everything you need is down there."

Just then, Nick heard Melissa screaming up at him from the parking lot.

"Nick, get your skinny ass down here! Let's blow this joint!"

Nick walked to the edge and waved down at her. He then turned back to where the little girl was standing. Predictably, she was gone.

Nick jumped back down the ladder and ran around the building to catch up with the girls.

"Bout time, Emo Boy. What were you doing up there, being emo?" Melissa commented with a smirk.

"Just thinking," he said. He then had a thought.

"Hey you didn't hear someone laughing a moment ago, did you?"

Melissa and Stacy both gave him an odd look.

"Nooooo," Melissa answered, her eyes narrowed and her head slightly cocked to the side.

Nick shook his head, "Just someone in one of the rooms upstairs, I guess."

Melissa seemed to shrug it off, but Nick caught the look of concern remain on Stacy's face a moment longer.

"So, who calls shotgun?" Nick said, walking around back to make sure his sword was tucked away in the trunk.

"Oooh, me!" Stacy said exuberantly, raising her hand and hopping up and down.

"No way, Rainbow Brite," Melissa said, shooting her down, "Emo Boy gets to be co-pilot. You get in back with the dog."

Stacy's shoulders slumped, but she obediently opened the door and got in the back seat with Blitz.

"I don't even like Rainbow Brite," Stacy muttered as she plopped down on the seat and reached for her seatbelt.

"What was that?" Melissa asked, sticking her head through the driver's seat window.

"Nothing," Stacy said, visibly pouting.

Nick grinned. Despite the circumstances, despite everything that had happened to them in the past 24 hours and the days and weeks before, there was a tangible air of excitement around the three of them. They were going on an adventure. Leaving their pasts and the burdens those pasts had brought them quite literally behind. New Orleans might as well be a whole new world.

They would save their friend. They would take down Raven. Nick would do whatever it was his Pull was asking of him. And then…just maybe…there might be a happy ending waiting for them.

Nick and Melissa got in the car. She turned on the ignition. Nick looked in the rearview mirror and saw that Stacy was smiling.

Melissa turned to him. He could see she felt the same excitement and hope that he did.

"Nick, Stacy, Fuzzy…. Let's go get our boy."

Six months later...

21

The tunnel was damp, and dark, and covered in filth. A stench of offal and refuse permeated the enclosed space, but its current inhabitant did not notice. A sliver of light shone through a mostly-clogged grate in the street above, casting just enough light to make out shapes in the dark. The drainage system in this part of New Orleans was labyrinthine, dangerous, and full of near-pitch darkness. Just like home, thought The Whisper.

He crouched against the wall of the sewer pipe, shrouded in shadows, only his flaming eyes and ever present grin were visible. A large rat, roughly the size of a small dog, scurried into the pipe. When it came within smelling distance, it shrieked and turned to run, but no creature was faster than the demon. A bladed finger slammed through the rat's spine, pinning it to the ground.

The Whisper watched as the creature squirmed and squealed in pain. His grin widened. Pain was the demon's truest source of pleasure. That and the thrill of the hunt.

The truth was, he was not a demon in any Christian sense of the word. He was a creature of the Threads, an entity drawn into creation by raw living emotion. In his case, that emotion was malice. The need to inflict pain. The Whisper reveled in his purpose. He stalked and then he hurt and then he devoured his prey. All had fallen before him in his centuries of existence. All but one.

The Whisper retracted his claw after the rat's struggle ceased. He was beginning to gain limited control over the shape of his vessel, the body he had been summoned into by those pathetic cultists; amateur manipulators of the Threads who had no idea the forces they were attempting to control. He could shorten or lengthen his blades to some degree, and he could mold his facial features into whatever horrifying visage he desired. He rather favored the grin though. His favorite aspect of his new body was that it was completely indestructible. This he had tested.

One night when the streets were particularly empty, he had jumped from the tallest buildings in Atlanta and landed without a scratch; though the pavement and the homeless vagrant he had landed on had not been so lucky. Weeks later, he had broken through the window of a police firing range in Alabama. The only thing more humorous than the looks of horror upon the officers' faces was the fact that not even their automatic weapons harmed him in the least. He tore the six men there to pieces after he allowed them to rain slugs upon his metallic form.

Once he had even stood in front of a train. It had plowed over him, and had dragged him several hundred feet before his metallic body got jammed in its gears and it screeched to a halt. He ripped his way out from under it an instant later, for as he had also discovered, his fingers could cut through anything as if they were slicing through paper. Almost anything, as he had yet to understand why the boy's sword wasn't damaged during their brief struggle.

Now, a full six months after he had followed Nick from Atlanta, he rested underneath New Orleans. This was only one of his many hiding places he had discovered in this city, but it was perhaps his favorite. The Dredd boy was here somewhere, that's why Nick and the others had come. Occasionally, The Whisper would climb up through the air-conditioning ducts in Raven's new building and watch Jason as he tested himself in his captor's gym.

Jason was changing rapidly, and the demon knew why. He laughed at the thought of it. Yet another victory for the darkness. Innocence lost. Hatred embraced. That's usually the way it went when a child underwent a dramatic tragedy in their life, as Jason believed he had. And to think his friends had no idea. The demon laughed his raspy laugh. They probably still thought he was the bright-eyed, intelligent youth they knew before. What a surprise they were in for.

Yes, The Whisper thought, they'll find him. Either that or he'll escape and find them. He knew this because he had noticed that he wasn't the only inhuman being keeping an eye on them. The little girl that had appeared to Nick. The Whisper had been watching.

Someone wanted them together for some reason. But why? The demon grinned as an idea struck him. Was it because of him? Are they trying to protect the boy by keeping him with others? Perhaps. But the question still remained as to why they were so interested in him in the first place. Yes, he had noticed that Nick's soul was different somehow. Very different. But that's why The Whisper wanted him, his soul had tasted so delicious for the time he had been inside him, before the boy had caught him off guard and pushed him out.

That above all had troubled him the most. He had sworn that he killed the boy. He had completely consumed him. He was not only spiritually, but also physically deceased. But somehow, he lived on; under a different name now and with different skills but alive nonetheless. Part of him had allowed The Whisper to win. It had curled up and died under the weight of its own rage; but then another part...a secret part of him, had emerged. This part was stronger. This part was stronger than anything The Whisper had seen before.

Now the boy was walking around as if he knew nothing of who he was before. He carried a sword that shouldn't exist, a warrior's instinct more on par with the demon's than with any humans, and a name that wasn't his. Or was it? Was this really the boy The Whisper had attacked before, or someone completely new?

It does not matter, thought the demon. New prey or old, this boy was something The Whisper had every intention of savoring. Every last bite, every bit of pain, every bloody swipe.... The demon would take his time with this one. Nick and his friends would never know peace. Not for long.

The demon stood up. He had been below for long enough. It was getting dark, and night was the time when he liked to roam about. If not following Nick or his friends, he would find someone else to inflict pain upon. This New Orleans was such a bountiful place. So many lost souls. So much delicious pain. So much fun to be had.

Stacy hummed a tune while she flipped pancakes for the tenth time that evening. It was a typical night at the diner, and she and Melissa were as busy as ever. The two of them made up nearly the entire kitchen staff plus the wait-staff. The only other employee was a part time chef named Bob. Bob hardly ever spoke. He just grunted and got to work whenever Melissa or Stacy called back an order.

Stacy watched Melissa out of the corner of her eye. The tall, athletic blonde looked comical in her apron and striped skirt. Her hair was tied back and there was a smudge of grease on her face. Stacy had thought of wiping it off Melissa's face about an hour ago, but then she had envisioned the punch in the arm that would likely have been the reward for her courtesy. Besides, Melissa didn't care about her appearance. Melissa didn't care about anything. That's why Stacy envied her so much.

In the months since their arrival in New Orleans, Melissa's attitude towards Stacy had softened little. She still seemed to view Stacy as an interloper, despite the fact that it was Melissa herself who had inadvertently brought Stacy into this. Maybe it was Stacy's fast friendship with Nick that unnerved her. Maybe it was the fact that Melissa still believed Stacy would weigh them down. Stacy thought it was more likely, however, that Melissa was just using her as a scapegoat; a convenient vent for her frustrations over having not yet found Jason.

It hadn't taken them long to determine that Nick would be the most effective tool at their disposal for scouring the city for clues to Raven's whereabouts. Melissa had lost her advantage when they had left the familiar underworld of Atlanta behind. She no longer knew who to ask and who to threaten. Nick, on the other hand, could keep an eye on more of the city faster than any of them could.

He spent his days and most of his nights darting about slums, rooftops, and street corners both with and without the mask. He listened, he watched, and he learned the ups and downs of the strange and sometimes threatening city they now lived in. Though not quite as crime ridden as Atlanta had been being the seat of Raven's power, New Orleans had a seedy side of its own.

Nick had soon installed the same reputation for himself here as he had three states over. The Masked Hero had appeared more than a dozen times in the past few months, stopping assaults before they happened, chasing down a kidnapper, even thwarting a bank robbery. It was as if a comic book vigilante had erupted from the pages of those adolescent serials and had burst into reality. The public was split over whether to believe he even existed. The nightly news was often peppered with interviews with witnesses either cheering him on or deriding him for the irresponsible example he was setting. Yet Stacy had noticed that the deriding was becoming less and less frequent, and there were more and more conversations in the diner about the good this strange masked fellow was doing.

But all of it amounted to nothing for the three of them. Jason was still lost. Not even the infamous Masked Hero could locate their missing friend's whereabouts. Raven was always two steps ahead of them; if he was even still in the city at all.

So they spent their days watching, working, and waiting. Praying for a new lead or for Raven to pop out of hiding and back into the public eye. It seemed unbelievable that the man and his entire staff of mercenaries could disappear within a city such as this, and yet the man had done it. At night they returned home to the house Melissa had bought with a big chunk of her savings. She claimed it was an inheritance, though Stacy's attempts to find out further details were always met with stone-walled silence.

The house was a four bedroom, two story lake house. They had gotten a deal on it because the realtor claimed the place was slowly sinking into the lake. Five years or so and it would be gone, she said. They didn't care. They only needed a base of operations, and the place was perfect.

Not only could it house all of them, including Jason when they found him, but it had a huge garage attached to the house. Previously a storehouse for boats, Melissa immediately set to work converting it into a gym. Without her daily, sweaty workout sessions, Stacy thought she would likely lose her mind. There was too much pent up aggression in that freckly blonde head to not let it out from time to time. Nick joined her most days and it had become a favorite activity of Stacy's to watch the two of them playfully spar, taunting each other and displaying their impressive skills, each trying to top the other.

The few laughs they did share were merely a distraction. Each of them had their own way of dealing with their worries. In addition to her training, Melissa had spent the rest of her money on an old motorcycle, which she took out into the city frequently, the engine leaving a roaring trail of sonic pollution as she went.

Stacy played den mother, cooking and watching out for the others. Nick and Melissa really were a bit like children. Neither of them knew how to cook, and Nick didn't know how to drive. It made her smile to think that the famous "Hero" of Atlanta and New Orleans relied on her to take him to buy new socks.

As if on cue with her thoughts, Stacy heard a familiar soft voice at the counter behind her.

"Don't suppose I could bribe one of those pancakes off of you, could I, gorgeous?"

Stacy turned around, grinning ear to ear. "Depends on what you've got to offer, handsome."

Nick smiled widely, laying his backpack on the seat beside him. Blitz sniffed the floor nearby for leftovers that might have succumbed to the laws of gravity.

A few of the customers, non-regulars, looked at the dog with disdain. One man opened his mouth, but Melissa pointed an accusatory finger at him before he could speak.

"That dog's probably cleaner than you are, Jack, so don't say a word."

The man's jaw snapped shut. Melissa's powers of persuasion were as effective as always.

"And speaking of gorgeous..." Nick said, turning to face Melissa, obviously barely able to contain a laugh at her out-of-character appearance.

"F you, A-hole," she said, giving Nick another of her fingers.

"And such manners," Nick said.

Stacy giggled. Nick and Melissa's banter was one of the only things that kept the three of them in high spirits these days.

Melissa strode up to them and sat down next to Nick, totally heedless of the needs of her customers. Stacy brought out a plate and slapped a pancake down on it. Nick winked at her and dug in greedily. For such a skinny guy, thought Stacy, the boy could eat.

"Well?" Melissa prodded, looking impatient.

Nick looked up at her with a mouth full of pancake.

"I didda fin areyink."

Melissa sighed. "No habla pancake. Speak English, Senor."

Nick smiled, and then swallowed. "I said I didn't find anything."

Melissa sat back in her chair. "Figures. I just...had a feeling tonight would be different."

Melissa had one of her "feelings" about once a month. So far, none of them had led to anything.

"We'll find him, Melissa," Stacy said, reaching her hand towards Melissa's but not quite touching it.

Melissa looked up at her angrily. "You're starting to sound like a broken record, Stacy."

"But it's true. With Nick out there, and you and I keeping our ears to the ground, we're bound to hear something sooner or later."

Nick nodded.

"She's right, Melissa. We can't give up hope. Raven's here. I know he is. Jason must be, too."

Melissa turned back to him. "And how would you know that?"

Nick shrugged.

She made a noise of frustration and got back to her feet, angrily spinning away from them and stalking back towards her customers. Some unlucky patron was about to get the most uncomfortable service of his or her life.

Nick sighed as he watched her walk away. Stacy could see the guilt in his eyes.

"You're doing the best you can, Nick," she said to him, "and don't forget the good you're doing out there. You may not be finding Jason, but you are helping people that need it just as much as he does."

Nick smiled weakly at her. "Thanks, Stace. You just can't ever let someone be down, can you?"

She smiled back at him, "Nope. Sadness is a pet peeve of mine."

He laughed, getting up from his chair. "Back into the night I go."

"Ooh, that sounds so mysterious," Stacy said, narrowing her eyes for dramatic effect.

"Mysterious…right," Nick said, amused at the fun Stacy often poked at him for his "hero" persona.

"See you in the morning?" she called after him as he walked away with Blitz following behind. She knew Nick would not be in until well after she and Melissa had gone to bed, and that when he did he would be as silent as always.

Nick nodded and waved at her, and then turned towards Melissa and her customers.

"Better tip her good, buddy. Unless you like trips to the emergency room."

He quickly darted the rest of the way through the door seconds before a salt shaker sailed across the diner towards him.

Back out into the night air, Nick breathed deeply as he turned the corner of the building, retrieving his sword from under Melissa's car. He strapped it to his back, pulled on his mask, and then broke into a run into the trees across the road, making his usual b-line towards the interior of the city. Blitz happily sprinted along behind him, sharing in the exhilaration of movement and purpose.

As his body moved, Nick let his mind wander. His first thought was not surprising, as the subject of it had not truly left his mind for months. Shimmering black hair and dark eyes, simultaneously compassionate and tantalizing. A laugh that made his heart feel five times lighter every time he heard it. The warmth of her as she sat so close to him on the couch as they watched TV at night. So close because she trusted him, as she trusted everyone; loved him as she loved everyone, for Stacy's natural inclination was to give. Affection, compassion, assistance; she always wanted to help and she always wanted to brighten the mood of those around her, and Nick loved her for that.

For six months he had harbored these feelings, and for six months he had pushed them...and her...away. Because every time he thought of pulling her closer, a different set of eyes superseded hers in his mind's eye.

Purple fire.

The Whisper hadn't appeared to Nick in a very long time. Not since the alleyway the night he met Patricia. In fact, the demon had only appeared to Nick once. But Nick felt with near-certainty that the monster had not left him. He was watching. Or, at least, he had been. As more time passed, Nick felt safer and safer, with more and more distance between himself and that dream-like encounter in the alleyway, and the half-remembered battle that had apparently taken place inside of him before he had woken up.

Woken up. That's what he called it now. The day he had woken up. The day that, for all intents and purposes, he had entered this world; for Nick still did not remember who he was or where he had come from. He did not know why he could do the things he could or where the mask and sword had come from. His origins were as much a mystery to him now as they had been those many months ago; and yet he found himself caring less and less, asking those questions less and less.

He had a new purpose now. Finding Jason was his mission in life, yes, but there was another reason to live. When he wore the mask and when he held the sword...it was as if something inside of him opened its eyes and saw the world anew. He helped people. He often found himself in the right place at the right time to stop some horrible thing from happening to someone. He supposed it was The Pull; that inexplicable draw within him that carried him forward towards...something. Sometimes he would just feel the need to go left at a street corner instead of right, and there he would find a mugging taking place or a gang fight about to erupt; and then his sword was in his hand and he was in the midst of battle, moving with ease and grace and...yes...joy at what he was doing. The looks on the faces of those he saved filled him with a sense of more identity than he believed he could ever find anywhere else. The past was not his goal. Not any longer. Now his reason to live lay in front of him.

Nick and Blitz erupted through the trees, running across a field with the speed of the wind. The city proper was only blocks away. Nick trusted that his Pull would tell him where he needed to go.

He saw the glimmer of headlights from the street below the bank in front of him. A giant billboard broke through the grass to his right, advertising some kind of soda to a public that no doubt would buy it in droves. A public that....

Nick stopped running so fast that Blitz skidded past him, coming to a stop several feet ahead and trotting questioningly back towards him.

Nick's heart nearly stopped. Standing on the billboard was the little girl. Same red dress, same dirty shoes, same smile.

She was standing there, not a hundred feet away, watching him.

He wanted to call out to her, but he didn't know what to say.

Before he could act, the girl turned her head towards an intersection behind the billboard, away from the direction Nick had been running. She watched it for a few moments, and then looked back at Nick.

And then he felt it. The Pull tugging at him, yanking him in the direction the girl had looked. He took a few steps in that direction before looking back up at the billboard.

The girl was gone.

His heart began racing again. Every time the girl appeared Nick ended up pulled into one of the most fateful encounters of his life. He knew better than to question.

Nick ran towards the intersection at the far end of the billboard. He reached the top of the bank and looked down.

Cars. There were just cars parked at a red light; nothing more.

Suddenly confused, Nick crouched down and surveyed the situation. In the four lane highway there were two white sedans, a minivan, and a maroon SUV. Nick sighed in frustration. What had the girl been trying to tell him?

He suddenly felt an urge to take a second look at the SUV.

Sitting behind the wheel of the vehicle was a large man with slicked-back hair. He looked like a football player or a professional wrestler, but he was dressed in a business suit. Something about him was strangely familiar.

Then it dawned on Nick. It was one of the men from the parking garage. The one Nick had fought the day they rescued Jason the first time.

The light turned green, and Nick sprang into motion. By the time he reached the road, the SUV was already moving rapidly down the highway. There was no way Nick could catch it in time.

Without thinking, Nick jumped into the air and landed soundlessly on top of one of the white sedans.

He looked back at Blitz. The dog barked and ran after him along the side of the road, but eventually gave up as Nick coasted too far away. He could only hope Blitz would know to go back to the diner and wait for him.

Deciding to trust the dog's considerable intelligence, Nick turned his attention back to the situation at hand.

He was riding on top of a car. The car was approaching sixty miles an hour. He suddenly was aware that what he was doing would be considered insane, not to mention impossible, by anyone's standards. Anyone's but his.

Nick did not question. He knew better than to do that. He just held on.

The driver of the car must not have noticed its new passenger. The radio was blasting beneath him. Nick did, however, notice the amazed stares of several men and women driving around him.

"Looks like I'll be on the news again tonight," Nick said to himself.

The SUV changed lanes several cars ahead of him. Its speed was climbing up to eighty. Nick would have to switch rides if he was going to catch up with it.

He noticed a red sports car approaching from the left. He took a deep breath, and then flipped sideways through the air from one car to the other, landing silently.

Almost silently. Nick laughed loudly as the wind whipped by him. No roller coaster on earth could beat this.

The sports car zoomed steadily forward, closing the distance between itself and the SUV. Nick was dismayed to see the SUV suddenly and quickly move three lanes to the right, approaching an exit to an adjoining road. He didn't think the driver had spotted him. No, Nick thought, this guy is just that reckless.

He jumped again, pulling himself onto the roof of a semi. In quick succession he jumped from the semi to a brown sedan to another sports car that was also approaching the exit. Now he was only two cars behind the SUV.

The road they exited onto was a two lane road running away from the highway. The lights of traffic gave way to darkness as they left the glow of headlights and gas stations behind them and entered the gloomy industrial district, nearly deserted at night.

About a mile later, the SUV turned off the road. Nick jumped off his ride and landed behind some discarded shipping crates, crouching low and surveying the scene in front of him.

"Well, crap," Nick said beneath his mask.

The good news was that he had probably just located Jason. The bad news was that they had likely just jumped out of the frying pan and into the fire.

22

Melissa paced back and forth across the hardwood floor of her room. Her heart was beating a mile a minute. If what Nick had said was true, then her best friend was likely only days away from rescue. Less than that if they got lucky.

"C'mon, c'mon girl. Focus," Melissa muttered to herself under her breath.

An idea popped into her head. She pulled open her top drawer and retrieved an item she had bought months ago in case just such an occasion arose. She dug at it with her fingernails, slowly ripping a hole in the fabric.

She sat down on the bed and made herself take three deep breaths. She would be no use to Jason if she ran in there proverbial guns blazing. Tonight would be about scoping out the situation. If they were going to rescue their friend, they needed to be prepared, and even she could admit that.

She slipped the item over her head and yanked her hair out through the hole she had just ripped. It felt strange and alien against her skin.

"How the hell does Nick do this every night?"

Stacy leaned against the doorway into the kitchen. Nick stood across from her, waiting at the bottom of the stairs for Melissa. He looked at her. A familiar guilt was in his eyes. Stacy had been seeing it for months, but had yet to pinpoint the reason for it.

"I know we can get him out of there, Nick," she said to him. She knew full well that the look he was giving her was not due to worry for Jason, but she wanted to lure the truth out of him.

He nodded. "Yeah. We saved him once. We'll do it again."

No dice. Stacy sighed. As often as she found his mystery appealing, she just as often found it incredibly annoying.

Nick looked at Stacy, his heart feeling like a balloon with a rock tied to it. How could he have dragged someone like her into this? He and Melissa were used to danger. Hell, they thrived in it. But Stacy was a gentle soul. Her weapons were kindness and laughter, not swords and fists. The path they had chosen was one of violence, and the longer Stacy followed them, the more likely she was to fall victim to that violence.

Nick realized the irony of his train of thought even as it occurred to him. Stacy isn't the only one he should be worried about. He or Melissa, or Blitz, or even Jason himself were just as likely to suffer because of their choice to fight; and because of his lifestyle.

When this was over…when Jason was saved…he wondered if the best thing for him to do would be to leave them.

He continued to watch Stacy, his eyes heavy above the mask he still wore. She knew something was wrong, and the concern radiated off of her. It would not be so easy to walk away this time.

Melissa came thumping down the stairs, and suddenly Nick forgot about everything else.

He burst out laughing.

"What?" Melissa said, throwing her hands up questioningly.

Stacy put a hand over her mouth and stifled laughter of her own.

"We're doing recon, right? I need to blend into the darkness," Melissa defended herself.

"I think you missed the point," Stacy giggled.

Melissa was dressed in black sweats and black sneakers. On her head she wore a black ski-mask. On the back of the mask, Melissa had ripped a hole, pulling her bright blonde pony tail into the open.

Realizing what they were laughing about, Melissa tugged at her exposed hair.

"Meh. More comfortable this way."

Nick gained control over himself, and put a hand on her shoulder.

"Good enough," he reassured her.

Thirty minutes later Nick was back in front of the factory that Raven's man had driven into. Melissa was at his side, crouched low and taking the scene in. They had left Stacy and Blitz back at the lake house. The two of them were the most agile, and therefore the least likely to be spotted.

"You weren't kidding," Melissa said under her breath, her eyes wandering back and forth across the building in front of her.

Between them and the building was a fence. Chain link with razor wire looped across the top. The only break in the fence was the entryway the car had driven into, which was flanked by a large wooden guard hut. Two men inside were dressed like ordinary security guards. Melissa could tell immediately that they were Raven's trained thugs. The way they carried themselves spoke of a confidence of someone with far more than a security guard's salary; plus they were well armed. Nick had seen two shotguns inside the hut when he had checked the place out earlier.

Beyond the fence was a huge parking lot lit brightly by flood lights. The building itself was a factory complex; large and intimidating. A good cover, and very ironic considering that the sign on the entrance said, "Bourbon Street Poultry."

Fitting that a Raven should roost among the chickens.

About a dozen more "security guards" patrolled outside the building; some around the ground-floor perimeter, some around the third story catwalk. The building was seven stories tall. A bit unusual for a factory in New Orleans. Nick and Melissa wondered what Raven was doing with all of that space, and why he was choosing to hide his operation. Surely it wasn't just from them, and it was uncharacteristic of Jacob Raven to not flaunt himself in the public eye. No, the man had to be up to something. Neither were comfortable with the possibilities of what that something might be.

Either way, they had to assume that Jason was in there, and that meant they had to get through all of Raven's protective measures. That would not happen tonight. They were not prepared. Tonight was all about information.

"I'm going to take the fence. Think you can follow?" Nick asked her quietly.

Melissa scoffed. "Does a duck shit in the woods?"

Nick scratched his head, and then nodded. He ran through the shadows to a nearby stack of crates. He jumped on top, then instantly shifted his weight and sailed a good three feet over the razor wire, landing silently and in the darkness against the side of the building on the other side.

Melissa steeled herself, and then ran at the crates as Nick had. She jumped atop them, and then turned her momentum to the left and jumped again. She inhaled sharply as her feet coasted mere inches from the razor wire below her. She landed with a muffled thump on the other side.

"Piece of cake," she said to Nick as she joined him against the building.

He pointed up. Melissa's gaze followed his finger.

"That's how we're getting in," he said.

"Oh this is just getting better and better," Melissa grumbled, looking at the small vent nearly ten feet above them.

Nick looked at her expectantly.

"Ladies first?"

Stacy sat on the couch, her hand absently stroking Blitz and her eyes staring at a blank television screen. Her mind was a million miles away. Her heart beat a little faster than normal. She chewed a little bit on the inside of her lip.

During times like these, she was tired of playing house mother. It's true that it had been her choice to tag along with Nick and Melissa on their search for their missing friend, but often Stacy wished she could be of more help than she had been.

Though Nick and Melissa were the true fighters, Stacy was no slouch herself. Her father's militant regiment had included three years of martial arts lessons when she was younger, but those days in the dojo were years behind her, and she had never learned anything like the moves she saw Melissa and Nick employ. There was a lot more jumping, flipping, and maneuvering where these two were involved. Not to mention screaming, in Melissa's case.

Often when the two of them were somewhere else, Stacy removed her crossbow from her room, the same one she had used to kill her father and several of the armed men guarding her, and shot at trees outside. Despite the recent terrible memories attached to it, she wanted to hold onto something from her old life. Melissa labeled her attachment to the weapon as morbid, but Stacy didn't care. It had been a gift from her father, in the days when she had still loved him like one.

Shooting it calmed her just as it always had before; before her life had turned upside down and her sheltered existence with her family had exploded into this current, admittedly bizarre state of affairs.

She was far removed from that old life now. Nick's calming presence and Melissa's amusing antics had given her something she hadn't felt since she was a small child: a sense of place and purpose. These were her friends. Nick seemed to care for her more than any of her "real friends" ever had. Heck, more than any boyfriend ever had. Melissa acted tough, but Stacy wondered sometimes if she wasn't grateful to have another female presence around; not to mention someone to vent to whenever she was frustrated at Nick, her job, or the apparent futility of their search for Jason.

A futile search until tonight, she hoped. Nick had seemed almost certain that he had found the place of Jason's captivity, and when that edge of determination crept into Nick's voice, it was hard to argue with him.

So she was excited, nervous, and terrified at the same time. Over the past few months, Stacy had become nearly as invested in Jason's rescue as the others had. She knew that he was there that night, helping them save her from a trap meant for them, a source of endless guilt on her part. Perhaps if she had been a bit more careful, perhaps if she had fled after flagging that false alarm instead of waiting around and choosing to trust her father.... Perhaps Raven's men wouldn't have found an opportunity to take Jason back.

Though she also knew that if things had not played out the way they had, she would not be here; among people and a purpose that had finally given her life a sense of meaning.

But also a sense of helplessness. Stacy shifted on the couch, and chewed her lip a little harder.

After about three hours of waiting and hand-wringing, Melissa finally shoved the front door open, and Stacy's nervousness was immediately replaced with a feeling of concern. Melissa's anger burned brighter than usual. Their recon mission had obviously not gone well.

She spun around and pointed a finger at Nick, who was following her into the entryway.

"Don't say it, Nick. Don't fucking say it. If the words, "there's still hope" come out of your mouth one more time, I'm going to punch you in your dumb skinny face."

Nick's eyes widened defensively, but he didn't argue. He just walked around Melissa, threw his sword to the ground, and sat down in the armchair, taking off his mask and looking defeated.

Stacy stood up. She then made the mistake of asking Melissa instead of Nick what they had discovered.

"A goddamn fortress, that's what," Melissa snapped at her, turning her angry blue eyes Stacy's way. "It's a factory, Stace. Just like Nick said. And it's patrolled by less than a dozen people outside, just like Nick said. But what the masked wonder here didn't know is that there are about five times that many men inside the building, plus all of Raven's elite guard, the bad-asses that gave Nick and I a challenge when we were just facing three of them."

She ran a hand through her hair, walking towards the stairs.

"It's hopeless, guys. We're good, but we're not that good. We'd need a goddamn army to get inside of that building."

She stalked up the steps. A few seconds later they heard a slam as Melissa shut herself in her room, likely to punch another hole in the wall.

Stacy looked at Nick. He seemed more deflated than she had ever seen him. The sight made her heart hurt.

"She's right, Stacy. We wouldn't stand a chance. Even if we went in with stealth like we did tonight, we could never get out that way. Any option would bring a fight, and it's a fight we couldn't win."

Stacy sat back down and sighed heavily.

"But...we can't just give up on him. Not after all this."

Nick looked at the floor, in that way he often did when something heavy was on his mind.

"She said we'd need an army..."

Melissa stared hard into the mirror in her room; an object she almost never used. In fact, she only used it in times like this; times when she needed to bore a cold hard fact deep within herself.

But try as she might, she could not bring herself to say those words; that Jason was lost to her; that Raven had won. Whether it was her father's stubbornness or her mother's optimism, Melissa could not say. All she knew was that her words downstairs were empty. She could not give up. She would not lose Jason like she had lost her mother.

She was strong, but not that strong. Jason had spoken to the last shred of compassion left within her. If that was gone....

Melissa watched herself take a deep breath in the mirror. It was time to swallow her pride and apologize to Nick, and then ask him to help her formulate a plan to get the two of them around Raven's daunting security force.

As she walked back out of the room and towards the stairs, she felt a pang of guilt rise up within her. She knew that Jason wasn't the only one that was keeping her sane these days. Nick had proven himself to be an unlikely best friend in Jason's absence...and loath as she was to admit it, Stacy too was beginning to feel like family. The girl's smile took the edge off of Melissa's worries, just as it had when Melissa had met her. She was glad now that Nick had been so insistent about bringing her along.

So when she got to the foot of the stairs, she was glad to see Stacy looking up at her, but that gladness turned to concern when she saw that Nick was no longer present.

"He left," Stacy said, the worry evident in her voice and on her face. "He said he thought he knew the only way we could make this work, and then he left."

Melissa crossed her arms and looked at the front door.

"Did he say where he was going?"

Stacy shook her head. "No. Just that we should wait for him."

Melissa leaned back against the wall and sighed. She looked over and saw Blitz staring up at the door. The dog uttered a pathetic whine, just as confused as they were over where his friend had gone.

"I think that's all we can do right now, Stacy. Wait and hope for a miracle."

23

Patricia reclined on the couch, holding a microwave burrito in one hand and the TV remote in the other. Her eyes were on the screen, but as usual, her mind was somewhere else. She flipped thoughts like she flipped channels, never settling for long on one problem because, after seven months, she had not found a solution to any of them.

She thought of her favorite problem, and a small smile crossed her face. The boy in the mask. The one she scanned the papers for news of every day. Lately he had been showing up in New Orleans. She was disappointed that he had moved farther away, but she still held onto the hope that she hadn't seen the last of him. Without him she wouldn't be where she was; lounging in front of a television, mooching off of her friend Kurt, but free of the monster she had once called her boyfriend.

Patricia took a bite out of her burrito. When she heard the voice from the window to her left, she thought her mind was simply conjuring a memory.

"Well...you weren't so hard to find after all."

Patricia turned her head, expecting to see nothing. Instead, she ended up choking on her burrito, her eyes widening with shock. Nick was standing there with one leg in the apartment and the other propped up on the open window sill.

Nick started making his way toward her, but Patricia beat him to the punch by jumping up off the couch and wrapping him in a big hug, her mouth still full of burrito.

"Good to see you too, Patricia," Nick said, smiling warmly beneath his mask. He reached up and took it off. Patricia swallowed and held his face in her hands.

"I thought you were in New Orleans. I wasn't sure I'd see you again. And...can't you use the door like everyone else?"

Nick laughed. "It was either that or use the buzzer, and where's the surprise in that?"

"So how did you get here?" she asked.

"Hitched a few rides," he said nonchalantly.

She grinned, and motioned him to the couch.

"Where's Blitz?" she asked after they were seated.

"Back home," Nick replied.

Patricia's smile faded a little.

159

"Home, huh?" she said.

Nick nodded. "Yeah. We're staying at a house in New Orleans. I've been trying to help rescue a friend of mine for the better part of a year now. His name's Jason. I met him not long after I met you. A…lot has happened since then, Patricia."

"And I expect you to tell me every bit of it," she said to him.

So he did. For the next hour and a half, Nick recounted the events of the past several months of his life, from meeting Melissa to discovering Raven's new place of operations.

"Jacob Raven," she marveled. "The Jacob Raven? That's incredible, Nick. Sam was a small-time thug compared to him. In fact, Sam told me once that Raven owned half the gangs in Atlanta. Probably still does. And now you're going to go up against him and his whole army?"

She looked at him, saw the determination in his eyes, and felt a new wave of admiration wash over her. This boy was something special. She remembered how he had stood up to Sam's entire gang without fear that day in the parking lot. If anyone could take on Jacob Raven, it was Nick.

"But how are you going to do it? And why are you here, if Raven's base is back in New Orleans?"

Nick smiled coyly. "I'm here because you are, Patricia. We need you, and we need your friends."

Understanding dawned on her. Raven had a small army at his disposal, so Nick and his friends needed one as well.

"But Nick," she said, "most of my friends from those days are scattered across the state…hell, across the country even. Some have even gone back to Sam. I know a few roughnecks, but not enough to take on a factory full of trained killers."

Nick shook his head. "I'm not asking you to storm the castle. I've got something else in mind. All you have to do is try, Patricia. Gather up as many of your friends as you can as quickly as you can. People who are able and willing to cause some trouble."

She thought she could do it. She didn't want to, but for Nick's sake, she thought she could.

"All right," she nodded, "Kurt and I will make some calls tomorrow. Between the two of us, we should be able to gather up a good number of people."

Nick smiled. "Thanks, Patricia. I know I shouldn't be asking this of you, but I honestly believe you're our only hope."

It made her feel good to hear him say that; that he needed her. She took hold of his hand and squeezed it gently.

"Right now I'd agree to just about anything, Nick. I'm just glad to see you again."

Nick smiled, but did not miss the hint of desperation in Patricia's voice. Plus the fact that she was still living in Kurt's apartment concerned him.

"So...enough business. Tell me what you've been up to," he said.

Patricia gave a forced smile and a small shrug.

"Still living here, obviously. I've tried to get a few part time jobs but...nothing's stuck. Nothing feels right. I spent so much time with Sam and his lifestyle that I don't really know what else to do anymore."

Nick squeezed her hand back.

"You have a lot to give, Patricia. You just have to find the right way to give it."

She looked up at him.

"Like what, Nick? What do I really have? I have no skills. I have no real interests to speak of. All I do is sit around here all day and try to think of where to go next, but...nothing ever comes. Nothing ever pops into my head and tells me, 'this is where you should be'. I just...feel so lost, Nick. I knew this would happen when I left Sam. It was the right thing to do, but that doesn't make it any easier on me."

Nick sighed and sat back, still holding her hand.

"I know how you feel."

Patricia raised her eyebrows, wondering how someone who graced the papers on almost a daily basis could feel as if he had no place in the world.

"I'm out there every night, Trish. I help people, I do good, I fight for my friends; but it always feels like...there's something else. Something farther than all this, and I still have a ways to go until I find it."

She folded her arm under his, suddenly realizing how hard it must be for him to journey through life having no idea what his true past was, or what his real purpose might be.

"I don't think I told you this before, Patricia, but I have this...feeling. I call it my Pull. It's a feeling that draws me towards something. I guess it's something from my past that some subconscious part of me is trying to find again. So everything I do and every step I take towards finding Jason and helping the people around me...this Pull keeps tugging me somewhere else. Somewhere far away. I don't know why. I don't even really know where. But until I find it, everything I do and everything I am will be incomplete."

Patricia suddenly felt silly. Her problems seemed trivial compared to his. At least she remembered her past. At least she had some idea of who she really was. At least she had a last name and memories of her family and her childhood.

"I'm sorry, Nick. I know it must be hard not knowing so much about yourself."

Nick looked over at her.

"Sound familiar, though?"

She thought about it for a minute. Yeah, it kind of did.

"You and I are a lot alike, Patricia. I was basically born anew when I woke up in the woods that day. You were born anew when you walked away from Sam. And both of us now have to find a new place in this world, and a new identity to replace our old one."

She looked over into his dark green eyes. Eyes she had thought of nearly every night before she fell asleep. She held his arm close to her and found comfort in his presence and his words. Her heart fluttered, the way it had that day when he had sat so close to her in the garage.

She leaned over and kissed him.

For one sweet moment, he kissed her back, but then Patricia felt him pull away. He looked at her helplessly.

She smiled, and knew then that his heart wasn't hers, and probably never would be.

"Tell me about her," she said, trying to hide her disappointment.

Nick looked at the floor and shook his head slowly.

"It's Stacy, right?" she asked him, recalling the way he had spoken about her.

He looked up at her. His expression seemed to ask if he had been that obvious.

"It's okay, Nick. I just…wanted to know what that would feel like."

He smiled and continued to hold her hand.

"Part of me did, too."

She grinned. That was good enough for her.

"How's Ben?" Nick asked, changing the subject.

Patricia perked up at the mention of her brother.

"He's great, actually! You want to see him?"

"Of course!" Nick replied.

She led him down the hallway into Benjamin's makeshift room. As soon as he walked in, Nick noticed a color in the boy's cheeks that hadn't been there before.

"He's been moving, Nick! Not a lot, but every once in a while I catch his arm shift or his leg twitch. It's like he's trying to wake up. Like he's finally really trying."

162

Nick moved over to the boy's bedside. Sure enough, the boy looked even more like he was just taking a nap than he had before. There was something in his face...in the set of his eyebrows and his mouth...as if he were fighting something only he could see.

Nick turned to Patricia and smiled.

"I think you're right. He does look a lot better."

She nodded emphatically.

"Nick, I don't know what I'd do if Ben actually woke up. I mean I know whatever this is has to be psychological, but to see him actually up and moving and talking again...."

He put his arm around her.

"It'll happen. He'll be a normal kid again. Looks like he's almost there now."

She smiled and leaned into him. His words had brought a troubled reminder.

"The dreams, Nick," she said to him softly while looking at her brother, "They're getting stronger; more vivid. They stay with me longer...."

"Dreams of what this time?" he asked, concerned.

"Ben's calling to me. He's awake and aware and he's trying to tell me something. Really trying, like it's something important. But I can never quite make it out. We're standing in front of a blue house. It's unfamiliar; not one I've ever seen before; and I get the sense the house is very dangerous. I think Ben's trying to warn me about it, but.... I always wake up not knowing what it means."

Nick looked down at Ben; at his strained expression. Patricia did as well.

"You don't think..." she began to ask, unable or unwilling to finish her thought.

"I don't know," Nick shrugged, "I've seen some very strange things, Patricia. Done some very strange things. I'm certainly not one to tell you what's possible and what's not."

Patricia shook her head.

"Doesn't matter, really. I don't want to think about it anymore. I'd rather just look at him and think about all the places I'm going to take him when he wakes up. All the things he's missed. Come on, let's go talk about tomorrow," she said. She reached down and caressed Ben's face before turning to leave the room.

Nick turned to go with her...and then stopped as he felt something brush his hand.

He looked behind him, and sure enough, Ben's small hand was lying against his. He was certain the boy's hands were both on his stomach a moment ago.

163

It was as if the boy had reached out for him.

Nick felt a chill run up his spine. The hand along with Patricia's dream and the expression on Ben's face made him uneasy.

He decided to say nothing to Patricia about this.

Three days after Nick's sudden departure, Melissa leaned against the railing of the front porch, twirling her staff around with her fingers and listening to the first crickets of the evening. The sun was just setting. The lake house sat upon a bank above most of the neighborhood, so they had a better view of the panorama than their neighbors. Despite the tall trees to the east of the property, the house faced a mostly open view to the west, and therefore was an ideal place to watch the sun go down. Once upon a time Melissa would have found such a view mesmerizing. Now she hardly gave it notice. All she could think about these days was her struggle to get her friend back.

She knew that she had been overly focused on conflict for the past five years of her life. Since running away from her father, she had held onto nothing but anger and violence. Jason had been a remedy to that in the short time she had known him, but even now, the thoughts of his return were interlaced with her eagerness to bring revenge to his captors, and her former employer.

Melissa wondered sometimes if she would ever be free of the dominant violence of her personality. She wondered if she ever wanted to be, for without it, she wouldn't really know what to hold onto.

She watched a van pull into the neighborhood at the bottom of the hill and begin winding its way towards the lake house. As it got past the second side street, three more vans turned in behind it.

Melissa smiled. She backed up a step and banged heavily on the door.

"Hey, Stacy! I think the cavalry is here!"

As the first van pulled up the driveway, Stacy and Blitz joined her on the porch. Blitz immediately began wagging his tail. Stacy, on the other hand, looked more confused than relieved.

The van parked, and they could see Nick sitting there in the passenger seat. A large, muscular bald man was driving beside him.

Nick opened the door and jumped out, grinning widely. Blitz took off down the porch step and began barking and wagging his whole body in excitement. The van's back door slid open and a girl in ripped jeans and a Ramones t-shirt stepped out. She was very pretty, with an olive complexion and platinum blonde hair streaked with red. Nick turned to her and motioned her towards the house. She smiled and followed him.

164

Melissa looked over at Stacy with eyebrows raised and a coy smile on her face. Stacy looked back at her with bewilderment.

"Well Nick, you brought us the A-Team," Melissa said, breaking the awkward silence.

He laughed.

"Melissa, Stacy, this is Patricia."

Patricia stepped forward and held out a hand. Melissa shook it eagerly enough. Stacy did as well, though with slightly less enthusiasm.

"I've heard quite a lot about you," Patricia said, giving Stacy a warm and appraising look. "Both of you, I mean."

That seemed to thaw Stacy's mood a bit.

"Nice to meet you," she said, finally giving Patricia a little smile.

"So Nick, where'd you dig up this band of hooligans?" Melissa asked, surveying the four vans parked in and around their driveway now. A strange assortment of tattooed, heavily pierced, denim and leather wearing people stepped out of them, stretching their legs on the lawn and in the cul-de-sac.

"These are my friends. As many as I could round up. We're here to help you save Jason," Patricia replied.

Melissa gave her an approving look.

"Looks like some of those guys could bust a head or two. Especially the big one there," Melissa motioned to Kurt.

"You know...he looks kind of familiar," she said, staring at him.

"That's Kurtis McElroy. Probably the best friend I've got," Patricia said.

Melissa's eyes widened. She looked at Nick, who seemed equally stunned.

"You say his last name is McElroy?" he said.

"Yeah," Patricia replied, seeming confused.

Nick looked back at Melissa. "Couldn't be, could it?"

Melissa stared hard at Kurt, who was lighting up a cigarette. He waved at them from across the yard.

"Well...if you gave him hair...and a business suit...," she noted.

"Who...?" Patricia asked Nick, mystified as to what they were talking about.

"Former co-worker of hers," Nick told her.

Melissa chuckled and shrugged. Nick just shook his head and walked up the steps towards the front door.

Patricia called back to Kurt.

"Call me if you need anything!" she said.

Kurt waved and smiled.

"Didn't think you would mind if they camped out on the yard tonight," Nick said to Melissa.

"No, it's the least we can do," she said, though she was obviously still surprised at the party now taking place on her front lawn.

"Now come here, you little genius!" Melissa called to Nick, wrapping an arm around his neck and pulling him down and tussling his hair as they walked through the door.

"They do that a lot?" Patricia asked Stacy as she followed them inside.

"When they're not fighting, yeah pretty much," Stacy responded.

Nick and Patricia took a seat on the couch after Melissa let him go, giving him a big kiss on the cheek and then shoving him away from her. Stacy and Melissa sat down in the armchairs on either side.

"So...how did you two meet?" Stacy asked, her curiosity readily apparent.

"Patricia was the first person to take me in after I wandered into Atlanta," Nick told her.

"Well...I didn't just take him in. Some of my friends out there actually jumped him and locked him in a cage. We were part of a gang then, led by my ex-boyfriend. I asked Nick for help, and he helped us take Sam down a peg or two. I left the group along with my little brother and most of those people out there in your driveway. We owe him big time, and that's why we're here."

"You sure Ben's going to be ok for a few days?" Nick interjected.

Patricia nodded, "Yeah. Sally and Joe will take care of him. I trust them almost as much as I trust you and Kurt."

Melissa seemed amused.

"So that's where you've been these last four days, Nick; calling in a favor."

"Why didn't you tell us about this before?" Stacy asked.

Nick looked at her, seeming surprised by the question. Patricia looked at him with the same curiosity Stacy was showing.

"I don't know. I guess I just was too focused towards the future, what with our search for Jason all these months."

Stacy nodded, but seemed unconvinced.

"C'mon, Stace. You know it would take a crowbar and a barrel of whiskey to get Nick to talk about himself," Melissa said, attempting to defuse the tension.

Nick gave a small smile.

"I told Patricia she could stay here tonight, so we can talk about our strategy in the morning. I've got an idea, but we're going to have to put all our heads together to make it work,"

Melissa grinned and tapped her fingers on the chair. "It's about to be clobberin' time, eh hoss?"

"Something like that," Nick agreed.

"Where is she going to sleep?" Stacy interjected.

They all turned towards her. Melissa's jaw dropped a little. Stacy's question had had a tone of desperation behind it, which they had all caught.

"In the empty room, of course," Nick answered her.

She visibly relaxed.

"Okay. I'll grab you some blankets, Patricia," Stacy said, immediately getting up and heading to the upstairs closet, obviously embarrassed.

Melissa stifled a laugh when Stacy was out of sight. Patricia blushed and smiled knowingly at Melissa. Nick just looked dumbfounded.

"Is she okay?" Nick asked, turning to Melissa.

Melissa shook her head.

"Nick, for such a smart guy, you really are as dumb as a rock sometimes."

Patricia burst out laughing.

24

"So tell me," Jacob Raven asked The Dark Man, "what exactly am I waiting for?"

The Dark Man's expression didn't change, but Raven could feel a palpable sense of annoyance radiate off of him. He looked at Raven with his currently green eyes.

"I've heard that patience is a virtue, Jacob," he said.

Raven scoffed. "And since when are we in the business of virtue?"

He stalked around the side of his desk, looking out his window onto the factory floor below him. Crates were stacked dozens of feet high. Each one was filled with weapons, drugs, and other things; things far worse than the contraband Raven was used to dealing with.

"I want to make my mark. I brought you in to help me do that. But all this waiting, all this building...it's starting to wear thin."

The Dark Man smiled.

"You have your distractions."

Raven turned and looked at him.

"Like the boy, you mean? Slowly tooling him into a monster? Yes, there's that. Jason was ripe for my little experiment, but the hatred has already set in deep. There's not much decency left in him to squeeze."

"So you've succeeded, then. You've done it. You've proven what I've known all along, that even the best of them can be turned. You know now that when the time comes and the proper factors are in place,...you'll have your army."

"They won't all be like him," Raven said scornfully.

"Then we'll kill the ones that aren't," The Dark Man replied, his tone icy and resolute.

Raven watched his eyes turn from green to red. Never before had the change taken place directly in front of him. It made his skin crawl.

Suddenly a voice crackled forth from the speaker on Raven's desk.

"Sir, we have a situation at the front gate."

Raven's face darkened with concern. He pressed a button on the receiver.

"What kind of situation?"

"Sir, there's a...mob gathering. I think they're protestors. Maybe from PETA."

Raven sighed. "Goddamn hippies think we really are a chicken factory."

He looked up, and was startled out of his anger when he saw the look of alarm on his mentor's face.

"No," the man in black said, "this is something else."

Raven waited for clarification. After several seconds, the guard called through the speaker again.

"Sir! They're getting awfully close to the...Stay away! I said stay away or I'll shoot!"

They listened as other voices joined the guard's. Voices of anger. Many voices.

"They're charging the gate! Sound the alarm!" the guard yelled.

Raven pounded his fist into his desk angrily.

"Hold them back, Johnson, or I'll have more than your job!"

There was no response; only static. The security alarm began to blare around them. Johnson must have pulled it before he had been cut off.

"Who do you think it...?"

"He's here," The Dark Man interrupted, and the Raven watched in astonishment as the man melted into a black mist, dispersing into nothing and leaving Raven alone in the office, with only the blaring siren for company.

He. The Dark Man had said he was here.

Shit, thought Raven. Things were accelerating faster than he had planned for.

"McElroy! Order the full force to the front entrance, call my chopper to the roof," Raven screamed into the receiver, "and tell your men to gear up. We're about to have a busy night."

"Yes sir," McElroy immediately responded through the speaker.

Raven grabbed his cane from the corner. He stared at it for a second, feeling his anger turn slowly into eager anticipation.

He hated having to improvise...but my, how he loved the adrenaline rush of walking into a fight he knew it was impossible to lose.

Raven laughed, and walked out of his office, slamming the door shut behind him.

Jason heard the siren echoing through the gym outside his door. The next sound he heard was the frantic shuffling of twenty or so of Raven's men dropping weights, yelling at each other, and running around like ants.

Francis McElroy's voice blared from the walkie-talkie of one of the men outside Jason's cell.

"We need every man to the front entrance. The compound is under attack. Repeat: the compound is under attack."

Jason jumped to his feet and looked out the small barred window of his door. He had learned long ago not to look out unless he had to. His eyes were so used to the darkness of his cell that it hurt to do so. He squinted, ignoring the pain, and saw nearly every man running out of the room, picking up guns and other weapons as they went. Only two men stayed behind, changing out of gym clothes as quickly as they could.

Jason's heart beat faster. Now was the time.

He turned and knelt down, reaching into a crack in the wall. He pulled out a fork he had managed to keep one day when the guard had not been paying attention while retrieving Jason's meal tray.

Jason crawled back to the door and set the fork against the steel hinge pin. He rolled his shirt around his fist, and then began to hammer on the end of the fork. He had done this during the rare opportunities when the gym outside had been vacant. The last time he had done so, he had managed to get each pin within a few strikes of popping loose. He had hoped that a moment would present itself sooner or later for him to make his escape. A security alert was one of the eventualities he had been waiting for.

The sound of the siren masked the tapping of the fork. Within seconds, the lower pin popped out of its hinge. He stood up and began working on the upper hinge. The two men outside were still preparing. Jason figured that they were procrastinating out of fear of action. Raven's workforce were mostly trained and hardened professionals, but a handful of cowards parading as bullies were peppered throughout the ranks.

Jason decided to take the risk now while he had the chance. The top hinge popped loose, and the door clunked to the ground, resting now only in Jason's arms.

He knew that Raven wouldn't have been so careless as to allow a door that could be removed from the inside. He knew that this particular escape plan would only be possible if Raven had allowed it. He knew Raven had probably been waiting for Jason to do just this, and walk into a trap.

But he had to hope that on this particular day, Raven would be too busy to spring that trap. He had to take advantage of the weakness, whether intentional or not, in Raven's cage. There was simply no other hope of escape.

Jason braced himself for the flood of light that was about to enter the cell. He shoved the door aside, and suddenly he was free.

The two men yelled in alarm, and Jason immediately sprang into motion. He broke into a full run and tackled one man, sending them both crashing into a table behind them. He heard the man's head hit the floor with a crack. One down, one to go.

Jason got to his feet, barely able to see his surroundings. The second man was fumbling on the floor, reaching for something amongst the contents of the table that had just fallen over. The weapons table.

Jason smiled when he saw a familiar metal glint near his foot.

The man finally grabbed hold of a bat. A cocky grin spread across his face as he stood up to face Jason.

That grin was then wiped off as a heavy metal chain smacked across the man's jaw, nearly breaking his neck as his head whipped to the side with the force of the blow. He dropped the bat.

Jason took two steps forward and punched the man in the face before he could recover. He fell to the floor as if he had been hit with a sledgehammer.

Jason stood there for a few seconds, looking at the unconscious man on the floor. His chain dangled in his fist. He clenched that fist tightly, feeling six months of pent up violence and anger course through him. The first blow of his revenge had been struck. Now he had to find Jacob Raven.

He saw something poking out of the man's pocket. Jason smiled. He reached down and picked up the pair of shades; a requisite accessory for most of Raven's men. As he put them on he breathed a sigh of relief. The world turned to more tolerable shades of grey. These were much more comfortable than the tinted goggles Raven had allowed him during his daily gym visits.

Jason looped the chain around his forearm, holding one of the weighted ends in his hand; the weapon he had been practicing with for months, chosen specifically because of its unusual nature and therefore unpredictability, prepared so he could easily lash it out when he needed to. There was also something enjoyably ironic about the thought of attacking his captor with a chain signifying his bondage.

Soon he would. Very soon. Jason stepped towards the door that led further into the compound, not pausing to realize that he was about to enter parts of the building he had never seen before.

The only thing Jason saw through those tinted glasses was the face of the man he intended to kill.

Stacy's back was pressed against a small Oldsmobile. She was in the midst of the second biggest adrenaline rush of her life. All hell was breaking loose behind her. Gunshots rang out. Two dozen angry street kids screamed and hurled bricks, rocks, and anything else they could get their hands on. Blitz was barking beside her.

She looked over and saw Patricia sitting next to her, looking just as scared and just as anxious. Stacy held her crossbow in her lap. Her brain told her to stand up and use it, but her arms didn't want to move. That day in the warehouse she had used it out of fear and despair. Today she was only astounded and confused. How did she get into this? Wasn't she just an ordinary high school senior with ordinary high school problems less than a year ago? Now here she was, crouched in a parking lot, dodging bullets and holding a crossbow that she was considering firing at someone.

Patricia looked back at her. They stared at each other for several long seconds. The look in Patricia's eyes calmed Stacy a bit and reminded her she was not alone. She managed a smile and grabbed Patricia's hand. Regardless of her petty jealousy over Nick, Stacy didn't really hold any ill will towards this girl. In fact, she kind of liked her.

"They need us, don't they?" Stacy said to her.

Patricia took a deep breath and nodded.

"Yeah. I guess they do."

Stacy smiled again.

"Then let's raise some hell."

Patricia laughed nervously. Stacy's bold front seemed to knock some of the nerves out of her.

Stacy put a hand on Blitz's shoulder.

"Go get 'em, Furball."

Blitz didn't even look up at her. He just ran out from behind the car, barking and snarling and pointing himself in the direction of Raven's besieged security force.

Stacy stood up, steeling herself.

The scene was not promising. Raven's men were positioned with strategic precision on catwalks, behind riot shields, and beyond windows. Some of the ones outside the entrance moved forward slowly, wearing full riot gear and holding batons and stun guns. She would have thought they looked like police if not for the brass knuckles quite a few of them wore.

The men on the catwalk above the entrance fired repeatedly into the mob below. Stacy watched several of Patricia's friends get hit. They kneeled or fell to the ground, but then got back up and kept going. Rubber bullets again, Stacy thought. Apparently Raven's men were trained to incapacitate instead of kill. Though this was somewhat odd considering the nefarious nature of the infamous crime lord, Stacy decided not to look a gift horse in the mouth.

Instead, she looked down the sight of her crossbow, and aimed at one of the men stationed on the catwalk.

She fired with little hesitation, and heard the man scream a fraction of a second after her finger pulled the trigger, her bolt buried deeply in his thigh.

A smile spread across her face. Nick and Melissa may be the ones storming the fortress, but she would be the one leading the charge at the front gates.

Stacy loaded another bolt. She strode out confidently from behind the car.

She felt Patricia staring at her. She felt the gaze of the mob around her. She saw every one of the security guards look at her, a teenage girl with a crossbow walking towards a building full of armed men. She had never felt more powerful in her life. For Jason, for her friends, and for herself, she had to be.

"Hey assholes!" she screamed as she brought her weapon to her shoulder.

The next sounds to echo across the parking lot were the twang of her bow followed by another of Raven's men screaming in pain.

She ran back to the car, skidding behind it just in time to duck a hail of bullets. Patricia looked at her in awe.

"Remind me never to fuck with you," Patricia said, a grin spreading across her face.

Stacy giggled. The sound made Patricia laugh loudly. Across the parking lot, Kurt led a large group of tattooed and angry anarchists in a charge towards the wall of riot shields in front of the entrance.

"C'mon," Patricia said. "Let's bust some heads."

In a room on the second floor of Raven's factory, Francis McElroy and six of his best men were suiting up for battle. The room contained the best of RavenCorp's security equipment, with items ranging from Kevlar vests to semi-automatic rifles. Two grenade launchers hung from the wall, though no one touched them. They were under strict orders to kill no one.

McElroy strapped a combat knife to his gun holster. He didn't need heavy weapons. His skills were more than enough.

He waited for the others amidst the sounds of clicking gun-clips and clanking metal. These men were all nearly as capable as he was, and though they all carried the stoic countenance of professional hit men, none of them could deny the palpable excitement of entering a fight on the scale of this one. This wasn't one or two street thugs that needed pushing. There was a full blown riot outside.

McElroy suddenly became aware of another sound. Scratching metal coming from above. He looked up at the air vent in the center of the room. Little metal shavings were raining down from the edges of the vent.

And then all hell broke loose. The vent dropped to the floor with a crash and after it followed a boy in a mask. The boy landed nimbly and immediately sprang towards one of McElroy's comrades, who had not even noticed the intruder yet.

With amazing speed, the boy drew a sword from his back in mid-air. He kicked out and sent his target crashing face first into a steel locker, and then rolled to the right and came up with a sword swipe at a second man, who brought his arm up soon enough to receive a deep gash in his forearm.

It was him, McElroy realized. The one from the warehouse. The one they had been warned about.

This was going to be fun.

Melissa shoved open the ventilation grate and climbed out into the hallway. She checked to make sure she was indeed in a vacant part of the building. Not a soul was seen at either end of the hall. Content she was alone, Melissa doubled over and wretched.

"Damn stinking chickens," she gasped. The vent smelled like burnt livestock, and she had been climbing through five floors of it.

Recovering herself, she pulled her staff from the vent behind her. Now she would set about the task of searching the building for Jason. Stacy and Patricia and the gang outside would distract the majority of Raven's men while Nick kept the elite force busy. Melissa trusted in Nick's skill, but she worried that even he would not be able to walk out alive from a room full of Raven's best.

But that didn't matter. Nothing else mattered. As long as Nick and Stacy kept them busy long enough, Melissa would be able to do her job and find her friend; wherever he was; in whatever shape he was in.

If she happened to find Raven first…that bastard would be introduced to whole new worlds of pain.

175

Nick moved faster than he ever had before. Springing left, then right...then straight up...then back towards the wall, he was a constant blur of motion, taking sword swipes and kicks where he could at Raven's men.

They were good. Melissa was right about that. They were right behind him everywhere he went, and he had only managed to take down two of them since he had entered the room. McElroy himself was still standing in the corner with his arms crossed, seeming to enjoy the spectacle. Nick supposed he would have to take the big man one-on-one; that is, if he survived the battle with the other four.

He rolled away from his attackers towards a wall. Up from his roll, he ran three steps up the wall and somersaulted backwards, slashing one of the men in the collarbone as he sailed above him. Completing his flip, Nick landed squarely on the chest of another man, knocking the wind from him. As he hit the ground, Nick followed by striking the man in the skull with the butt of his sword.

And just like that, two more men were down.

Not even winded, Nick immediately spun back around and put the remaining two men on the defensive. The man whose collarbone he had slashed lay on the floor bleeding and writhing in pain. Apparently his sword had cut deep.

So this is what he was capable of. His body flowed seamlessly from one motion to the next, sometimes performing two or three maneuvers at once. His mind whirred like a clock, constantly taking measure of his surroundings and the right strategy to employ with every situation. It was mostly his body, though, that did the work. Instinct drove him. The strategy was really only an afterthought.

Though no real opening presented itself in either of his opponents' defenses, Nick created one. He jumped straight up and kicked both men in the face, then whirled and slashed them both across the arms. He landed in his defensive crouch, hoping the ferocious attack was enough to end the skirmish.

For ordinary thugs, it might have been; but Raven's elite guard were trained to get their job done with no regard for personal safety. One man circled left, clutching his bleeding right arm, while the other man circled right, stumbling from the force of Nick's blow to his head.

Nick faced the man on the left, and then, to the surprise of both men, jumped backwards, kicking out at the man on the right. He hit him full force in the chest, sending him flying backwards into the wall. Nick, on the other hand, flew like a bullet towards the left, smashing the last remaining enemy directly in the face with his fist.

McElroy watched in bemused awe. As Nick landed and looked around the room at his fallen enemies, McElroy stepped forward and clapped his big hands together in applause.

"That was really something, kid," he said, not seeming afraid of Nick in the least.

"You beat up a whole room of B-list thugs in what...," McElroy looked at his watch, "five minutes? Pretty damn cool."

Nick backed up a step and re-entered his defensive posture. He could sense that Melissa's stories about Raven's right-hand man were true. He was a lot stronger than the others.

"But," McElroy continued, "beating up losers doesn't make you the shit...Hero." The title rolled off of McElroy's tongue with obvious contempt.

"It just makes you another loser."

He slipped on a pair of brass knuckles and brought his body into a fighting stance.

"This is what I do to losers," McElroy said threateningly, and then crossed the last few steps between himself and Nick with surprising speed.

Nick shifted to the right, then to the left, then backwards as McElroy threw several right and left hooks at him. One hit with those brass knuckles and Nick knew he would be facing a fractured skull.

But fists were apparently not McElroy's only weapons. He moved into a series of roundhouse kicks. Two left, one right, and then a low spin kick meant to knock Nick's legs out from under him. Nick dodged and jumped mere milliseconds ahead of each strike. He knew this was not going to be easy.

McElroy was backing him into a wall, attempting to take every last inch of tactical maneuvering room away from him. Nick didn't see an opening in the fury of McElroy's attack, but he knew he had to move anyway. He dove and rolled to the right, barely coming up in time to avoid crashing into a table.

McElroy followed him, smashing a fist into the table behind Nick's head. Nick jumped onto a chair and kicked it backwards, sending it into McElroy's knees. The projectile barely slowed the man, however. He just flung the object out of his way and kept coming.

Nick knew his only choice would soon be to trust his skills and go on the offensive. McElroy was a viciously strong opponent, and Nick was aware he may not make it out of this room in one piece, but as long as he bought Melissa the time she needed, that was all that mattered.

He ran at McElroy. The big man swung a left hook at Nick as he approached. Nick brought his arm up and blocked the blow, grimacing in pain at the force his slender arm was absorbing. Truly his strategy of "less blocking, more moving" was still the right one, but in this case…getting close to his enemy was his only shot at success.

Nick tried to knee McElroy in the chest, but the well-trained man deflected Nick's leg with his right hand. Nick tried again, this time kicking high, but again McElroy blocked. He slashed his sword in two alternating arcs, which finally seemed to put McElroy on the defensive, causing him to back up quickly and lean away from Nick.

Nick used the opportunity to take advantage of McElroy's lost balance. He swung his sword vertically, and then as McElroy backed up another step, he quickly jumped into the air and kicked him in squarely in the chest with both feet.

McElroy crashed backwards into a gun rack, splintering it and falling to the ground. He immediately got back up just as Nick was nearly on top of him, leading with a knee at McElroy's face. McElroy was quicker than Nick had hoped, however. The man planted his legs and shoved forward, grabbing Nick's arm with one hand and smashing Nick in the upper chest with his elbow.

The momentum of the elbow combined with the yanking of his left arm sent Nick flying into the table he had narrowly avoided earlier. Nick felt his ribs crunch underneath him as the table splintered and collapsed.

McElroy stood up, dusting his hands off. He then ran his fingers through his mussed-up oily hair.

"You're better than most, kid; but still not good enough."

Nick lay among the shattered remnants of the table, clutching his side and grimacing him pain. He looked up at McElroy.

"She told me…you were afraid of her," Nick said to him.

McElroy paused. "What?"

"Melissa," Nick continued. "She told me you were scared of her. You should be, you know."

Though momentarily taken off guard, McElroy threw his head back and laughed.

"Yeah…she thought she was the best. But I could have taken that annoying bitch any day."

Nick chuckled. McElroy's face darkened with anger.

"I seriously doubt it," Nick said, slowly getting to his feet and circling to the other side of the room, away from McElroy.

"I've fought her, you know. Just like I'm fighting you now. She's quicker than you, stronger than you, and smarter than you," Nick continued, smiling beneath his mask as he saw McElroy's face grow redder and redder.

"Especially smarter than you."

McElroy's fists clenched and he took a step towards Nick.

"Big words coming from the skinny prick I just threw into a table."

Nick shrugged.

"True. But I do know one thing, Francis," he said, pausing while still slowly moving away from McElroy.

"And what's that?" McElroy asked condescendingly.

"You'll never get to do it again," Nick said, and then ran towards the far wall.

McElroy ran after him, having no intention of allowing the punk to get away. Nick ran at the wall, jumped and kicked off of it back towards McElroy.

McElroy smiled. The stupid kid thought he could bull rush him. That would be his last mistake.

But Nick didn't collide with McElroy's charging body. Instead he did something that McElroy wouldn't have thought possible.

He curled himself around McElroy in mid-air, grabbing the arm of the man's jacket and simply pulling and twisting his body underneath and around it, bringing himself behind McElroy's back. At that point, the combined momentum of McElroy's charge and Nick's strange acrobatic feat left nothing between McElroy and the wall but several inches of air.

The man smacked into the wall with such force that Nick was afraid McElroy's neck had broken. Nick dropped from his piggyback-like hold on McElroy and backed away.

McElroy stepped away from the wall, spinning around with his arms held limply at his sides. He looked around the room, seemingly searching for something he could no longer see. His mouth hung open.

Nick backed away another step, amazed that the man was still standing after the face-first collision.

But after two more stumbled steps, McElroy's eyes rolled back. He collapsed, first to his knees and then to the floor, the sweet realm of unconsciousness wrapping him up in its embrace.

Nick waited a moment longer, making sure the fight was truly out of this dangerous opponent. Satisfied that McElroy was down for the count, Nick stood up straight and looked around the room. Discarded guns, splintered wood, and the unconscious bodies of seven trained killers littered the floor.

And he had done it.

Nick couldn't believe himself. Sure, he had taken a beating in the process, but he had only expected to delay Raven's elite guard while Melissa rescued Jason. He had expected to block their passage for a while, and then make his escape, not clear the room of them.

He couldn't help but give an exhilarated smile. Because as dangerous and as life-threatening as this had been...he had fun doing it.

After giving the mostly-destroyed room one last satisfied look, he turned to walk out the door. A needle-sharp pain shot up from his injured side, and Nick was forced to remind himself that this wasn't a game.

Bruised rib today...bullet in the head tomorrow.

Still, he thought...what a rush.

Melissa turned another corner, her pace becoming quicker and more frustrated. This was the third empty floor she had searched and she had still seen no trace of Jason. Luckily she had not run into any resistance either. Every man in Raven's employ was either quelling the riot outside or being distracted by Nick on the second floor.

There was only one place left to search. The roof. Somewhere on this floor would be a service ladder, though Melissa did not like the prospect of finding it. If Jason was up there, it would be for one of two reasons. Either Raven would use him as a hostage to bargain for his own safety, or Jason was being herded into a helicopter right now for another escape.

She didn't think she could take losing him again. A repeat of McElroy's helicopter escape six months ago was almost the worst thing that could happen. Almost. Melissa didn't want to think about the alternative.

She turned another corner and saw the ladder. She also saw someone enter from the opposite end of the hall. A large black man with thick dreadlocks and sunglasses, wearing a black sleeveless shirt and sweatpants with no shoes. A chain was wrapped around one of his bare forearms.

Melissa froze in her tracks.

The man looked up and noticed her. He slowly came to a stop as well.

The two looked at each other for many long moments.

"Jason?" Melissa heard herself gasp in disbelief.

His shoulders slumped. If the chain hadn't been wrapped around his arm, he would have dropped it.

"He lied. You're not dead," the man said, his voice sounding hollow.

Melissa took a step forward. Was this really Jason? He was a skinny boy when she lost him. The person standing before her had about fifty pounds more muscle and nearly eight inches more hair.

"What has he done to you?" she found the courage to ask.

Jason shook his head.

"He lied. The bastard lied about what happened to you. What else did he lie about?"

She walked closer.

"It doesn't matter now, Jason. I found you; that's all that matters."

He looked up at her. His shoulders rose again and his brow darkened above his glasses.

"No, Melissa. That's not all that matters. The son of a bitch lied to me. He kept me locked in a cell for six months. He told me you were dead. He told me my mom was dead. He told me I had nothing. And I believed him. He tried to rip my soul out...and he came pretty goddamn close."

She looked him up and down. Jason must have done this to himself. He must have changed himself out of anger and grief. Oh god, if only she had found him sooner.

"I'm so sorry," she whimpered.

Jason seemed surprised at her show of emotion, but he made no move to comfort her.

"Where is he?"

Melissa looked at the ladder.

"He has to be up there. I've looked everywhere else."

Jason nodded and looked up towards the hatch leading to the roof.

"Then that's where I need to be," he said, and started climbing.

Melissa watched him go. She wanted to follow him. She knew she would, but she also knew that Jason had no intention of letting her or anyone else interfere. She could not see his eyes, but she had a feeling there was murder in them.

As Jason disappeared through the hatch, Melissa heard someone else come around the corner behind her. Nick walked into view, holding his side and looking like he was in pain. His eyes widened when he saw her.

"Did you..." he started to ask, but stopped when he saw the defeated look on her face. She pointed upwards, towards the hatch.

"He went up there to find Raven. Nick, he's...."

Nick walked over to her.

"Is he hurt?"

Melissa shook her head.

"No…. Maybe worse."

Nick started to ask her what she meant, but before he could someone else approached them in a hurry from behind. He turned around and saw it was Stacy.

"What the…are you okay?" he asked, surprised to see her. The plan was for her to stay outside with Patricia and the others.

Stacy nodded, out of breath.

"Most of Raven's men broke off and came back inside. They're re-arming downstairs. I snuck past them to warn you."

Nick nodded, glad she had made it safely.

"Are Patricia and the others ok?"

"A little banged up, and there's still some fighting going on out there, but things are about to get a lot worse in here, Nick. We need to leave. Now."

Nick looked behind him. He saw Melissa's feet disappearing up the ladder.

"Jason's up there. We have to go help him."

Stacy looked behind her nervously, but nodded in agreement.

"Then let's get what we came for and get as far away from this place as we can."

Jason heard Melissa come up behind him. He heard two other sets of footsteps as well. He supposed one of them was Nick. If Melissa was alive, he likely was too.

But Jason didn't turn to look. Right now his eyes were locked on the object of his every vengeful fantasy for the past several months of his life. Right now his eyes were locked on Jacob Raven.

There was no helicopter on the roof. There were no bodyguards and no weapons. There was only Raven, himself, wearing a white leisure suit with a garish purple tie and standing with his cane propped in front of him. He wore a contemptible smile and a devious twinkle in his eye.

"Well the gang's all here," Raven noted, grinning.

Jason finally turned to look. Nick was indeed standing next to Melissa, in full Hero regalia. Next to him was the girl they had saved in the warehouse that day. The day Jason was captured. She was holding the same crossbow.

"Stay out of this," Jason told them, his voice deadly serious.

They said nothing. Nick only seemed shocked at Jason's transformation. Melissa seemed just as helpless as she had in the hall below.

Jason turned back to Raven.

"You know what's going to happen now, don't you Jacob?"

Raven nodded, his grin turning back into that ironic smirk.

"You're going to try to kill me," he answered.

Jason said nothing. He didn't nod or offer any verbal affirmation. He just let his chain drop from his hand, its weighted end clanking to the gravel rooftop below.

Raven looked at the weapon.

"I'm genuinely impressed by what you've done with your time here, Mr. Dredd. You could have hidden in that room like a coward, like all the others did. But instead you ventured out, and used every moment I allowed you to turn yourself into this fearsome specimen I see today. You even picked a weapon I never could have guessed. The slave faces his master with chain in hand. How truly poetic."

Raven glanced over at Melissa.

"Isn't he impressive, Miss Moonbeam? I was thinking of making him my personal bodyguard. He would have given you a run for your money."

This shook Melissa out of her depression.

"I'm going to kill you for this, Raven," she said, her voice trembling in anger.

Raven laughed.

"Not if he kills me first," he said, pointing his cane at Jason.

Nick spoke up.

"Why are you so flippant? Shouldn't you be running for the hills right now like the coward you are?"

Raven smiled hungrily at Nick.

"Ah, The Hero. Finally we meet. A friend of mine has told me a lot about you, Nick. Seems you're a pretty important piece in this chess game; though maybe not in the way you might think. In fact...that name they've given you might turn out to be a little bit ironic in the end."

This seemed to startle Nick. He took a step back and Stacy grabbed his arm.

"You're a monster!" she yelled at him. "You only exist to hurt people and take from everything around you! Jason should kill you."

Raven shrugged comically.

"You call it like you see it, Miss Cross. I am a monster. I do only want to hurt people and I do want to take from everything around me. That's what I do. That's what I'm here for."

"Why?" Jason screamed. "Why did you do this to me? Why did you take my family?!! Why did you tell me everyone I cared about was dead?"

Raven gave a look that told them all how pleased with himself he was.

"You want to know why, little rat? You want to know why I hurt you and why I took everything you ever loved from you?"

They all looked at him. Every one of them was ready to beat him to a bloody pulp.

"Because I could," Raven replied. "I did it because I could."

Jason's fists clenched. The rage boiled inside of him like a furnace.

"I wanted to hollow you out. Take all the hope from you and replace it with anger. And here you are. The product of my experiment. Once a boy with stars in his eyes. Now a man with murder in them. You proved my point, Jason Dredd. You have proven to me that any man can be turned into a monster."

Jason roared and ran forward, swinging the chain above his head.

For a moment, Raven just seemed to stand there, still grinning; but then he sprang into motion, stepping away from the range of Jason's weapon and pulling a long thin blade from the handle of his cane.

"Let's see which one of us is the bigger beast, shall we?" Raven yelled in excitement, happily swiping forward with his blade and meeting Jason's advance.

Melissa started forward, but Nick grabbed her arm.

"This is Jason's fight, Melissa," he said.

Melissa started to argue, but then she saw Stacy facing the hatch with her crossbow pointed downwards.

"Besides," Nick continued, "We're about to have problems of our own."

The sound of dozens of rushing feet thundered up from below. Raven's men were coming to their leader's aid.

Melissa gripped her staff tighter, gave one last look back at Jason, and gritted her teeth.

"Then let's do our job, people. Let's keep these monkeys off of Jason's back so he can kick that runt's ass!"

Nick nodded and drew his sword. Behind them, the sounds of Jason and Raven's battle began to echo across the rooftop.

Jason was taken aback by Raven's nimble movements. In all the time he had known him, he had only thought of Raven as an impotent dictator who let others do the dirty work. Apparently that misconception was also one of Raven's weapons.

"Surprised?" Raven said, obviously sensing Jason's alarm. "I'm a billionaire in the illegal weapons trade, Jason. Surely you didn't think I had never spent time learning how to defend myself."

Jason stepped aside from a swipe from Raven's cane. Raven moved fast, but not nearly as fast as Nick or Melissa. Jason would still be able to defeat him. It would just take a little more work than he had thought.

"It doesn't matter," Jason said, swinging his chain high and watching Raven barely duck in time. "I'm still going to kill you."

Raven cackled.

"And I'm going to enjoy watching you try."

Raven's arrogant defiance only spurred on Jason's anger. He pushed forward, taking a slash in the arm from the blade while throwing a left hook at Raven's chin. Raven knelt back, feeling the wind from Jason's fist brush against his face. Jason momentarily saw worry in his eyes.

Good. Worry would come first. Then fear. Then pain. And then nothing but the cool kiss of death.

Melissa moved with a fury, passing her staff from one hand to the other over her shoulders, bringing it swinging low at the feet of the two men attacking her. She pressed forward, kicking out at one man and hitting the other one with a staff thrust. Both hobbled to the ground. She looked for her next victims.

Nick was doing his usual pinball routine, alternating his attack between four different men, though Melissa noticed he seemed more on the defensive than usual. She didn't know if that was because of his injury or because he was distracted by watching Jason's battle with Raven. Though they were not a part of it, none of them had any intention of standing by while Raven killed their friend, personal vendetta or no.

Stacy was doing quite well on her own, to Melissa surprise and approval. The girl moved and swayed defensively as one of Raven's men came at her with an iron baton. After dodging another swing, Stacy fired a bolt point-blank into the man's ribs. He went down like a light, and Melissa could see Stacy already looking for another place to aim her weapon.

Melissa screamed her usual joyful and fearsome battle cry, diving at three more men who had emerged from the building below them. Despite her bravado, and despite the fact that the men seemed terrified of her, Melissa was wracked with confusion and doubt. She had found her best friend again, but in a way her worst fears had been confirmed. She had been afraid she would find Jason too late. Now she knew that she had. Raven's damage had been done. He would never be that boy she would once spend hours talking to any more. He would never look at the world with wonder the way he once did. Now all he was was a weapon, just as Raven intended. No matter what happened on this rooftop, no matter who won the battle…Raven still had what he wanted.

Jason risked a look back to see how the others were doing. Melissa was roaring like a banshee as usual and busting heads with her usual abandon, though Jason did not miss the uncharacteristic quiver in her voice. Nick and the girl were holding their own as well.

Raven took to the opening eagerly. He thrust low with his blade, stabbing Jason in the calf. Jason yelled in pain and bent over just in time for Raven to smash him across the face with the handle of his cane.

Jason stumbled back, his nose bleeding.

"That's really all you Dreddowskis are good for, you know. Bleeding," Raven taunted.

Jason straightened back up, locking Raven in a death-stare beneath his dark glasses.

"You lied about that too, didn't you?" Jason said, "My mom. She's still alive, isn't she?"

Raven shrugged sheepishly. "Eh, so I fibbed a little about a thing or two. Like who's dead and who's not. Besides, I'm not really in the business of murder. If I was, you'd be dead. No," Raven continued, his eyes flashing a dangerous look as he stepped forward with another swipe at Jason.

"I much prefer torture."

Jason knocked Raven's blade away with his chain-wrapped hand. He shoved out with both hands, hitting Raven in the chest and sending him back, flailing his arms to keep from falling over.

Jason suddenly became aware of running footsteps very close behind him. One of Raven's men must have broken loose from the fight and was rushing to defend his employer. He was too close. Jason wouldn't be able to defend himself in time.

The next sound Jason heard was a grunt and the sound of stumbling feet. He turned in time to catch the man, coming down to his knees and sinking to the floor of the roof. A crossbow bolt was buried in his back.

Jason looked up and nodded at the dark haired girl who had possibly just saved his life. She gave a cheerful grin and a wave in return. Despite the circumstances, Jason found himself stifling a smile at the girl's excited expression. He made a mental note to thank her later, if he got out of this alive.

He heard Raven scrounging forward to strike at Jason's open defenses once more. He decided to beat him to the punch.

Jason whipped around, swinging the chain in a forceful arc. Raven was indeed charging forward with his blade descending for a blow, but the chain met the blade and wrapped around it.

Jason smiled, and yanked back with all his might.

Raven's thin sword snapped in half with the force of Jason's pull.

Raven gave a comical shriek of alarm, his eyes wide and his mouth pulled taut in a shocked grimace.

Jason jerked the chain, sending the top half of Raven's blade clattering to the ground. He walked forward, thoroughly enjoying the expression of fear on Raven's face.

Nick landed from another back flip away from the foe he had just struck. He watched the man fall to the ground, and then turned his attention towards Melissa and Stacy. Melissa was wrapping up a fight of her own, and Stacy was standing with her crossbow lowered, watching the struggle between Jason and Raven. It seemed that they had finished off the last of Raven's men.

From the look of things, Raven himself was not faring much better.

Jason stomped towards him, and then punched Raven squarely in the face. Raven fell flat on his rear on the gravel beneath him.

Jason picked him up by the shirt collar and dragged him to his feet.

He head-butted him, sending Raven's head rocking back and nearly making his eyes roll back in his head.

"You thought you were safe up in your tower, didn't you Jacob?" Jason screamed into Raven's face, carrying his nearly limp body across the rooftop.

"You thought you could play with me and my family like we were toys, didn't you? Like the dolls you used to pull the heads off of?"

Blood trickled down Raven's face, but a smile managed to form across his lips.

Nick suddenly noticed with alarm where Jason was taking him.

Jason held Raven with as much difficulty as he would hold a bag of laundry. He was so much stronger now. His hate made him so.

"Smile all you want, shit-head. You'll still be smiling when you hit the pavement."

Raven chuckled, causing a bubble of blood to pop between two cracked teeth.

"Jason, no! That's enough!" he heard Nick scream behind him.

But Jason didn't care. Jason didn't care about Nick, or about Melissa, or even about himself at that moment. All he cared about was tossing Raven off the edge of this roof.

Raven knew what was going on. He even looked below him and laughed again when Jason carried him over to the edge of a seven story drop. A Mardi Gras float was parked below at the rear of the building, apparently abandoned there by the previous owners of the factory. The head of a huge chicken stared up at them with wide eyes and an open mouth, seeming to ask for Jason to drop Raven like a mother bird would drop a worm into the mouth of its young.

Raven continued to laugh.

"You can't kill me, Jason Dredd."

Jason shook him, holding the top half of his body over the drop.

"Watch me," Jason replied.

Raven fixed him with a steel-cold glare.

"You can't...boy. I'm bigger than you. More important than you. A rat can never kill a lion."

Jason heard Nick call out again behind him, but he was too focused on what he was about to do to even hear what it was Nick said.

He felt his mind send the signal for his hands to let go. He was going to prove Raven wrong. Now was the time for his vengeance.

But his fingers would not respond.

"I have a destiny, Jason. Something a useless punk like you can never understand. I have a calling."

Jason snarled in anger, but still did not let Raven go.

Something was wrong. The moment he had fantasized about for what seemed like an eternity had come, and he could not make his fingers let go.

"Eh heh," Raven chuckled, "See? Too weak to do it."

Jason's face clenched up and his teeth gnashed together. A tear fought to course its way from his eye. His entire being was in turmoil. His heart screamed at him to kill the man, but his body simply would not move.

Raven slowly shook his head, giving Jason a condescending look.

"You can't. You…can't…kill me. No one can."

Raven's prodding only made Jason angrier. Truly the man was insane.

Raven grabbed onto Jason's arm with his left hand. His eyes went wide in a crazed glare and Raven pulled himself closer to Jason's face.

"Wanna see?" Raven whispered.

The next series of events happened so fast that they were nearly over before Jason had time to register them.

Jason had been too blind in his rage to remember that Raven was still holding the broken bottom half of his blade in his right hand.

In a quick motion, Raven buried the jagged piece of steel deep into Jason's thigh.

Jason howled in pain, and in that moment his body finally did what it could not moments ago.

He let go.

Raven's mouth opened in a wide carnival laugh as he fell backwards. His arms stretched to his sides and his legs made no effort to stop himself from careening over the edge.

Nick was there in an instant, but too late.

Raven plummeted, emitting a half scream, half laugh the entire way down. His crazy eyes stayed locked on Jason the whole time. It was a scene that would remain burned in his memory for the rest of his life.

Raven's body smashed into and through the carnival float far below. The sound of broken metal and breaking bone instantly cut off the sound of his laughter.

And then there was silence.

Jacob Raven was gone.

25

Jason sat in the armchair in Melissa's living room. He was leaning forward with his elbows on his knees. His sunglasses were still on. The light still burned his eyes. It probably would for a long time.

There was a commotion in the room around him. Patricia was leaving. He had been introduced briefly in the van last night as they had fled RavenCorp, but he had only barely nodded a hello and offered a thank you. A part of him hoped he hadn't come across as ungrateful or rude, but the truth was a majority of him didn't care. He had spent the last six months of his life thinking of nothing but revenge and murder. Suddenly being thrown back into the world of politeness and social contact was startling to him.

He was aware that Stacy was watching him out of the corner of her eye. He had properly met her in the van as well. She had quite possibly saved his life during the rooftop battle. For that he really was grateful, regardless of how incapable of showing it he was at the moment. Her concern for him was obvious. He had a feeling he would enjoy getting to know her, if he stuck around much longer.

Melissa was playing an odd game of caution and avoidance with him. She was obviously hurt and unsure of what he had become. He imagined a fair amount of guilt was involved. Nick told him earlier that Melissa had jumped off of a roof trying to catch the helicopter McElroy whisked Jason away in. She had been frantically searching for him ever since. What she was going through now was a kind of regret. She felt she had been too late to stop most of Raven's damage from being done. Jason believed she was probably right, though it had not truly been her fault.

No. It was no one's fault but that of the man who he saw fall to his death less than twenty four hours ago.

Jason looked down at his hands. They were steady as a rock now. His whole body was. He felt as if he could wrap those hands around the throat of anyone he wished and squeeze until they breathed no more. They did not seem like hands that would hesitate. Yet at that crucial moment, when he should have done what he had focused his life towards doing, those hands would not let go.

He could not kill Jacob Raven.

Maybe Raven was right. Maybe he was just too weak. Maybe even those countless hours of honing his body and his mind had been for nothing. Deep down inside of him, he was still a scared, skinny, ghetto trash kid.

His fists clenched so hard his fingernails nearly drew blood from his palms. His weakness should not have been an excuse. He still should have been the one to toss Raven off of that rooftop, or beat him to death or strangle him with his chain or smash his face into the gravel so many times that his skull collapsed.

But because of his hesitation, he had instead watch Raven basically hurl himself off of that rooftop. The lunatic seemed to truly believe he was invincible. He would not have escaped past Jason and his friends. The only way out of his situation was to take a route they could not follow. So...he chose to trust his insanity and plunge to his death.

Jason knew that scene would trouble him for a long time. Now the object of his hatred was not only malicious and cruel, he was also completely beyond the grasp of reason.

Jason sighed and sat back. Nick was hugging Patricia behind him and telling her he wouldn't be far if she needed him. Nick...always the hero. Jason wondered if Nick didn't carry his own breed of insanity. No one could be there for everyone, all the time. No one could ever protect you in every situation. No...sometime...somewhere...the cruel hand of fate would always find you, no matter who swore to be there for you.

As morose as he felt, there was a glimmer of hope on Jason's horizon. He truly believed now that his family was still alive. Raven had stowed them away somewhere else. Though the man was dead, his empire was not. Jason would find them. He would hunt the remainder of RavenCorp to the four corners of the earth until he found the truth. He would bring to them the same pain he had brought to their employer.

Jason looked around. Nick and Stacy walked Patricia out the door. Patricia gave one final wave to Jason as she left. He managed a smile and a nod. That seemed to satisfy her.

Melissa was propped against the arm of the couch. She watched Patricia go. Jason thought it was more of an excuse to keep from looking at him than it was genuine interest in Patricia's departure.

He had to talk to her. He had to make her know somehow that what had happened to him had not been her fault.

He looked around the house. Melissa and the others had stocked it with cheap but usable furniture. The yellow armchair. The almost-matching yellow couch. An old wooden coffee table in front of a 25 inch TV on a wooden stand. A small kitchen adjoined to the living room and a smaller den with a fireplace adjoined to that. A back porch overlooking the lake outside. Melissa and Nick's garage-turned-gym. And Jason's small but comfortable room upstairs; three times bigger than the cell he had spent every night in before, and with a real bed.

He thought he could stay here a while. It would be difficult. He wanted to start looking for his family, but at this point…he really had no idea where to start.

Melissa needed to feel that she had truly saved him. It was important to him to make her feel that way. The others too.

Blitz trotted up to him and put his head on Jason's leg. Of all of them, himself included, Blitz was the only one who seemed to think that Jason was the same.

He smiled and ran a hand through the dog's fur. This was not as he had imagined his escape from Raven would turn out…but he thought he could live with it just the same.

"Is he going to be alright, Nick?" Patricia asked, standing at the bottom of the stairs in front of the house.

She saw the worry wash over his face. Stacy, too, looked unsure.

"This isn't what we expected to find when we saw him again. I didn't know that Raven would have…toyed with him like that. Given him enough freedom to vent his anger and build his hatred. Jason ended up doing exactly what Raven wanted him to do; embracing his primal desire for revenge."

"But we saw what happened on the roof. Jason couldn't kill him," Stacy chimed in optimistically. "So…I guess that means he's not all gone."

Patricia smiled and nodded. "He's a good person. I can tell. He just needs some time to remember."

Nick and Stacy nodded in agreement.

"And Melissa?" Patricia asked. "Will she be okay?"

Nick shared a look with Stacy.

"Melissa is nothing if not resilient. This is tearing her up inside, but I think she'll fight through it like she does everything else. Besides…we'll be there for her. For both of them."

Patricia took a deep breath and smiled. Nick truly cared for these people. She believed he cared for her as well, but this was where he belonged.

She looked at Stacy. "Take care of him, girl," she said, motioning her head towards Nick. "His heart's in the right place, but he needs people more than he thinks he does."

Stacy grinned. She punched Nick in the arm.

"Hear that? Told you so."

Nick smiled and rubbed his arm.

Stacy nearly hopped the few steps between her and Patricia and wrapped her in a big hug. Patricia shared a surprised look with Nick, and hugged Stacy right back.

"Are you going to be okay?" Stacy asked in her ear.

"Yeah," Patricia answered. "I'll figure things out. And if I don't, you'll be seeing a lot more of me."

"Good," Stacy said. "We need another girl around here. Melissa doesn't count."

The two of them shared a laugh. Stacy stepped away. She looked between Patricia and Nick, and then started up the steps.

"I'll be inside," she said, giving them time to properly say goodbye.

"She's really something," Patricia said after Stacy had closed the door.

Nick nodded.

"Yeah. Never lets anything faze her. Not for long, anyway."

"That's strange, Nick. Considering what you told me happened to her."

She watched his smile fade. Obviously the thought had occurred to him as well.

"I think that's how she's dealing with it. By being happy and by watching out for us. In a way we're distracting her. I don't know if that's a good thing or a bad thing. Time will tell, I guess."

A sly smile crossed Patricia's face.

"Well one thing is obvious. The girl adores you."

Nick went a little pale. His eyes went distant and his shoulders slumped. Strange, thought Patricia, it was almost the same helpless look he had when she had asked him to stay with her nearly a year ago.

"She is something special. But there are certain things I can't..." he trailed off, not knowing how to continue.

"I know," Patricia finished for him. "Nick the noble loner."

He looked up at her, seeming to acknowledge that she understood.

"You're going to stay with them for a while then?" she asked, changing the subject.

He nodded, the resolve suddenly coming back into his face.

"Yes. At least until Jason gets back on his feet and Melissa and Stacy find a proper place for themselves."

Suddenly Nick seemed to remember that Melissa and Stacy were not his only friends out of place in the world.

"What about you?" he asked her, "What will you do now?"

Patricia shrugged.

"I don't know yet; but I know I'll keep searching. I may not be cut out to be a waitress or a shop clerk, but there's something out there with my name written on it. A calling that's all my own. I'll find it."

Nick smiled and nodded. "I know you will. And if you need me..."

"You'll be there," Patricia said warmly, "I know."

She looked at him for a long moment. She understood now that Nick was just as confused and out of place in life as she was. Maybe more so. He was still her hero, but now she knew him for the vulnerable human being he was also.

She stepped forward and hugged him fiercely.

"You're doing the right thing, Nick. They need you."

Nick held her back, closing his eyes and enjoying her nearness. Patricia was someone special to him. She understood him in a way the others didn't.

"I have faith in you, Trish. You are meant for something important, and you'll find it. Sooner rather than later."

She smiled. "That's good to hear."

She reluctantly stepped away from Nick, still holding his hands for a couple of steps before letting them go.

"Be who you are, Nick. Your past can't define that. Your Pull can't define it. It's what you do now that does."

He looked at her, taking in her words.

"And take care of yourself. Try not to piss off any more crime bosses for a while," she called out.

He laughed loudly.

"I'll try."

She waved and began walking away towards the caravan that was waiting for her in the cul-de-sac.

"Call me when you get home," he yelled after her.

She turned and grinned at him.

"Will do."

When Nick walked back in, Jason was in the same spot he had been before. Still propped in his armchair. Still wearing his shades. Still looking far away.

Melissa was sitting with her arms crossed on the couch attempting to ignore Stacy, who was play-punching her in the shoulder.

"See? He's back. Now get up off your duff and let's cook dinner," Stacy said to her, attempting to prod her into doing something other than sitting there looking depressed.

"Stacy, you are annoying the hell out of me, now go away," Melissa muttered, though without any real emotion.

Stacy stuck her tongue out at her. She sat back and looked up at Nick.

Nick looked at the two of them, so wounded and confused. Maybe Stacy was on to something. Maybe they needed something to take their minds off of things.

"How about we go out for dinner?" he suggested.

Stacy brightened up immediately.

"Yeah! Dinner and a movie!"

Nick walked around the couch and sat down on the coffee table in front of Melissa and Jason.

"We all had one of the roughest nights of our lives last night. We need to celebrate now that it's over."

"Celebrate, Nick?" Melissa asked, looking skeptical that there was anything to celebrate.

"No," Jason suddenly spoke, "Nick's right."

Melissa looked up at him in surprise.

"We're not doing anyone any good moping around here. There's a time to know when to act and a time to know when to relax. Besides," he said, looking up at Melissa and offering a small smile, "I haven't had a decent meal in a long time."

Melissa smiled back, some of her worry seeming to fall away.

"So come on!" Stacy yelled, tackling Melissa on the couch.

Melissa – finally - offered a laugh.

She shoved Stacy off of her and sighed.

"Okay then," she said, a little bit of her trademark spirit back in her voice, "Let me go get my party shoes on."

Nick and Stacy laughed. Nick understood why Jason had truly volunteered. He saw it in the way Jason watched her as she walked away.

Maybe their friend wasn't so lost after all.

26

To everyone's surprise and delight, the moment the four of them arrived at the restaurant and sat down at one of the patio tables overlooking Bourbon Street, it was as if the events of the past six months hadn't happened.

Melissa seemed to finally shove her way past her uncertainty and allow herself to come out again. The first thing she said when they sat down was a comment about how many "greased up douche-nozzles" were prowling that night. By that, of course she meant the mass of frat kids that often prowled the French Quarter. They all had a laugh, even Jason.

He ordered three different entrees after taking a long time to study the menu. When the meals arrived, the others watched him tear apart a platter of fried crawfish, a bowl of gumbo, and a rack of honey glazed ribs.

It was strange seeing him sitting there stuffing his face with his sunglasses on in a dimly lit open-air restaurant at seven o'clock at night, but truth be told they all thought it was a glorious sight. All of their work, all of their worrying, all of the stress had not been for nothing. Jason was back.

Melissa, who just hours before had seemed almost as if she wanted to run away from her best friend, was now beaming, unable to keep her eyes off of him and a smile from crossing her face.

At one point Stacy reached under the table and squeezed Nick's knee. He looked at her and smiled, sharing the pleasure at watching their two friends be something close to happy again. But Nick also couldn't fight back the way his heart seemed to beat faster while her hand was there; and how when he looked at her...he was happy about more than just Melissa and Jason.

After dinner they walked a few blocks to the movie theater. Melissa picked a revenge flick about a cop who lost his partner. Jason seemed pretty interested in seeing a movie again. He hadn't had anything close to entertainment for the entirety of his stay in Raven's cell. This was almost like being born again. He even took off his sunglasses in the dark theater. To their relief and despite the drastic changes the rest of him had undergone, Jason's eyes looked just the same.

As they sat there in the dark, Nick noticed that Melissa was leaning more towards Jason than she was towards him. Every time gunshots rang out her eyes seemed to sparkle and she inched a little closer to him. Jason himself wore a slight smile on his face the entire time.

On Nick's other side, he noticed Stacy shuffling nervously a few times. When he looked over at her he placed his hand on the armrest between them.

"Are you okay?" he whispered.

She looked at him, smiled serenely, and placed her hand over his.

"Yes," she whispered back, "I really am."

Nick felt her loop her fingers around his, holding his hand and not taking her eyes off of him.

She was telling him something. He knew her well enough to read what was behind those brown eyes. Stacy was thanking him. She was telling him that, like Jason, she had once been lost. Nick and the others had found her. They had saved her not only from violence, but from a life that she could never have been herself in.

He didn't question how he knew that. He didn't question why. He didn't question the touch or what it really meant. He knew. He knew and he wanted her to know. He wanted her to know that she meant as much to him as he did to her.

Nick turned his hand over and wrapped his palm around hers, holding her hand more intimately. Without saying a word she moved the retractable armrest and scooted closer to him. He placed his arm around her and took her in.

The warmth of her. The way she smelled. The soft cascade of her hair against the side of his face. Her breath on his shoulder. The way he could almost imagine he could feel her heart beating; and what that heart felt for him.

He took her in. All of her. And at that moment, Nick regretted nothing. He regretted nothing and he feared nothing. All he felt was wonderfully, perfectly, unquestionably…right.

"I'm just saying, the human mind doesn't work that way. The guy wouldn't go from Johnny Law to Dirty Harry in the space of a week. His whole career he never questioned his orders and he never questioned the methods of his superiors. Now all of a sudden he decided to throw all of that out the window and go guns blazing through the Latino criminal underworld?"

Melissa looked frustrated at Jason's tirade.

"Listen Jack, if someone killed your partner, the past wouldn't matter. Your training wouldn't matter. All that would matter would be a chamber full of bullets and a hit list filled with the names of the guys that did it."

Jason shook his head.

"No. Someone from his background would have gotten his revenge from within the system. He would have used his police resources to bring the guys down, not a couple of sawed off shotguns and a crowbar."

Melissa shrugged.

"I would have used a crowbar."

Jason looked at her with one eyebrow raised.

"I know you would have."

Melissa made an angry noise and elbowed him in the ribs.

"Melissa, you would have done that if the guy stole your sandwich," Stacy said.

Melissa pointed an angry finger at her, then smiled and looped her arm around Jason's.

"Walk me to my chariot, Spartacus," she said smugly.

Jason looked over at Nick.

"She still has a nearly infinite supply of nonsensical one-liners, doesn't she?"

"Almost," Nick replied, "that's the second time she's called someone 'Spartacus' this month."

Stacy laughed so hard she spit a mouthful of Coke all over herself.

"God damn mother fucker!!!" Stacy exclaimed, still laughing a little, but looking down at her stained shirt in dismay.

Melissa started laughing uncontrollably and pointing at Stacy.

"I always knew there was a sailor under that 'Hello Kitty' exterior!"

Nick nearly doubled over with laughter. He grabbed Stacy's hand after a moment.

"Do we need to find you someplace to clean up?"

She looked up at him with puppy-dog eyes.

"Yes, please."

Then she kicked Melissa in the shin.

After a few more moments of play-fighting and hurling of insults, the four of them followed a sign towards the closest restaurant to get Stacy cleaned up. Melissa and Jason couldn't help but notice that she and Nick held hands the whole way. Of course, Jason and Melissa themselves were arm-in-arm, so they couldn't say a word.

Nick led them around a corner.

"Must be one of those places where you go in the back door," he noted.

"That's what she said," Melissa chimed in.

The others were starting to wonder if the signs had led them in the wrong direction.

"Or not," Nick said as they came to a dead end behind the building. All that was there were stacks of big wooden crates and a dumpster surrounded by the rear walls of two adjoining buildings.

"That's why you come home late every night," Melissa said. "You can't find your way out of a paper bag."

Nick stood there, suddenly feeling a sense of déjà vu. The dumpster. An alleyway. Stacks of newspapers instead of crates.

The body of a mangled teenager.

He suddenly let go of Stacy's hand and turned around.

"Let's try another way."

Stacy looked after him with concern. She started to walk after him...but then she heard something. Scratching from above. Like a rat scurrying on the rooftops.

A big rat.

"Do you guys hear that?" she said.

Melissa and Jason, still standing there, looked up.

Nick froze in his tracks. His eyes widened and his heart nearly stopped.

He hadn't brought them here by mistake. Something had called him here. Dear god...he had almost forgotten.

He whirled around.

"Run! NOW!!!" he screamed at the top of his lungs.

Before the others could react, another sound followed the sound of Nick's voice.

A raspy, inhuman laugh echoed from above.

Nick, Melissa, Stacy and Jason watched as a man-sized shape stood up against the moonlight, its silhouette casting shadows below. It then stepped off the roof, raising arms that seemed to be holding large objects in each hand.

As it landed a mere two feet from Stacy, she suddenly felt very much as Nick had seconds before. Like her heart would never beat again.

"Nick," Melissa said in a low voice, "what...the...hell...is that?"

Nick pushed past her violently.

"I said run! Get out of here now!" he pleaded with them.

The Whisper stood up to its full height, towering over Stacy by a foot and a half. She looked up at it like a snail standing before a steamroller.

The…thing…was human-shaped, but bore characteristics that no person possibly could. For one thing, there was no face behind that metal mask. All she could see was fire…flickering and waving like a living thing behind that jack-o-lantern grin. Purple fire. A color she didn't even think flames could be.

And its hands were so…big and sharp. Every finger looked as long as Nick's sword. How would anyone lift an arm with weight like that? Why would anyone want to?

And the way it was looking at her. The way it seemed so…hungry. Not in the way she was before she bit into a cheeseburger, but in the way she had been as a child; just as eager to play with her mashed potatoes before she devoured them.

Finally she took a step back, then another. Nick grabbed her and yanked her behind him.

"It's…just some jackass in a suit…right?" Jason muttered, not sounding entirely convinced.

The Whisper opened his razor-toothed maw and uttered a soul-wrenching roar. The sound was part animal, part machine, and almost human. Almost.

Nick knew what The Whisper wanted. He was telling them it was play time.

"Not now. Not here," Nick stepped forward, eyeing the demon with a murderous glare.

"Not them!"

"Bullshit," Melissa said behind him.

"If Shredder here wants to party with us, let's give him what he wants."

Nick turned to her, praying that The Whisper would not make the first move.

"Melissa, you don't know what this thing is."

"And you do?" Melissa replied angrily. "Lucy, I think you got some 'splainin to do."

"I know what it is," Jason spoke up. The others watched as he took a step forward and let his previously-concealed chain fall from inside of his shirt sleeve.

"It's some asshole with a special effects degree and a bad sense of humor."

Melissa grinned. Jason's bravado washed the last of her fear away.

"And a death wish," she added.

Nick looked more terrified than ever.

"No! You can't fight this thing! He only wants me!"

"If he wants you..." they heard Stacy say quietly from behind him, "then he gets us."

Melissa grinned even wider.

"Damn straight, sister!"

Jason began to swing his chain above them.

"Giddeyap, cowboy!" Melissa screamed, and ran at The Whisper full speed.

Nick wanted to move, but couldn't. He wanted to shove her out of the way, but all he could feel was numbness in his arms and legs. He was certain he was about to witness the bloody demise of his closest friend.

Melissa launched herself into the air, leading with a kick that would have taken the head off of a linebacker.

The Whisper was no linebacker.

The demon moved with a speed that seemed to deny his enormous size. He turned sideways and stepped forward, leading towards Melissa with his right shoulder. His bladed hands came up.

For a split second, Melissa saw the hands and wondered if she was about to be sliced to ribbons in mid-air. Instead, the monster grabbed her leg in one hand and wrapped a huge paw around her shoulder with the other. It pulled her forward, mostly allowing Melissa's own momentum to carry her. And then it head-butted her so forcefully she felt the entire world go black.

The Whisper tossed her like a rag doll into the crates behind him. She smashed into and through several of them, bringing the others piling down on top of her.

Jason roared. His chain whipped through the air with enough force to smash a cinderblock.

The Whisper, his attention already towards his new attacker, reached out and grabbed the weighted end of Jason's chain. If an ordinary man had done that, his hand would have been shattered into a million bone fragments. The sound of metal clanking against metal echoed in the alley.

Jason pulled back, trying to free his weapon.

The Whisper laughed, and yanked the chain hard.

Jason stumbled forward, propelled by The Whisper's strength and entangled by the end of the chain that was still wrapped around his arm.

Before Jason could raise an arm in defense, the demon thrust his own arm out and wrapped his bronze palm around Jason's face. He lifted with ease, and suddenly Jason, all six feet and nearly 200 pounds of him, was hovering above the ground.

Nick and Stacy watched as The Whisper walked two steps to the left, carrying the struggling Jason. The demon pulled his arm back, and then smashed Jason's head into the brick wall in front of him. When Jason fell to the ground, they both saw the crater his skull had just made in the brick.

Jason was no longer moving, and Melissa hadn't stirred from beneath the pile of rubble.

"Oh god," Nick said beneath his breath. "Why is this happening?"

The Whisper turned and began to slowly approach Nick.

"Why is this happening to me? Why are you taking them away from me?"

Stacy tore her eyes off of the monster and looked at Nick. Something odd was happening to him. His face was twisted in terror and confusion...but also anger.

"What did I do? What did I do to deserve this?" he yelled.

His panic only seemed to make The Whisper's grin widen.

"Why is this happening?!!"

Nick's chest was heaving. The fear in his eyes was fleeing. In its place was a look Stacy had never seen in them before.

Pure, unfiltered rage.

"Why?!!" Nick screamed one more time, and leaped into the air towards the object of his fury.

Stacy's eyes widened.

The Whisper stepped back in alarm. For one second it was facing a panicked victim...and the next it was facing a howling adversary with a sword.

Stacy didn't know what to think. Nick had been unarmed the whole night. There was nowhere he could have hidden it, but somehow his sword was now in his hand.

And dear god, she thought...the mask...

Nick landed on The Whisper's chest, his sword kept from the monster's throat by one bladed finger that had made it just in time. Nick glared at his enemy, his green eyes burning with fury above his mask.

The Whisper, at first startled, now seemed enthralled by what he was seeing. The almond shaped slits that were his eyes seemed to grow larger with excitement. He held Nick's angry stare for a moment, and then snapped his face forward, biting at Nick like a trapped dog.

Nick somersaulted off of The Whisper, but the moment he hit the ground he was charging again. The demon hissed gleefully and met Nick's sword with three of his blades.

Stacy didn't know what to do. She couldn't magically make her crossbow appear in her hands like Nick had just done. She had a basic knowledge of combat, but how the hell could a judo throw be any good against a nearly seven foot metal monster with blades for fingers?

But as Stacy watched Nick and his enemy do battle, it became more and more clear to her that the only thing she could do was stand aside. She could no more affect the outcome of this battle then she could stop a tornado with a dust buster. The two of them crashed into each other like dueling tsunamis. Forces of nature that man could only run from.

It was like watching gods do battle.

Nick was a blur of motion. Spinning and slashing and kicking off of walls, jumping up and over and around with a speed Stacy's eyes could hardly keep up with. But though her eyes could not, The Whisper's hands could.

The monster was just as fast as his opponent, slicing and cutting and maneuvering its powerful legs to always match and beat Nick to his next position. Ten fingers moved in different directions. Three at Nick's head. Two at his stomach. Four at his weapon and one at his heart.

Yet somehow Nick dodged or blocked them all. Again and again the monster attacked, and again and again Nick avoided getting speared or diced by mere nanoseconds.

Nick's kicks, furious as they were, were obviously useless against the beast, slowing him down for moments at best. And when Nick did happen to land a sword blow, all Stacy saw were sparks shearing off of the monster's bronze hide. There seemed to be nothing Nick could do to inflict harm upon this terrifying creature.

And so Stacy began to see that it was only a matter of time before Nick, despite all of his speed and grace and power, was unable to stop one of those fingers from slipping through his furious defense and piercing his flesh. For Nick, unlike the demon, could be hurt.

Or at least, she thought he could. It was becoming clear to her now that for all her feelings for him, she really knew nothing about this man. Who he was. What he was.

Seeing the monster, and seeing Nick's recognition of the monster.... Stacy finally understood why Nick had never returned her advances until tonight. The monster followed him; and Nick's own...otherness...followed him as well.

"Dear god, Nick," Stacy said breathlessly, "None of us had any idea."

Then the moment Stacy had dreaded occurred. In the midst of a back flip dodge through the air, the monster was able to slash Nick across the back.

Nick yelled in pain, landing carefully; one hand going to his wounded back while the other hand attempted to block further attack. The Whisper took the opening, battering Nick's sword to the side and slicing another wound into his chest.

The demon kicked out with a taloned foot, catching Nick in the upper torso and smashing his body into the dumpster behind him. Nick's head smacked into the metal object. The demon, unrelenting, slammed a knee into Nick's throat, and then picked him up and smashed his body into the cobblestone ground beneath him.

Nick lay very still. His hand was still wrapped around the sword, but that sword did not rise up to strike back.

And all of a sudden, Stacy realized she was alone.

So did The Whisper.

The demon placed a foot on Nick's back and stepped over him, beginning to slowly walk towards her.

"S....st....stay back," she said, her heart beating what she believed might be its last panicked tempo.

The Whisper laughed. The raspy, dry sound of it made her sick to her stomach. She noticed now that the sound echoed not across the alleyway, but inside of her mind.

It was getting closer. Only a few more steps and it would be upon her, tearing her to shreds with those endlessly long bladed claws.

She could have run. She knew the thing would have caught her, but she also couldn't stop looking down at Nick. He was starting to stir now, but only barely. He wouldn't be able to help her in time.

Stacy put up a semblance of a fighting stance.

"I'm warning you. Stay back," she tried to sound menacing, but her voice was trembling too badly to allow for much threat.

Then the monster was upon her; standing right in front of her, as close as Nick had been not even thirty minutes before. Her knees threatened to buckle beneath her, but still she held her ground. She would not give this thing the pleasure of killing her on her knees.

Smiling almost tenderly, The Whisper reached a finger out and gently pushed Stacy's arm aside. Staring into those eyes of purple flame, she found she could not make herself move any further.

Nick raised his head from the cobblestones. He saw The Whisper standing in front of Stacy. He saw the hateful thing move her hands away. He saw the demon look back at him to make sure he was watching.

And then he watched helplessly as The Whisper pulled back his arm and swiped a bladed finger across Stacy's stomach.

Nick knew he was screaming, but he did not hear it. He knew he was struggling to get to his feet, but he did not feel it. All he experienced at that moment was the terrible sight of Stacy's eyes widening, her hands wrapping around her stomach...and blood seeping through her fingers.

Nick was barely aware of The Whisper giving him one last satisfied look before tearing off back into the night. He was sure that evil laugh followed him, but Nick did not hear it.

He was at her side almost instantly, scooping her up in his arms just as he had the first time he saw her, tears streaming down his face. His face which bore no mask. His arms which held no sword.

Her eyes closed and he felt her go limp. Her hands fell to the pavement. There was blood everywhere.

"Not her. Please not her," Nick wept. He held her face to his chest, mindless of the blood.

"Why did you take them away from me?" he asked helplessly, speaking only to the night air, it seemed. But Nick knew who he was speaking to. The same source he had been feeling was leading him. The same intelligence he had come to believe was the source of The Pull.

The source that had now allowed his friends to die.

"I thought you were looking out for me! I thought you made me something special so I could help people. Not watch him kill my friends!"

Nick shook his head, feeling Stacy's hair against his skin again. The sensation brought a fresh sob from his lips.

"He wanted me.... He wanted me because I'm so god...damn...special," Nick said with contempt. Never had he hated himself as much as he did then. Whatever he was. Why-ever he was. It had brought the monster that had taken his only real home away.

But then he did feel something. A hand on his shoulder.

Nick turned around, and there, standing above him, was Melissa. She wore a few bruises on her face and arms, but she seemed otherwise alright.

And behind her, Nick saw Jason sitting on the ground, holding his head in his hands and looking pained. His skull was not crushed. His neck was not broken. Hell, even his glasses had fallen off early enough to remain undamaged. No, he just looked like he had a headache.

"It's not your fault, Nick," Melissa said to him.

He stared at her, not knowing whether or not to believe she was alive. Jason got up and walked over to them. He knelt down and picked one of Stacy's limp hands up off the ground. He studied it for a moment.

"She's not dead, Nick."

Nick's head tilted and his arms loosened their death-grip on Stacy a bit.

"What?"

"She's not dead," Jason repeated, lifting her wrist in front of Nick. "Healthy heartbeat."

Nick lowered her body and looked at her wound. Jason pushed her shirt up a bit and looked at her stomach.

"Ooh," he noted, "Might leave a nasty scar, but it didn't break through to anything important. Just enough to bleed."

Nick allowed himself to breathe again.

"Then...?"

"She just passed out," Jason smiled.

"Wouldn't you?" Melissa added.

Nick laughed a little through the remainder of his tears.

"Thank you, God. Thank you, God," he said, looking up into the sky and smiling at the stars.

Melissa looked up with him, following Nick's gaze before giving Jason a skeptical look.

Nick stood up, lifting Stacy in his arms. Jason took off his shirt and placed it on her stomach to stop the bleeding, but also to disguise the wound. They still had to walk back to the car.

"Most people that see us will think she just had too much to drink," he reasoned.

Nick nodded and started off.

Melissa stopped him by grabbing his shoulder.

"This isn't over, pal," she said, not a hint of friendliness in her voice, "Not by a long shot."

The look in her eyes told Nick that before this night was over, he may lose his friends after all.

He knew what she was asking...no...demanding of him.

The time had come to tell the truth.

207

27

When Stacy awoke on the couch, Melissa was on the floor in front of her.

"Melissa," Stacy smiled as she sat up, "You're okay."

"And so are you, thankfully," Melissa answered. "Jason, too."

Stacy swung her legs to the floor, suddenly alarmed.

"Where's Nick?"

Melissa motioned towards the window. Jason was standing in front of it, looking out.

"He's out there, on the porch. Has been since we got back. Jason's been watching him. Making sure he doesn't take off."

Stacy looked confused.

"Why would he…"

"I've never seen anyone look so guilty in my life," Jason said from in front of the window. "You'd think it was Nick that tried to kill us tonight, from the expression on his face."

"The thing didn't try to kill us," Stacy said, "It was playing with us. Using us to get to him."

Melissa's eyebrows lowered and anger entered her eyes.

"Maybe he should feel guilty," she muttered.

Jason moved towards the door.

"I'll call him back in, now that Stacy's awake."

Stacy watched Nick walk in the door with his arms crossed almost protectively around himself. His face was as pale as a sheet and his eyes wore a broken expression, as if he had just lost something of great value to him.

Jason closed the door behind him.

"Let's do this in the kitchen," Jason suggested.

"Why?" Melissa asked.

"Because we're about to have a hard talk, and it's no good having a hard talk in a place that you don't want to leave hard memories."

Melissa and Stacy got up, leaving the comfort of the living room behind and entering the kitchen. Stacy, Melissa and Jason all sat around the kitchen table. Nick followed them in, several steps behind, and propped himself up against the counter. Blitz sat nervously at the door, knowing something was wrong.

209

The three of them sat there, staring at him; waiting for an explanation they knew would never suffice for what they had experienced that night. Nothing could explain it enough to bring any sort of relief or closure, no matter what fantastic tale Nick had to tell.

He just stood there, his arms still folded, his head down towards the floor and his eyes somewhere far away.

"Tell us the truth Nick. You owe us that. Tell us who you are, where you really came from, and what that thing was that attacked us tonight," Melissa said to him sternly.

Finally Nick nodded, and began to speak.

"I call it The Whisper," he said, barely speaking above a whisper himself.

"I call it that because that's the way it spoke to me, before I woke up."

Jason crossed his own arms and sat back in his chair.

"Woke up? You mean the earliest thing you can remember?"

Nick nodded.

"I woke up in the woods that day, about three weeks before I met Melissa. I was alone...I think...and all I had with me was my sword and the clothes on my back. I don't know why I had the sword. I don't know where it came from, but I've learned since then that I know how to use it."

Stacy thought of the titanic battle she had just witnessed. Nick's simple claim of "knowing how to use it" was an extreme understatement.

"I didn't remember who I was or where I had come from. I didn't remember who my family was or where they lived. I did remember my name, however."

Nick trailed off. He looked like he was conjuring up something that was painful to think about.

"And I remembered something else."

The others waited while he mustered the courage to speak further.

"I believe, before I lost my memory, that something attacked me. Not an animal or a person. Some...thing. A monster with purple eyes. And it didn't attack my body. I think...I think it attacked me from the inside."

Melissa cocked her head.

"Like a parasite?"

Nick looked at her as if that word had hit the mark.

"In a way, yes. But not like a living parasite. More like a...spirit. Like something had found its way inside my soul and was feeding off of me."

Melissa raised an eyebrow and looked over at Jason. Jason just kept staring at Nick.

"You believe you were possessed by a demon?" Jason asked.

Nick sighed and shrugged.

"Maybe. Something like that. I think that might be what caused me to lose my memory."

"But you said it was there before you lost your memory," Jason said. "Was this demon no longer in you when you woke up?"

Nick shook his head.

"No. Whatever happened before I lost consciousness that day…I must have beaten it. I must have forced it out. Maybe that's why it hates me so much."

Nick paused, as if he was considering whether or not to share the next bit of his tale.

"There was…something else. Aside from my name and the vague recollection of this thing that attacked me, I also had a feeling. I had a sense of where I was supposed to go. I guess it was lingering memory. Some part of me that knew where I had been heading before. It tugged at me. It called to me, in a way. It still does sometimes. A voice without words. Like a homing beacon that's always on, sometimes stronger than others. I call it The Pull."

He paused again. Stacy could tell Nick was afraid they were all thinking he was crazy.

"And The Pull brought you to Atlanta?" she asked him.

"Yes," Nick nodded.

"Where did it tell you to go then?" Jason asked, obviously intrigued.

Nick's face darkened with uncertainty.

"I don't know. When I got to Atlanta, it seemed to be pulling me in every direction at once. Almost like it didn't know where to direct me. Like it was just as lost as I was. It stayed that way for a while, until I met all of you."

Melissa looked at him sternly.

"So where is The Pull telling you to go now, Nick?"

Nick looked up at her, looking helpless again. He seemed to not want to answer.

"Somewhere else. Far away, I think. Back east. There's still something in or around Atlanta I have to find."

"So why don't you go there?" Melissa asked coldly.

Stacy shot her an angry glare, but Melissa's eyes were fixed solely on Nick.

"Because I didn't want to follow it anymore," Nick answered.

He looked at Jason, then at Stacy.

211

"Because, for the past six months, my past…maybe even my future…hasn't mattered so much to me."

Stacy smiled at him.

"None of this explains tonight, Nick," Jason said. "Tell us about the person that attacked us in that alley."

Nick shifted uncomfortably.

"It wasn't a person," he said, "It was the thing I remembered from before. The thing with purple eyes. It was the demon that was inside of me."

Stacy was entranced, not knowing whether to believe him or not, but somehow feeling as if she had no choice.

"How?" she asked.

"I don't know," Nick said. "The day I walked into Atlanta, that thing came for me. It killed a kid right in front of me. At first I didn't know what it was, but then I got close to it and…it was like I could still feel it…inside. I think we're still connected somehow. When it's close to me, I know what it's thinking."

"And what was it thinking tonight?" Melissa asked.

"That it wanted to show me that it could hurt me," Nick answered without hesitation.

Melissa leaned back in her chair.

"So you're saying that the 'demon' that possessed you somehow gained a body and is now stalking you in real life?" Melissa asked.

Nick nodded.

"Yes. I don't know how, but he somehow gained a physical form. A metal shell of some kind. I think he's possessing it just like he would a person; and he's using it to come after me."

"Why doesn't he just kill you?" Jason asked.

Nick seemed to think for a minute.

"The times I've been near him….only twice now…I've gotten a sense that he's toying with me. I think there's almost a childlike level of playfulness to him; but he doesn't play like a person would."

"He plays like a tiger or a crocodile," Melissa said. "He tears his prey to ribbons before he eats it."

"Yeah," Nick answered. "Something like that."

"And tonight, he used us to get to you. To hurt you," Stacy said.

Nick looked at her.

"Yes. He hurt you in order to hurt me. He doesn't want to kill me. Not now. He just wants to take away the things I love. He wants me to know that I'll never be safe, and neither will those around me."

A long moment of silence came then, as the three of them took in Nick's words and his strange story.

"And that's why I have to leave," Nick said suddenly. "Tonight."

Stacy looked up in alarm.

"No," she said.

"Yes. What happened tonight will happen again. Probably worse next time. He'll keep hurting you in order to hurt me. That's what he wants. That's probably why he waited so long to attack me again. He wanted me to gain friends so he could use them against me."

"Nick, you took out a room full of the best fighters money can buy," Melissa said, referring to McElroy and Raven's elite guard. "Are you saying you're afraid of one psycho in a tin suit?"

Jason nodded.

"I know what you think happened, Nick, but memories can be deceiving. Maybe this is just some guy with too much time on his hands and a fascination with knives and monsters. He probably just dresses that way to scare his victims before he kills them. Besides, does anybody really believe in demons these days?"

"Oh yes," Melissa suddenly said, surprising them all. They all looked at her and were further shocked to see the vacant expression in her eyes, as if she was being assaulted by a memory, herself.

"You'd be surprised," she said, offering no further explanation before bringing her attention back to Nick.

"Why don't you think you can beat this guy? Sure, we messed up tonight, but that's just because we underestimated him. If you know what he can do...why are you so sure you can't beat him?"

"You didn't see what it's capable of, Melissa," Stacy spoke up. "That thing...it's so," she struggled to find the right words.

"Nobody can move like that. And did you look into its eyes? There's not a person in there. It's like a metal shell filled with nothing but fire. Fire and malevolence."

Jason studied her for a moment, and then turned back to Nick.

"Well...regardless of what it is...regardless of what it can do," he said, "we can find a way to beat it."

Melissa turned to him angrily.

"What do you mean 'we'? What makes you think I don't want this asshole to leave?"

"Because he's our friend, Melissa," Jason replied just as forcefully.

"But he lied to us!"

"No. He didn't lie. He just didn't tell us everything. And would you have believed him? Until tonight, would you have thought such a thing was even possible?"

Melissa seemed to want to continue the argument, but obviously could not think of a reply. Jason was right. None of them would have believed him.

213

"It doesn't matter," Nick said. "I have to leave. I can't put any of you in danger anymore. Who knows what else is going to come after me? I don't know what I am. I hardly know what I can do. What if this is just the tip of the iceberg? What if The Whisper isn't the only horrible thing from my past out there?"

Melissa snickered.

"Worse than Mr. Ginsu Knife? I kind of doubt it."

"Then what if I'm worse?!" Nick suddenly screamed.

They all looked at him in shock.

"I don't know who I am, Melissa. You've seen what I can do. Can you even really say what I am?"

Stacy thought of the scene between Nick and The Whisper earlier, and wondered if he wasn't right. She wasn't going to tell Melissa and Jason about the fact that Nick seemed to materialize objects out of thin air, or the fact that his movements in battle seemed to be far beyond human limits.

"Bullshit, Nick," Melissa yelled back at him. "You're good, but you're not that good. I've beaten your ass a time or two. Yeah, I've never seen anyone jump over my head before or run as fast as a car, but I can't say that it's not possible. Hell, I bet I could do those things too if I tried hard enough. You're just a kid with skills, Nick. It doesn't matter where those skills came from. You're just like everyone else."

Nick seemed unsure, but in a way he also seemed encouraged by the thought.

"Nick," Jason said calmly, "I know you think this thing can't be beaten, but I can tell you that no matter how big or how bad your enemy is...there's always a way to bring it down. Demon or not, this thing has a weakness, and we can find it."

Nick looked at him.

"He could have killed you. You're not afraid of him?"

Jason smiled slyly.

"Fear and I parted ways a while ago."

Stacy stood up.

"Jason's right, Nick. We can beat this thing. The next time he shows up we'll be ready. I know he's scary and I know he's strong, but as long as we stick together, he'll never be as powerful as the four of us are combined."

"You don't know that," Nick said.

"I do!" Stacy said passionately. "You move like a force of nature. I saw that tonight. Melissa is the best female fighter I've ever seen and Jason is stronger and smarter than any three men combined."

"Female fighter?" Melissa chimed in, "Honey, you haven't seen the trail of broken Joes and Toms and Butchs I've left over the years."

214

"I trust you, Nick," Stacy continued, ignoring her, "I don't care who you are and I don't care what you're capable of. When I look at you, I don't see danger. I don't see a man that's going to hurt me. I see a friend. I trust you. And despite what Melissa says, I think we all do."

Melissa looked embarrassed, but didn't bother to contradict her.

"Now I ask you to trust us," Stacy said to him. "Let us help you."

Nick looked around at them. Jason was smiling and Melissa was looking at him with a lot less venom than she was before. Blitz was wagging his tail. Nick raised his shoulders a bit, feeling less deflated and more hopeful.

"Alright," Melissa sighed. "Now we have three things on the to-do list instead of one."

Melissa raised her fingers, counting off as she went.

"Find Jason's family,"

Jason looked at her, surprised.

"Kill your monster," she continued, "and help you find your past. What's a little extra work going to hurt us?"

Nick's eyes were wide. The color had returned to his face. A hint of a smile was forming on his lips.

"I...don't know what to say."

"Say thank you, dumbass." Melissa told him.

He laughed a little.

"Thank you."

He looked around at them with pride and gratitude.

"Maybe you're right. Maybe together...we will find a way."

Epilogue

Nick stood outside again, staring up into the night air, watching the stars twinkle and the treetops sway in the breeze.

He hadn't been entirely forthcoming in there. As hopeful as he was now that he knew his friends were behind him, he was not as confident in himself as they seemed to be. If The Whisper wanted to hurt him, the demon would find a way. Nick was no match for a supernatural monster. Sure, he could fight, but what good were those skills against an enemy who had no flesh to pierce or no bones to break? What good was it against an opponent that was so fast and strong that, no matter what Nick did, the demon was always one step ahead?

He had almost fought The Whisper to a standstill in that alley, though the memory of the battle itself was a bit of a blur. How could he seem to remember having his sword and mask with him when he had not gone out with them that night, and they had not been there when the demon left? Regardless, even with every ounce of ability Nick believed he had, the demon had still won. Whatever he had…whatever he was capable of…it would not be enough.

Would it?

The truth was, Nick didn't know what he was capable of. Every time he stepped out into the city with that sword in his hand and that mask on his face, he surprised himself with some feat or another. Car surfing? Who on Earth could do that?

Who on Earth, indeed?

Nick snickered. He didn't think he was an alien. He didn't think he was a supernatural force like The Whisper. But still…he had a feeling he wasn't normal, either. There was something about him that was different. Something that frightened him.

He remembered how Stacy had felt in his arms after The Whisper had left. So lifeless. He was developing strong feelings for her. Nick couldn't deny that. And the feeling he had experienced upon holding what he thought was the corpse of the woman he loved was a sensation he never wanted to feel again.

With great regret, Nick decided then and there to put that love aside. Stacy deserved someone normal. She deserved someone who would not bring her into harm's way. He wouldn't think of her anymore. Not in that way. It was for her own good.

He had surprised himself earlier, calling to God. Asking God why. Did he really believe in God? Is that who he thought was behind The Pull? Was the little girl that kept appearing to him really a manifestation of something divine?

It sounded ridiculous. But could it really be any more ridiculous than being chased by a demon? Or being able to enter a room full of trained killers and walk out nearly unharmed?

He didn't know. He didn't know what was true and what wasn't; but he did know that he liked the thought. He enjoyed feeling that there was something watching out for him. That there was a reason for his existence. That there was a reason for...everything.

Melissa stood at the window, staring at Nick as he slowly paced around the yard, apparently deep in thought.

Could she trust him? Yes, he had neglected to tell her about a psychotic killer that was tailing him, but he hadn't really lied to her. And Jason was right. She wouldn't have believed him.

Melissa had always had trouble trusting men until she met Jason. Jason had seemed so innocent and sincere that Melissa found herself unable to put up her usual rough exterior and dismiss him as a typical male. And then Nick came along and further chipped away at her image of what men always wanted and what their desires stood for.

She had been hurt many times in the past, and always by men. She could never tell the others that. Two men in particular had taken every bit of innocence from her and filled her full of the anger and mistrust she used as fuel to get her through life. From the moment she had left those men behind, she had nothing to rely on except that anger. It drove her forward. It gave her strength. Like Nick's Pull, it was her reason to keep moving.

But now she was in a place where she didn't have to be angry anymore. She didn't have to fight all the time and she didn't have to defend herself. She was with people that would fight for her, not against her. That was something she had not experienced since her mother died.

In a way, Stacy reminded Melissa of her mother. So kind and always smiling. Always with a kind word to say and an encouraging hand on her shoulder. She would never tell her so, but in a way, Melissa loved her for that. She still felt like an annoying kid sister sometimes, but even that trait was endearing.

Jason was back with her, and she still felt safe with him. He was different now. Most of that innocence that had attracted her before was gone, and it had been replaced with the same kind of anger that Melissa herself carried. Jason had transformed from one kind of kindred spirit to another, though Melissa still had a feeling that Jason's innocence was buried in there somewhere. It may just take a while to find it.

And Nick.... As strange and as different as he was, he was her friend. Her brother in arms. When she fought beside him or sparred with him, she experienced a union of movement and anticipation that she had never felt before.

Or had she? Why did she still have the feeling that Nick reminded her of something or someone that had crossed her path before?

She supposed that was just part of his appeal. He made people feel things they couldn't quite explain. Melissa had been lying earlier. Nick wasn't just like everyone else. When that sword was in his hand, he could be outright frightening. She wondered sometimes if the only reason she could keep pace with him was because he was aligning himself to match her on purpose, however subconsciously. If she ever had to face him...truly face him...in battle, she wondered if those unbeatable skills of hers would still be so unbeatable.

Thankfully she did not believe she would ever have the chance to find out. Nick felt the same sibling union with her that she did with him. Like a twin brother that would just as soon throw himself off a cliff as harm his sister.

So she would trust him. For the first time in her life, she would allow herself to trust. Nick, Jason and Stacy would be something to her that she hadn't had in a long, long time. A family.

Melissa shuddered at the sappy notion. She turned and headed towards the gym, feeling an overwhelming urge to punch something.

Jason sat in front of the fireplace in the den, watching the waves of flame dance in front of his eyes. Red flame, not purple.

Could Nick's story be true? Could a demon really exist? And if so, could they really find a way to defeat it?

Jason suddenly realized that he hardly cared. He had spoken the truth when he told Nick he thought there was a way, but in fact the situation with Nick's supernatural stalker was just an afterthought in Jason's mind.

In that fire, it was green eyes Jason saw, not purple.

He still could not shake his desire for revenge on a man that was already dead. He wanted to find Raven's body and fling it off of that rooftop once more, just so he could say he had done it this time.

Would he ever be free of this? Would he ever stop fantasizing about the death of a man he could no longer touch? Raven had ruined his life. He had stripped his youth and his dreams away. His mother was gone. His brothers were gone. His home was gone. And now his face was gone. When he looked in the mirror, it now felt like a strange and unfamiliar person looking back.

Jason looked at the muscles of his arm, so much bigger than they once were. His brothers used to make fun of how skinny he was. Now Jason's arm was nearly as thick as Colin's thigh. The workout regimen and the diet Raven had provided him had allowed such a transformation, though Jason thought those were not the only reasons. He suspected almost from the beginning that the drugs Raven gave him were some form of steroid. Raven did, in fact, view him as an experiment, but he had been impatient enough to try to speed that experiment along. Perhaps the drugs also helped fueled his anger. Maybe when their effects wore off, he would calm down a bit. In the meantime though, the fact remained that he could now punch a hole through a brick wall if he wanted to.

And he did want to. Often. The only thing keeping him in check was the distraction of being surrounded by other people with problems of their own. As dead as most of his emotions now felt, Jason still found himself offering Nick solutions or saying something to Melissa he knew would make her feel better. There was still some part of the decency he once carried left inside.

He didn't want to stop, either. Being here with them felt good. He would not stop looking for his family, but until he found them, this would be as good a place to hang his hat as any.

He ran his hand through his thick dreadlocks, something else that was unfamiliar to him when he looked in the mirror.

He would fight Nick's demon. He would protect Stacy and Melissa. But when the time came…he would move on, whether to strike at the remains of Raven's organization or to follow a lead towards his missing family.

In the meantime…all he could do was wait, and get used to his new body, his new emotions, and the new face that looked back at him from the mirror.

Stacy stood in the doorway between the den and the living room, aware of Melissa and Jason and knowing that both of them were deep in thought.

Hah, Stacy laughed to herself, it seemed that all of her new friends were "deep in thought" nearly half the time she was around them.

But the truth was that the gears of Stacy's mind spun just as often as theirs did. She just hid it better. She used humor and compassion as a mask to shield the things that troubled her.

She was bothered by how little she missed her family. Yes, they had treated her like dirt, but it didn't seem natural for her mourning phase to have come and gone in the short period of time she had been in Melissa's hotel room in Atlanta. Nick and Melissa had whisked her away on a grand adventure, but even that distraction shouldn't have banished her feelings altogether. Her father had betrayed her and she had killed him for it, yet nearly a week later she had found herself laughing and cavorting with two strangers half way across the country.

Maybe she had simply let those feelings out in one violent burst? Maybe her suicidal attack on her captors that night was her way of shedding those tears in fast-motion? She still didn't like to think about that night. The feelings and thoughts she had experienced were so different from the person she now was that it almost felt like it had been someone else entirely standing there, holding that crossbow and covered in the blood of her father.

Could she really blame herself? All her life she had craved acceptance for who she really was and what she really wanted. Nick cared for her deeply in a way her past boyfriends never had. Melissa thought she was a dork, but still seemed to be grateful for her presence. Even Jason seemed appreciative of her, and he had only just met her.

These people needed her. All three of them were messed up in ways Stacy could barely imagine, much less identify with. Melissa had obviously come from a violent past. Jason was kept in a dark cell for six months by a violent lunatic. And Nick was being stalked by something that wasn't even human.

They needed her. She had to keep up this brave front. She had to smile when none of them would and laugh when they were too afraid to. If she didn't, they would crumble. And she felt that she would crumble too. If she didn't offer them light in the darkness…they would all drown in that darkness.

She looked down at Blitz, curled up near her feet. His body was pressed up against something Nick had left inside. His sword propped up against the doorframe. That strange sword that had appeared from nothing in his hand earlier that evening, and yet had been exactly where Nick had left it when they got back.

Everything she knew about Nick should have terrified her. Whatever he was before he lost his memory was obviously something dangerous. The things he could do now all had to do with violence and battle. The look in his eyes as he had fought The Whisper was nearly as inhuman as The Whisper's own eyes had been.

But she wasn't afraid of him. No...quite the opposite. She felt herself wanting to walk out that door, walk over to him, and wrap her arms around his back and tell him it would all be okay.

She was falling in love with him. She knew she was. It was a feeling no man...no human being had ever given her before. She didn't know why she was, exactly, but she knew that she was. She loved him and she would keep on loving him no matter what the truth of his past was, or what he was capable of. When he had told her to trust him that day that he saved her from herself in that warehouse, with the bullets flying past them and the sound of death all around, she did trust him, and she knew she would trust him until the day she died.

So she would stand beside him, and Melissa and Jason and Blitz and even Patricia if she needed it. She would stand beside them and give them the love they were afraid to give themselves. That was the weapon she would use. No crossbow, nor any bolt fired from it, could ever be as powerful as that.

She only hoped it would be enough.

The Dark Man stood above the broken body of his protégé, eyeing it disdainfully.

"What were you really trying to prove, Jacob? Were you taunting me? Were you taunting the forces that gave you all that money and power? You acted like a spoiled fool."

The Dark Man shook his head, his eyes now a sickly yellow.

"This is the age of change, Jacob. I told you that. This is our chance to take what is ours, and cause the greatest harm to those that have taken from us."

He looked down upon Raven's body.

"The boy has come. I was right. Even I wasn't sure it would actually happen, but...it has. Now...all we have to do is wait. If he doesn't realize what he truly is and what force he truly serves; if he doesn't decide to aid us...," The Dark Man smiled, "then he will die."

The Dark Man looked at the bandage-wrapped form beneath him.

"Like you almost did."

On the hospital bed in front of him, Jacob Raven opened his eyes.

The Whisper crouched in a tree half a mile away from where Nick now stood. Any closer and the boy would have sensed him. The Whisper didn't want that again this evening. No...he only wanted to study him.

The sheer possibility of what Nick was excited the monster in ways it had never felt before. Centuries had passed since the creature had first begun stalking humanity. Many men and woman of great strength and character had fallen before the insidious and corrupting influence of The Whisper, nor was this the first time it had been called into a physical shell and given a chance to bathe itself in the blood of its prey.

But this...this freak of nature that stood before it...would give The Whisper more of a challenge than it had thought possible. Never before had it witnessed something as strange and as unexpected as it had that day that it had been cast out of the boy's body in the woods. Never before had it been defeated at all.

Nick was a force worth watching. The Whisper would stalk its prey from the shadows. It would follow the boy and his friends wherever they went. It would threaten them and attack them when it pleased, always reminding them that they were marked, and that their doom was inevitable.

For when the time was right, The Whisper fully intended to kill them all.

In the meantime, however, he planned on taking full advantage of all the bloody delights this city had to offer.

The Whisper smiled in the darkness, and even the shadows fled in terror.

"Where are you taking me?" Nick called into the night.

It was The Pull he was talking to now. It was the sensation of purpose and direction he still felt tugging away at him.

It was calling him east now. Far, far away; beyond New Orleans, beyond Atlanta even, he suspected, and away from his friends.

But he would not follow it. Not now. Not with people who loved and needed him so close. He would stay here and protect them. He would die protecting them if need be. Pull be damned. Purpose be damned. Nick was in charge of his destiny now, and he would not fear it anymore.

"I'm sorry," he spoke to the stars, "but this is my home now."

Nick didn't know if there truly was a God, and he didn't know if that God had anything to do with his reason for living. But if there was...Nick wanted to believe He...or She understood.

Nick turned around, and saw that he wasn't alone.

The little girl was there, standing in front of a small oak tree. She looked exactly the same as she had before. Same red and brown dress. Same scuffed up black tennis shoes.

Nick looked at her. He waited for her to speak. He wanted her to, but she didn't. She just kept looking at him with those mischievous blue eyes, so full of understanding.

"Are you...Him?" Nick found the courage to ask.

She giggled.

"Or Her?" Nick asked, chuckling a bit himself.

She did not answer. She flashed her little white, slightly crooked teeth in a smile, but did not speak.

Nick looked at her. He watched her standing there, not saying a word, but in a way...not having to.

"Thank you," he said, feeling himself suddenly filled with hope, "Thank you."

Finally she spoke.

"Trust," she said simply.

Then with a smile, she stepped back into the shadows and was gone.

Nick watched the trees where she had disappeared for a very long time.

"Trust," he echoed.

He looked around at the stars. He looked down at his hands. He looked back at the house that contained his new friends.

"Trust."

Nick smiled, and turned to walk back home.

Look for Book 2 of The Pull Saga:
Home is Where the Monsters Are
Available Fall 2013
http://followthepull.com/

19347986R00136

Made in the USA
Charleston, SC
19 May 2013